NO LONGER PROPERTY OF
SEATTLE PUBLIC LIBRARY

D1164703

THE ATLAS OF US

Also by Kristin Dwyer

Some Mistakes Were Made

For the first storyteller I ever knew.
Who taught me the magic of words.
How to love them, how to use them, and most important—
how to hear them.
This is for you, Daddy.
The river is a little colder without you.

And still not for Adrienne Young.
Who always helps me understand the value of my magic.
This is NOT a dedication.

HarperTeen is an imprint of HarperCollins Publishers.

The Atlas of Us
Copyright © 2024 by Kristin Dwyer
All rights reserved. Printed in the United States of America.
No part of this book may be used or reproduced in any manner whatsoever without written permission except in the case of brief quotations embodied in critical articles and reviews. For information address HarperCollins Children's Books, a division of HarperCollins Publishers, 195 Broadway, New York, NY 10007.
www.epicreads.com
Library of Congress Control Number: 2023935670
ISBN 978-0-06-308858-0
Typography by Corina Lupp
23 24 25 26 27 LBC 5 4 3 2 1
First Edition

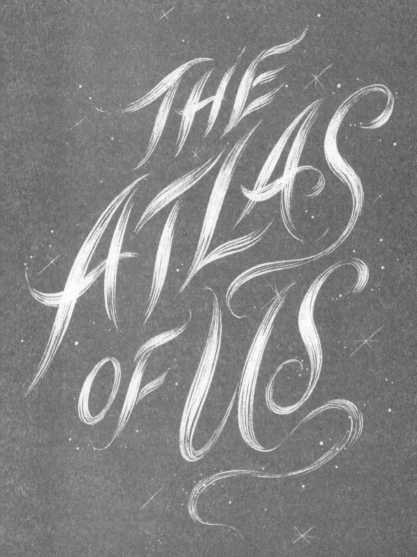

THE ATLAS OF US

KRISTIN DWYER

HARPER TEEN
An Imprint of HarperCollinsPublishers

THE END.

HE STANDS ON THE STREET.

The sunshine gone from his skin, and hair a little longer than before. It curls into the collar of the dark flannel shirt he's wearing. I can count all the ways he's different under the light from the lamppost instead of the light from a summer moon.

But the look in his eyes. That's the same.

It hurts to meet them, like pieces of jagged glass pressing against my heart, so I focus on his hands. He's holding the journal. Worn leather that's pockmarked from water and pages softened by touch. I want to reach out and open it because I know on those pages are words I want to read again.

And words I don't.

"You still have it." I'd hoped my voice would sound surprised, but all I can hear is the sadness in it.

"Yeah." He says it simply because of course he still has it. And I can feel my heart bend and break in that one word. Like the spine of a new book.

"Why?" I ask, but really I *hope*.

For what exactly, I'm not sure.

Gentle fingers run over the word etched on the cover; the one I watched him carve with a knife in short blunt strokes as we sat under the stars. "I didn't want . . ."

But he trails off, leaving me wondering. He didn't want what? Anyone to know about what happened?

About how he shattered my heart into pieces that bled onto those pages without my permission?

He didn't want his lie to unravel?

With a step forward, he practically whispers, "*Maps*."

"It's Atlas."

Bang. The two words are like a shot fired into the dark, cracking against the quiet. Words I know will hurt him. The way he's hurt me. "People call me Atlas here," I repeat—justify.

There's something different in his eyes now. "I don't call you that."

No.

No, he called me something else. A name that meant something different. In a place so unlike the one we stand in now.

"Please." It almost seems desperate. "Don't run. Not again."

But running seems to be the only thing I'm good at.

1

The beginning.

MY EYES ARE CLOSED.

I don't open them, even as the light filtering through the trees strobes against my eyelids. If I keep them closed maybe I can pretend.

Pretend that this drive is one I want to take, like it had been so many years before. Pretend that I'm with my dad. Pretend that when I open my eyes, he'll be tapping his tanned fingers against the steering wheel to the music.

But I know all the things I've been pretending aren't real. *Pretending* is just another word for lying. And I've been doing that. To my mother, to my friends, to myself, because this *drive* is something I've been dreading. And my dad is dead.

Things no one can pretend away. Not forever.

Most people say *gone* or *passed away* when they talk about my dad. It seems so gentle; almost soft and completely inaccurate. Cancer is never gentle.

I open my eyes to the reality I've been avoiding. My mother sitting next to me, her sunglasses a little too far down her nose and one arm propped up against the window as she drives down the windy mountain roads with sheer drops just off the side. I can't ever remember a time when she was the one who drove these roads. It was always my dad.

But the cliffs don't seem to bother her, which is a surprise, since everything seems to bother her now. Especially me.

I look down at my lap. The paper in my hand says WELCOME TO BEAR CREEK COMMUNITY SERVICE. Letters that are printed in a big, bold font feel a bit like handcuffs. Something I can't wiggle out of. On it are things like my new name, *Maps*—so clever—a rundown of safety requirements, dates of committed service, and an agreement.

> *I, _____ , from the dates of 7/23–8/25 agree to respect the trail, my fellow hikers, and nature. I understand fighting, weapons, drugs, and/or fraternization with other hikers can result in expulsion from the program. Upon expulsion, zero hours will be awarded even if service is compulsory.*
> *Signed,*

I haven't signed yet. Because I do not *agree*. Because even though this isn't compulsory, it doesn't feel like a choice. And because putting my name on this paper would make everything feel final. Like all the things I've been running from are finally here for me to deal with in black ink. Failures I have to admit.

Failed to graduate from high school. Check.

Lost my job at a family friend's floral shop. Check.

Antisocial. Depressed. Anger issues. Directionless. Check.

But I can boil all those things down to two words.

Father died. Check.

My mother doesn't know what to do with me, but in her defense, I'm not sure what to do with me either.

Bear Creek is the thing she has been hoping will fix me. Save me.

Now she gives me a tight smile from the driver's seat. "Sweetheart?" Her voice sounds concerned and gentle. Things I know she's not.

Since my dad died she's been something else completely. More like a wild animal backed into a corner.

"I'm fine, Mom."

"Fine?" she repeats, like I've just said a word she's never heard before.

I'm not fine. I had plans to spend my summer being sad and trying to find ways not to be. Or as my mother likes to say, "getting up to trouble."

How does someone get *up* to trouble? But this was the thing we agreed on—Bear Creek. And then I get what I want—her to stop asking me what's next.

If I say I don't know, she gives me a *list* of things. I should make new friends. I should start my new normal. I should be enrolling in a GED program and trying to find a job.

But she doesn't know about the other list.

I close my eyes and when I do, I see it by my father's bed. Written in his own chicken scratch handwriting were all the things he wanted to do before he died. And at the bottom . . .

Hike the Western Sierra Trail with Atlas.

It's the real reason I agreed to this and only put up a minimal fight, but it's also the reason I don't feel like I have a choice. This summer is the last thing my dad is asking me to do. Finish his list. Hike the trail.

Which is why Bear Creek feels compulsory.

I look back down at the paper again and my eyes snag on the last day of the program. August 25.

I have somewhere I need to be on the thirtieth.

With a deep breath, I push a smile onto my lips. "I'm not worried," I tell her. "It's only four weeks."

I can't remember exactly when I started lying. Maybe sometime after my dad died. Now it feels like the only thing I do.

My mother pulls off the highway and onto a dirt road that eventually opens to a beautiful valley. She stops and we get out of the car at a footpath that disappears between pine trees and heavy bushes. A dark wooden sign says, BEAR CREEK CAMPGROUNDS with a simple carving of a tent and a crescent moon above it.

I remember these hills and trails from a hundred different summers. It's like my body still carries the memories of this place. I shake out the feelings that seem to ignite on my fingertips.

Tiny wood buildings dot the valley along with gigantic white firs and gnarled ponderosa pines. They all compete with the large granite mountains that sparkle in the light like someone dropped glitter onto them. A beautiful river cuts through the center, with aspen trees growing out from its edges. I pull my phone from my back pocket and check it.

No signal. Not a single bar.

My mother looks at me and frowns. "You won't need that thing."

The truth of her words chews at the loneliness I feel inside my chest. There's not really anyone to call.

My mother pulls my suitcase from the trunk and sets it down on the dirt road with a thud. The silver luggage shines in the bright California sun as it sits on the baked earth announcing to everyone that it doesn't belong. I can't help but notice the similarities between us.

It's the beginning of the hottest part of the California summer. When the heat builds and never breaks, even in the darkness of night. I can feel the traitorous sun reaching down from the blue sky above as we stand in front of the gate.

"Like you said, it's only four weeks. Anyone can do anything for four weeks," my mother tells me, and then she repeats my lie, "You'll be fine."

I absolutely will not be, and hearing her say what I've just told her makes me angry.

"Four weeks." I say it as if I could count each one of the hours against the syllables. It feels like an unfathomable amount of time.

My mother takes my hand and rubs her thumb over it like she's brushing away the untruths I've pressed into my palms and can excavate how I really feel. With a deep breath, she looks around. "At least it's pretty here."

I make a noise like I agree, but I keep my eyes on the dirt at our feet. I don't want to look at the *pretty* valley.

"I'll be at the end of the trail to pick you up and we can go—"

I swallow, feeling her getting close to the nerve of my pain. "Mom." Her name is firm in my voice. I don't want to argue with her. Not about what happens after this. Not right now.

She pushes her glasses up on her nose and then lets out a sigh. "Right, right," she whispers, almost to herself. Something she's taken to doing since she started grief counseling.

"You won't even know I'm gone," I tell her. And then I add, "I'll be good."

I don't know why I say it. Maybe it's just a leftover reflex from when my dad was sick and I spent so much time trying to keep her from falling apart. And the truth is, despite the canyon between us, I'm worried about her. She's going back home, alone. I search her eyes for the mom I used to know, the fighter, but all I can see are the cracks and fractures and splinters of a woman who used to be invincible.

Staying busy is a powerful dam for your emotions, and when that's gone, you're left with nothing. It's something I understand intimately.

A tall boy with a fade passes us and a piece of metal flashes in the light. His septum piercing. He's the third person to walk up the trail toward the camp, so I know it's time to say goodbye.

My mother wraps her arms around me and I take a breath, smelling the things that are just her. Knock-off Chanel perfume and something sweet.

My fingers bury into her light blouse. I put my face against her shoulder. Even though my mother and I don't seem to understand each other, she's still all I have.

I won't cry. I won't show her how nervous I feel. I take my

fear and wear it like armor. Because if I break, she will break, and then what? What happens when our sorrow drowns both of us?

Nothing.

No one comes back, so what's the point?

When she releases me, my mother runs a hand down the side of my face, cupping my cheek. "Okay." With a deep breath she says, "Go be good."

Good.

Not bad.

Like I am.

2

I DRAG MY SUITCASE against the bumpy path, knowing with each jolt that I made the wrong choice in bringing it, until I end up at a courtyard.

A gigantic tree sits in the center surrounded by a few long and squat buildings. Branches reach up to the sky and spiral out in a tangled web. They cover a large patch of faded grass with benches scattered along the walkways. People move around but no one really settles. The entire place feels transient, not permanent.

This is a place where people begin, not where they end.

There are folding tables with signs taped to the front of them saying things like START HERE and TRAIL SUPPLIES. Several kids stand around talking to each other with stiff shoulders. I stand in the "start here" line behind the boy with the nose ring.

When it's my turn, a woman holds a yellow highlighter like a sword. "Name?" She looks physically incapable of smiling as she continues. "Nickname. *Not your name.*"

"Got it." I lick my lips and the name on my tongue feels

heavy. This is part of the test. My new identity given to me on a contract I still haven't signed. "*Maps.*"

She scans the paper in front of her and highlights something before she frowns. "It says you need to see Joe." Her eyes rake over me and her head tilts, curious.

"Joe?" I have no idea why I'm playing dumb. I know who *Joe* is. But something about her expression makes me feel like I shouldn't.

She points her pen to the end of the courtyard and a small A-frame building that sits apart from the others. The sign above the door reads OFFICE.

As I walk toward it, I pass several people standing under the large tree trying to hide from the heat. Some have small duffels, some have backpacks, but no one brought a suitcase. Just me.

I push open the sliding glass door and let the cool sensation of air conditioning hit my skin. My eyes adjust to the darkness and my ears to the silence.

Joe's office. I've been here before, but never like this.

Never as someone doing *his* program.

Dated furniture and ancient relics of technology fill the room and on the desk is a massive cream-colored monitor. The enormous map tacked onto the wood-paneled wall is drawn in muted colors of browns and blues and greens to make it look vintage. At the center is Bear Lake with a giant X for Bear Creek Campground. Over the X is written *Paradise on Earth.*

But this map isn't old, it just looks like it is. I know because I've never seen it before. This fake-old map is a liar.

It's apparently a theme in my life.

11

On the desk, turned away from the door, is a silver metal framed photo. My stomach tightens and twists as I realize what it is.

A picture of Joe. My dad. Me.

I'm not more than six, sitting on the ground between them, my dad wearing the olive-green fishing hat he was never without. There's a buzzing sensation in my fingertips like there always is when my dad's memory finds me unprepared.

I reach out to pick up the frame, but before I grab it, I hear—

"Don't touch my shit."

Joe comes out of a small door and frowns at me. "Atlas."

My fingers ball and I tuck a fist behind me. "My name is *Maps*. Remember?"

The head of the program, and my dad's best friend, stands behind his messy desk with his hands on his hips and his eyes narrowed. The blue bandanna around his neck is sweat stained and his cargo shorts have a gaping hole toward the bottom. Joe doesn't look like the director of a million-dollar state-funded park program. He looks homeless.

His gaze moves over me to my silver suitcase. "You know you're hiking, right?"

I stand in front of my suitcase, blocking it from his view. "I know."

"How are you?" Joe asks but it's stilted. Like he knows he's *supposed* to ask but doesn't really want to hear the truth.

"I'm fine."

"Fine," he repeats.

For a second, I think he's going to say something else. He'll make me admit I'm lying and twisting the meaning of the word *fine* till it's like the pine trees that grow in knots here. Or worse, ask about my father. My throat tightens and I look anywhere but at him.

"Really? You're fine?" He looks at me. "You're not mad? About the . . ." His hands wave around without a real direction.

Oh. Joe means about Bear Creek.

"Of course I'm mad. My mother basically extorted me to do this fucking program." But my hand goes to the list in my pocket. My dad's list. I wrap my fingers around it like Joe has X-ray vision and will find it.

He shakes his head. "Extortion is a little much. From what I heard you've been a real shit show."

"*Shit show?*" I let out a laugh. "Do people use that word?"

"Are you gonna give me trouble, Outlaw?"

My jaw clenches. It's my dad's nickname for me, the one that reminds me of a thousand spaghetti westerns watched on his lap and finger guns at tea parties.

"Maps," I correct.

"You're not Maps till you sign the agreement." Joe leans forward with his fists on the table. "If you don't want this, if you don't take it seriously, you'll get sent home. And it will waste my time and yours."

"Right. No fighting, or drugs, or sex." It's ridiculous that he's asking me to *want* this. I don't *want* to be here. I don't *want* to hike my entire summer. I don't *want* a dead dad. But no one cares what I want. "I'm here, aren't I? At your free labor camp?"

"Free?" Joe laughs. "It's not free. This is the number one

conservation program in the country. People come from all over to do this. I have a waiting list two hundred people long. I moved you to the top because your dad is one of my best friends and he . . ."

Is. God I hate the way I can't stop hearing the past and present in conversation.

Joe clears his throat. "Which reminds me." His eyes look down at the photo on his desk almost like it's an impulse. "Don't tell people that you know me. Or that your dad—"

"Why?" I interrupt.

The phone rings and he picks up the receiver just to set it down again. "I don't want anyone to think I'm doing you a favor."

"But you are," I push. Also, he's just hanging up on people?

"Because—" The phone rings again and he repeats the motion of hanging up the receiver.

"You don't need to get that?"

"Oh my fucking god, Atlas. Are you done?"

"Maps."

"Not yet." He sighs at me. A long thing that fills the air. "Can you just follow the rules and pretend you're not . . . you know, *you*?"

You. It hurts, so I force myself to smile.

"First rule of a cult is to strip someone of their identity."

He's not smiling and I feel mine fade in response. Joe takes a piece of paper and puts it out on the desk. It's the Bear Creek volunteer agreement.

He holds out a pen. "If you sign it, you're here. And if you're here, you're Maps."

"The nicknames are stupid." I toss the insult at him.

"The nicknames were your dad's idea." His words come back at me, spiked. He takes a deep breath. "Who you are, what you've done, none of that matters here. The nicknames are a blank slate. No past or history or judgment."

The last word sticks in my mind like gum on a shoe. But I can hear my father's voice in Joe's words.

Maps. How ridiculous. I take the pen and in big block letters, I write MAPS in the blank space reserved for my name. And I stare at it. Maps. Who is she? Does she have friends? Does she have a dead dad? Is she a fuckup who gets sent to community service?

I decide Maps can be anything I want her to be.

With the pen, I sign the agreement and decide, Maps is *fine*.

3

THE STICKER IN MY hand reads *Hello! My name is MAPS* with a bright blue dot next to it. I adhere it to my chest and instantly it feels like cosplay.

Strangers with cans of soda or sparkling water and name tags like mine fill the courtyard as they make small talk about the nicknames on their stickers like River and Cookies and Bucket.

I chat with someone named Key. Her circle sticker is red and she tells me it's her trail assignment. "You're blue." When she says it, she sounds disappointed and oddly it makes me feel good that she'd hoped I was on her trail.

Key points to a person without a colored sticker. "Trail leaders," she tells me. Key goes on to explain they're people who've done the program before. A girl without a sticker and wearing double French braids laughs at something the woman from earlier with the highlighter says.

"How do we know which one will be ours?" I ask.

"We don't. They assign them before we go out."

I nod as Key excuses herself, probably to find someone with a red sticker, and then I'm standing there in the middle of a crowd, alone with a can of Sprite in one hand and my dignity in the other.

I'm used to feeling out of place, used to feeling like something is happening just beyond me, but here, it's physical. The color sticker on my chest doesn't seem to match anyone else's. I hear someone whispering about my suitcase, and I just . . . I need a second to myself.

A second to think.

I pretend I'm walking with purpose toward the building with a sign that says OUTHOUSE, but instead of going in, I toss my mostly full soda in a trash can and walk to the back, leaning against the wood-paneled siding.

"Okay," I hear myself say out loud. "It's fine." My new favorite word.

One deep breath. Two. Three. This is not a panic attack, despite what my therapist keeps calling them.

I open my eyes and pull a pack of smashed cigarettes out of my back pocket. They aren't mine but something I found at the bottom of the center console of my father's truck. I didn't know he smoked. I remember pulling them out and just staring at the yellow packaging. This part of my dad's life that I couldn't place or understand. Like a puzzle piece that didn't fit anywhere. Why were they there? Had he always smoked? Did that cause the cancer?

But he wasn't around to answer any of those questions. And when my mother came outside, I hid them behind my back. I don't know why I didn't tell her. Or why I kept them, except the cigarettes felt like a secret between my dad and me. One that let me pretend—

"You can't smoke here."

When I look up, a boy is walking toward me. Golden hair matches his golden tan, and he wears a dark gray T-shirt over his broad shoulders.

He stops, and I notice how his beat-up hiking boots are pointing toward my brand-new and pristine ones. The real versus the pretend. He looks at my name tag and the pack of cigarettes in my hand. When his eyes meet mine, they feel heavy.

"Oh, I wasn't— I'm not—" *Fuck.* I let out a little laugh. "It's . . . they aren't mine."

A small crease forms between his dark brows. "Not yours?" he repeats.

"It's . . ." How do I even explain? "I wasn't going to smoke. I don't smoke."

He nods at me and looks back down at the pack. I search his chest for a name tag but there isn't one and suddenly, I'm not sure why I'm justifying myself to him.

"I didn't light it." My words sound petulant.

"There's no smoking anywhere on the trail or in the mountains." The boy plucks the cigarettes from my hand. "And you can't be back here."

My hands reach for the pack but he's already moving toward the crowd.

"Hey!" I shout, but he doesn't even turn around as he crushes the American Spirits in his fist. "Fuck."

I lean back against the wall and press the heels of my palms into my eyes. I don't want to cry, but more than that, I can't cry. Too many people will notice. And I absolutely can't stay here forever. Taking a deep breath, I walk back to the group.

A girl with soft green hair watches me curiously. Her eyes are defined with heavy black liner and she wears expensive athletic gear and fashionable hiking boots, but they're broken in and worn. She is not pretending.

The girl takes three long strides in my direction before coming to a stop directly in front of me. "Blue." She points at my tag with a smile and then points at her matching dot. "I told Joe to give me someone cool, and you look cool."

"Cool?" I do not look cool. I'm wearing denim shorts when everyone else is wearing expensive leggings. I have on an oversize T-shirt and my brown hair is messy and mousy. Next to her I look boring, and I tell myself not to shift and straighten my shirt, which has fallen down my shoulder.

But the girl ignores my question. "I swear Joe loves to punish people. Last year he wouldn't let me hike. Said there were too many boys and it wasn't *safe*, as if that's a fucking thing. It's called misogyny. Do you know Joe?"

"Joe?" I try to keep up with her.

"He runs the campgrounds and trails. He seems mean but he's not. Mostly. Just someone who's been in a bad mood since the eighties." She smiles at me. "I'm Sugar."

"Maps," I tell her, pointing to my name tag.

"Have you met anyone else in blue?"

I shake my head. "Have you?"

"Just you." Her lips press together. "Which is concerning. What *is* Joe up to?"

But before I can offer a theory, I see the boy with the septum piercing.

Broad and tall, I recognize him as the person who passed

us as we walked in and who stood in front of me at check-in. He approaches us with purpose and a smile. "Is this where the revolution takes place?" He hands us each a can of Sprite, and his pink glittery nails catch the light. On his chest is a name tag that reads *Junior.*

"The revolution?" Sugar asks with eyes narrowed. She takes the can from him and the lid pops when she pulls the tab open.

Junior arches one perfect eyebrow. "The girl with the head-band over there says that you volunteered last year and you're known as a bit of a troublemaker."

Sugar only sighs. "*Jacks* is jealous because she wasn't smart enough to get out of ditch duty. She's a troll. And a terrible kisser." She grumbles the last part into her soda.

"Jacks does look like she'd be a sloppy kisser," he says thought-fully and then looks at me. "She didn't know who you were, so I'm assuming you're new too?"

"To Bear Creek," I answer. "But not to revolutions."

He smiles and it's the kind of beautiful that makes you want to lean toward it. "I'm Junior."

"As in Mints?" I ask.

He doesn't smile.

"Or Junior High," Sugar asks. "Wait, or is it like Carl's. Are you Carl's Jr.?" Her face is serious, which only makes the mock-ing worse.

"Are you done?"

"It's an interesting name," Sugar tells him almost apologeti-cally. "Doesn't really fit you."

Junior shrugs. "Neither does Sugar, it seems."

"Maybe it's opposite day?" I suggest.

"What's the opposite of Maps? Lost?" Junior asks.

My jaw tightens but that sounds right. *Lost.*

We spend the next hour, in the hottest part of the afternoon, under the big tree, talking about the nothing only strangers have the patience for. Sugar mentions a trip to the ocean and Junior tells her he's never been.

"You live in California," she says, appalled. "It seems impossible that you've *never* seen the ocean."

"It's a big state." He only shrugs, distracted, like something has caught his attention.

Or someone.

Two boys stand over at a picnic table. One with golden hair that curls around the edges of a ball cap and the other with black hair that he keeps pushing out of his eyes. And in the blond's back pocket are *my* dad's cigarettes.

"Who are *they*?" Junior asks.

Sugar lets out a sigh. "Actual trouble," she tells us. "The blond is King and the one with dark hair is Books."

"Do you know them?" I ask.

"Everyone *knows* them." She looks a little sheepish. "But if you're asking if they know me? Not really. They rehabbed the river with Joe last year." Sugar is thoughtful for a long moment before she stands. "But they're not the trail leads *we* want."

"Really?" Junior asks, but he's not really asking. "Because I don't understand an argument against the one in the manga shirt teaching me to use tools."

I snort laugh.

"Jesus Christ." She stands in front of Junior. "Trust me. Those two boys are . . . they're . . ." Sugar groans.

Junior looks at her patiently. "Examples. Please provide me with reasons why I don't want the hot one as my trail leader."

"Books—the hot one—" She practically rolls her eyes when she says it. "He made a kid wake up every morning at four a.m. to clean the public restrooms all along the river. Do you have any idea what happens in a state park public restroom?"

"Why?"

"Why are the bathrooms—"

"Why did he do that?"

She shrugs as her fingers flick the tab of her soda can. "No one really knows. And the blond is Joe's pet. Last year he was sentenced to do this program by the courts. Apparently this year he's using this program to get an internship with another conservation program."

"Like an interview?" I ask.

"More like a test, I think. If he does well, he gets the internship. Which means if we're with them, it'll be horrible and hard and *not* at all cool. We want that girl. Ivy." Sugar points to a girl with a face full of freckles and a messy bun of red hair on top of her head. "Her trail partner is Pidgeon, and I promise you they will be on the hike that has toilets."

"She looks nice."

"She is, but mostly, she doesn't live for this program like some of the others. Which means an *easy* hike."

Easy sounds good. It sounds like exactly what I need. But I doubt that's what I'll get.

As the afternoon wears on, Joe tells us that we will learn how to report and rehabilitate damage on the trails, along with how to safely hike and camp over the next four days.

We watch five safety videos under a stuffy covered patio. They range from dramatic CGI forest fires to a woman falling down a trail and off the side of the cliff. Littered in between are speeches about why it's important to keep trails safe for hikers and the power of nature to heal the human soul.

Halfway through the most boring day of my life, everyone stands in a line for ice Popsicles. A girl behind me practically shoves another girl out of her spot.

"Am I missing something about the ice pops?" I ask as a girl in all black runs to stand in front of me.

Sugar doesn't answer, just motions for me to look at the front of the line.

Books and King dig into giant white coolers and pass out pops without any enthusiasm. Junior smiles at Books, who hands him a blue pop. King hands me a red one without even looking at who he's handing it to. I don't say thank you.

I wish he would hand me back my dad's cigarettes.

Then we're back to watching videos that explain terms that we'll need to know. Everything has silly names like *blowdowns* and *spring poles* and *widow-makers*.

Sugar looks like she's asleep sitting up and Junior narrates with inappropriate comments. He's decided that these are actually instructional videos on how to avoid STDs. "I knew this guy who got a *widow-maker* but he called it—"

I push his shoulder before he can finish his thought.

He earns us a stern look from Joe.

The trail leaders demonstrate how to prepare water with a pump, or the ratio of bleach to water and how long you need to let it sit before you can drink it. I make a face. It's hot and my skin feels like paper. The water in the bottle I've been given is warm and I just want this to be *over*.

Then finally it's dinner. We stand in a long line at the barbecue grill and have our choice between a veggie dog or a real hot dog.

"I'll give you my chips if you give me your cookie," Junior tells Sugar. She nods and they trade. We eat, sitting on the ground under the shade of the tree, silently.

Something about the heat that sticks to your skin and the dirt that layers on top of it feels familiar and sad.

Out here my father's memory is loud. It shouts over the breeze and the rush of the river and the quiet conversations. I can't help but think of all the meals I ate with my dad on hikes here while listening to the nothing that only happens in stillness. *"Your mind can't work if there's too much noise."*

I hate the quiet. I don't want my mind to work.

My throat clears. "If you could have any animal as a pet, what would it be?" I only ask so that someone is talking. But as soon as it's out of my mouth, I regret it. *Weird.* I'm weird. They're gonna think—

Junior looks at me thoughtfully and I brace myself for what he's going to say next. "Does it love me? Or does it want to eat me?"

It takes me a second to realize he isn't responding with teasing.

"Loves you," I tell him. "Obviously."

"Alligator," Junior answers right away.

"Elephant," Sugar says.

I nod. "I want a tiger."

"Boring," Junior teases. "People actually have tigers. All you've told us is that you're a cat person."

"Fine." I roll my eyes. "An orca."

"Where are you gonna keep a whale?" Sugar points her hot dog in my direction.

My mouth falls open. "You picked an elephant. I'll keep my giant mammal the same place you keep yours."

Junior counters, "Your whale will die on land."

"This game is abstract by nature!" I groan. "I am not answering *literally*."

"Also," Junior continues. "Clearly you've never seen that documentary about the serial killer orca."

"You picked an *alligator*!"

Junior shrugs. "But an alligator who *loves* me."

After dinner we're instructed to find a place to sleep in the bunkhouse, which is just an enormous room with rows of rickety metal bunk beds. Junior, Sugar, and I find some near the back and I undo my suitcase to pull out my toothbrush and face wash.

"What's with the suitcase?" Sugar asks.

I shrug. I'm not willing to talk about how it sat by the front door of our house every day for a year, waiting for a trip my dad would never take.

On my way to the bathroom to change, I pass King and Books. They're both walking back to the bunkhouse, King with wet hair curling against the nape of his neck and a shirt sticking to skin.

I offer a small smile, but neither of them return it, and when I look back, Books is saying something to his friend, who just shakes his head.

I can't help but feel like they're talking about me. About the cigarettes. I tell myself it doesn't matter. In four more days, I won't see them—or my dad's cigarettes—again.

When I get back to the bunk, Sugar and Junior are sitting on Junior's bed together with their legs out and backs against the wooden wall that lets light through the places the wood has shrunk over time.

I take a seat on the other side of Junior. "Is it always like this?" I ask Sugar.

"Kinda." Her head hits the wall gently behind her. "It all changes when everyone gets on the trail. Less chaos. Less everything. More work."

Junior lets out a low whistle. "Better than being at home."

Sugar makes a noise like she agrees. "Anything is better than home."

And as we sit there, I think of the things that could be better than *home* for them. None of us ask though, because those are the things strangers don't talk about.

Strangers don't share the truth.

4

IN THE PAST THREE days at Bear Creek, the most important thing I've learned has nothing to do with nature.

In between lectures about *trail eyes* and *erosion signs*, I've been educated in the secret meaning of Popsicles. Which seems to be the most important thing here. The long plastic tubes of frozen juice in artificial colors and flavors are the only thing that seems to keep everyone going during mind-numbing tutorials in the heat.

Cold ice and sugar that's passed out twice a day. They're meant to be a reward. But to Junior, they're a sign. A secret message.

He stands in front of us holding out a bright red pop. "Red. Fucking *red*."

Sugar gives him a patient look as she bites off a chunk of her pink one. He makes a disgusted face as he watches her chew. We sit underneath a wide oak tree, not bothering to use the picnic bench seats but sitting on top of the table.

"I don't get it," I tell them. "Red? Does that mean something?"

Junior narrows his eyes at me as if I'm saying the most

ridiculous thing. "Mean something? Yes, Maps. It's red. *Red*. As in the most coveted of all Popsicle colors. And this is the fourth time, *in a row*, that he's given me red."

I look back to the line of people still waiting as the two boys pass out pops.

King and Books.

They wield some kind of mysterious power because they've been assigned to hand out our treats.

And because they don't talk to anyone but each other. They're all mystery and hushed stories about cleaning bathrooms and coveted internships.

We watch Books hand someone else a yellow pop and Junior's hands go wide. "See?"

"So, it's official," I tell him. "He loves you. When are you getting married?"

Sugar's face turns serious. "You'll look amazing in white."

Junior waves his pop between us. "I hate both of you and I can't stand straight people."

Sugar frowns. "How *dare* you assume my sexuality."

Junior ignores her. "Red. It has to mean something, right?"

"Are you sure he's . . ." I trail off.

"*One of mine?* Yes. He's too hot to be that into manga and not like boys."

"I don't think that's a thing. Sounds like a stereotype."

Junior gives me a smug look. "Says the girl with the blue Popsicle."

"Again, I don't understand your color hierarchy. Is blue *good* or *bad*?"

Sugar puts a cold hand on my bare leg. "Everyone knows blue is the second-best color."

"Is there like a Wikipedia page that everyone has read?"

"Oh!" Sugar says to Junior. "This afternoon, whatever color he gives you, just mention that it's your favorite color."

"Yes!" Junior says, clearly understanding some plan I don't. "And then if he gives it to me on the last day, we'll know he's doing it on purpose."

There are many flaws in this plan. So many. "What if you end up in the other one's line?"

"The *other* one." Sugar raises an eyebrow. "You mean *King*?"

Sugar caught me watching King as he carried the heavy coolers out of Joe's office the second day we were here. It isn't my fault he doesn't like sleeves.

"Did King give you the blue pop?" Junior asks, biting his.

I feel my face heat. "I don't know."

"What color did you get yesterday?" Junior asks.

"I don't know! Yellow?" When did this conversation turn on me?

"You *liar*, you got red!" He's acting like a lawyer who just caught a witness in cross-examination. "I remember because your teeth were stained till dinner!"

I stand. "I don't remember because they're just Popsicles!"

Except their words lodge themselves inside my brain like worms slowly eating away at all the reasonable and rational thought I have.

And later that day, when King hands me a pink pop, I stare down at it trying to discover its meaning.

Junior gets green.

He groans. "I am an idiot."

Sugar can't stop laughing as we sit together on the table that I'm now beginning to consider our place. It's only marginally cooler than being in the direct sunlight. "Green is lime! No one likes lime!"

Junior speaks slowly, as if he's still trying to figure out what happened. "He handed it to me and I said, *Thanks, I love green.*" His eyes go wide. "*Thanks?* I said *thanks.*" His whole face transforms into horror.

"I doubt he even heard it," I say, trying to be helpful.

"That's worse!" He sits down on the tabletop next to me with his elbows on his knees and his head in his hands.

"How is that worse?"

"That would mean he wasn't even paying attention to me." Junior lets out a deep breath. "I guess I will just walk into the river, slowly—"

"And dramatically," Sugar interjects with a serious nod.

"—with rocks in my pockets, and let my beautiful, young ghost tragically haunt this campground."

"That's pretty serious commitment," I point out.

The next day Junior stands in line and . . . he gets green.

With a shake of his head, he looks down at the pop. "I hate green." But a smile has carved itself against his features.

"Wanna trade?" I ask, holding out a red pop to him.

Junior makes a face as he bites into the lime one he holds. "King give you that?"

"I don't know," I lie.

Junior opens his mouth, but before he can respond, Sugar is standing in front of us with a grave look on her face. "I have bad news."

"What is it?" I ask.

Her head shakes back and forth. "It's bad."

"Just say it," Junior tells her.

"We got assigned a trail and trail leaders. And I'm not sure which is worse." We wait in suspense for her to tell us. She takes a deep breath and says, "We're doing the Western Sierra Trail. And. We're doing it with Books and King."

I look at Junior, who is still staring at Sugar, and slowly his face breaks out into a smile. "Is this my main character moment in the romance novel of my life?"

Sugar rolls her eyes. "This is no romance. Think thriller. The Western Sierra Trail has been closed for the past seven years since a fire came through it. Hiking it is going to be . . . awful. It's probably haunted."

Sugar and Junior argue back and forth about ghost wildlife and wondering if maybe Joe will change our trail, but I'm not surprised that this is what we've been assigned.

It was the trail my dad never got strong enough to hike again.

The one that is on a list in my back pocket.

And I know this is Joe's way of making that right.

5

JOE STANDS AT THE head of a picnic table with his hands on his hips like an old Peter Pan.

On one side of the bench seats are Junior, Sugar, and me.

And on the other are Books and King.

As if we are opposing teams.

We all look down at a piece of paper with our names, our trail assignment with a map, and a list of what we'll need on the hike.

"Divide all the equipment between you five to carry," Joe is telling us, and I can't help but stare at the people I'm about to disappear into the mountains with.

Books seems almost nervous and King rubs at a spot behind his ear. I try to catch his eye, wondering if I'll be able to tell if he's going to say anything about the cigarettes and wondering what kind of judgments he's already made about me. Am I a bad kid? A troublemaker?

Does he think I'll be a problem?

When I was a freshman, my teacher accused me of cutting

class and using my dad's cancer as an excuse. I could feel the anger and the rejection building up because this person couldn't see the way I was hurting. Instead of trying to be better, I was worse.

"*You don't have to double down on every bad thought someone has about you*," my mother told me.

But my dad just shook his head.

And now I can't stop trying to read King to find out what he thinks of me because that will determine what kind of person I'll be on the Western Sierra Trail for the next month. If I'll double down on his judgment.

A month with strangers.

What if we end up hating each other? What if we get hurt? What if there's a snowstorm and one of us dies and we have to eat them to stay alive?

Apparently I'm the only one with questions because a moment later Books pulls the list toward him and clears his throat. "King and I can carry the shovels and saw. Junior looks like he can carry the extra water." He pauses and looks up at Junior, who raises his eyebrows. I think Junior's arms flex, but I can't really tell.

"Junior can carry the ropes too," King continues. "Sugar can carry the food and cooking supplies."

"Because I'm a woman?" she counters.

"You wanna carry the water?" Books asks her with a challenge in his voice.

"I wanna carry the saw." She never takes her eyes off him.

Joe knocks his knuckles on the table twice. "Play nice. I'm gonna check on the other groups."

As Joe walks away, King looks back down at the list. "Maps, can you carry the tents?"

He *asks* me. A question.

"Why are you asking her?" Sugar adds. "You didn't ask me."

King meets her eyes. "Because if she carries the tents she's in charge of putting them up at camp and packing them when we leave. So, I'm asking if she can handle that."

Everyone looks at me, waiting. "Yeah. I can carry the tents." How hard can putting up a tent be? I watched my dad do it hundreds of times.

"I'll carry the compass," Books says.

"No, you will not." King laughs and Books's face transforms into another smile that whispers of a memory the rest of us don't share. It changes Books and King into something softer, something less separate. King shakes his head.

"Fine. Give it to Tent Girl," Books says. "She looks like she has a decent sense of direction."

I don't say that I'm lost even in this conversation, that I can't find north if my life depends on it. I don't admit I can't tell the difference between a star and a satellite. So I say, "Don't call me Tent Girl."

"Sorry, *Maps*," Books replies, but he doesn't look sorry.

"It's a little on the nose," Sugar complains. "Maps. Compass."

King continues. "On the trail, we'll wake up, eat and take down camp, and then head out hopefully before the sun is all the way up to avoid most of the heat. All the rehabilitation we will do on the trail will be small and we'll take note of bigger things for forestry services. At night, we'll cook but you're responsible for your own dishes. If you're not comfortable sharing a tent, say so now."

No one says anything.

Joe comes back and tells us to grab our things. When we meet him in front of his office he hands us each a green canvas hiking pack and instructs us to fill them with our essentials.

"Only take what is absolutely necessary. Understand?"

The pack already has things like a toothbrush, toothpaste, and a shampoo bar. I feel like an idiot with my suitcase sprawled out on the dirt as I try to determine what is worth it to carry with me for the next four weeks. A collection of my most essential things laid bare and open for anyone to see.

When I look up, King has his arms crossed. Judging me. I stuff my pack as quickly as I can and fold up the giant silver monster.

"All right," Joe says. "Empty everything from your bag and show us what you think you're carrying around."

"I just packed it," Sugar grumbles.

But we do.

Almost instantly, Books and Sugar begin to argue.

Her expression is indignant as she moves for something that he snatches from her reach. "Joe said we could bring it if we could carry it."

"Not this," Books says, dangling a gallon bag full of skincare bottles and pots an arm's length away from her.

"I need those."

Joe walks over and takes the bag. "Where are you gonna do a ten-step skin care routine?"

A scoff leaves her. "Skincare is important."

"None of this . . ." He squints at a bottle, reading the label. "Hydrating serum? No."

"Come on," she groans. "The elements are going to destroy my face."

"You're too young to be vain."

"It's *never* too early to practice self-care!"

He looks down at a bottle on top of her bag. Hot sauce. "*No,*" she tells him, diving for it. "I'm keeping this. It's essential."

"Fine. Sunscreen. Hot sauce. That's it," Joe says before moving over to Junior.

Sugar curses, but I watch her slip eyeliner and mascara into a front pocket of her pack. Junior only has clothes and Joe nods. "You have too many underwear. You only need two pairs."

"Gross," Junior whispers.

"More than you can even imagine."

And then my view is blocked by King, who crouches in front of my pack. He's looking at all the things I've decided are necessary with pinched brows. And for some reason all I can think about are the red Popsicles he's given me. Did they mean—

He clears his throat, and I know I've been caught staring.

"Large animal mace, Swiss Army knife, flashlight, batteries," he lists off the things in front of me. "Cell phone, charger, screwdriver." He lets out a heavy breath. "Did you even read the rules?"

"Yes?" I did. I don't understand what he's saying.

"Half of these are weapons."

"Yes. To protect me from predators," I tell him, seriously. Men never worry about shit like this.

"Three pairs of shoes?"

"What if something happens to the ones I'm wearing?" I ask.

His face breaks into confusion. "Like what?"

I don't actually know, and now Joe has come to stand next to my pack, looking down at it with a frown, so I say the first thing that comes to my mind. "What if a bear eats them?"

Joe pauses and cocks his head like he's trying to figure me out. "This makes me think you don't know what a bear is."

"I know what a bear is." Probably.

"Maps, you *know* none of this shit is necessary. Where do you think you're going? The zombie apocalypse?"

"I've never packed a bag on my own before." I press my lips together because I've just reminded Joe that I've never hiked without my dad. In truth, I don't know what the fuck to bring. I don't remember what he packed. I don't remember . . . anything, and it makes me unbelievably angry that he's not here to ask.

Joe looks me in the eyes and then back down at my pack with a softer expression. "All of your weapons have to go." He pauses and adds, "And goddamn it. No cell phone. How are you gonna charge this? The fucking sun?"

He walks away and I'm left with King. I expect him to look smug or arrogant because Joe sided with him, but his expression remains neutral. "None of this," he says in a deep and quiet voice. "One pair of shoes."

In addition to our own stuff, we're given communal items to divvy up, like bug spray, some kind of eco toilet paper, a giant thing of socks. King and Books have backpacks strapped with shovels and shears, even a hammer. No one points out that those could also be used as weapons.

I strap the tents, one blue and one red, into my pack and by the time I'm finished, it's stuffed and overflowing. Everyone is picking up their backpacks and testing the weight, so I slide my shoulders into the straps and haul it onto my back. It's awkward and not great. But Sugar really struggles to pick hers up, so I count standing as a win. Junior looks like a puppy trying to see his tail as he spins around.

Books and King have no problem with their weight. Of course.

I'm shifting, trying to get used to the heaviness on my back, when Junior walks over to me. "Here," he says as his tanned fingers adjust the straps by my shoulders. "How does that feel?"

"Actually?" I move around. "Better. Still massive but . . . better."

He pats the top of my head and smiles down at me. "Good." Junior turns, showing me his pack, and looks over his shoulder. "Do you see—"

But before he can finish, Books walks over to him. His hands reach out to the buckles by his shoulder.

"I don't . . . I can do it." Junior's face turns a light shade of pink as Books ignores him and steps into his space. Junior's face darkens to red. "I got it."

But Books, for his part, doesn't seem to notice his protest as he pulls on the tabs. "Like that? Does it feel good?"

Junior is still blushing when he says, "Yeah." A little low and a little breathy.

"One of you could help *me*," Sugar says, and Books drops his hands from Junior.

"Here." King adjusts one final strap at my waist. His arms

circle around me as he pulls the bands forward, and then he steps back. "It's just to keep it . . . steady."

He turns, flexing his hand once.

Sugar holds her arms out wide. "Seriously?"

Eventually, after our luggage is stored and our packs have been sorted, Joe gives us a pep talk.

"Tomorrow you'll want to quit. Every part of your body will tell you it's not worth it and you should go home. And every day after that you will work harder than you think possible. You'll be hiking anywhere from ten to fifteen miles a day with a thirty-pound backpack. And when you're stopped, you'll be doing manual labor. Digging, raking, shoveling, sawing, clearing, hauling."

"So many verbs," Junior says quietly.

"You will hurt all day, and then one day, you won't. Don't neglect your body. Take care of your feet and hands. If those go, you'll be miserable. You'll hate your meals and want to talk about In-N-Out and your mom's cooking, but don't. Be present on the trail. You all can do this."

Having Joe tell us he believes we can make it in the wilderness for four weeks feels a little like someone handing you a snorkel before diving with sharks. We all nod and pretend like we understand.

Joe puts a hand on King's shoulder. "Remember to make notes of everything. You're gonna be okay with—"

King nods, and his eyes dart to the side.

"'Kay. Just stay focused and if anything comes up, let me know. You're gonna do great."

I look over to Sugar and make a questioning face. She just rolls her eyes and mouths, *internship.*

And then Joe starts to hand King the compass but he shakes his head and points to me. Joe runs a tongue over his teeth. "Here, Maps."

The plastic is made to look like brass, and it's lighter than I expected. It sits in the center of my palm and I hear my dad's voice whispering over my shoulder. *Hold it steady and it will point you in the right direction.*

North, it seems, is behind me.

You got this. His voice is a whisper in my mind and I close my fingers around the compass and look up to the trees trying to distract myself. But he's there too. He's all over these hills and I have to spend a few weeks hiking with my dad's ghost.

"I need to go to the bathroom," I tell everyone.

Joe shakes his head but says, "Hurry. You're about to head out and you should get used to going on the trail."

"Right." I'm already shrugging out of my pack and fisting the compass in my hand. I'm not sure where I think I'm going but my feet take me toward the outhouse.

I walk through the courtyard and past the bunks, which are all empty. It seems like everyone is already at their trailheads getting ready to hike out for the day. The rows of sinks outside the outhouses all have dirt-speckled mirrors, and I catch my refection in them. My face is pale. Because of a compass. By the time I step into the small building with a dozen stalls, emotion catches in my throat like barbed wires. I'm not sure I'm going to make it. The overwhelming need to hide, to cover up my pain so no one can see it, feels insurmountable. At the very end of the room, I find a stall and flip the toilet lid down before sitting on it.

As soon as the door shuts, I feel my brokenness ripped from me in bloody cuts that are pushed out in a sob. Grief is like that. It slowly stabs at you, burrowing itself inside, until eventually your body tries to get rid of it, and it ends up tearing through you. *Destruction.* That's all death does.

I try to stay angry that missing my dad can be so inconvenient, but then I'm just angry and broken. My sadness falls down my face in heavy tears as my breaths crash against my chest.

I wish I could anticipate what's going to upset me. Instead, I find myself crying about a fucking compass.

It's so stupid and nonsensical.

I don't know how long I sit there, crying on the toilet about nothing, alone in the deserted silence of the empty bathroom, but I eventually hear voices outside. Clear and perfect. Which means whoever is outside can hear me.

Clear and perfect.

"What's going on?" The words are from someone male. Books maybe? "Where is she?"

Shit. I wipe at my face, hoping I can make myself look presentable in the next three seconds before—

"It's fine," comes the answer. King's voice. "I sent her back to the bunkhouse to grab something she forgot."

A groan. And then, "Why are you standing here? We're all *waiting*. We aren't even on the trail yet and you're already—"

"Books," King cuts him off. "Just go back to the group. We'll leave in a few."

I wait in the silence that follows.

Ten, twenty, thirty seconds.

I breathe deep and tell myself King is probably gone now. With Books. Maybe he didn't hear me crying. Maybe he doesn't know . . .

Wiping my face on the bottom of my shirt, I step out of the bathroom. King leans against a tree with his ankles crossed.

His eyes meet mine, but only for a second before he inclines his head back to where I know the group is. King waited. Maybe so that I understand no one can leave until I'm back. Maybe to be sure I make it out of the bathroom. Maybe because he was bored.

I nod, trying to tell him without words that I'm okay. He turns around and walks toward the others and I splash my splotchy face with cold water from the rusted sink.

He didn't say anything. He didn't rush me. Or ask. He . . . let me have the moment.

And I wonder what color Popsicle that would be.

6

HIKING HAS A SONG.

The rhythm of your steps on the ground. The sound of the wind in the trees. Birds and bugs telling you their secrets.

I look up at the sky and see the sun is already making her ascent over the valley. We start walking. King and Books in front. Junior in the back. It's fifteen minutes before we stop hearing other voices on the trail. Another forty-five before we can't look down and see the camp. But eventually we are alone.

As we head deeper onto the trail, we listen to that sound. Every so often we pause and King writes something in a leather notebook while Books ties a red string onto a branch or a tree or some brush.

The miles are marked with small metal signs that read WESTERN SIERRA TRAIL in red. They look like the Eye of Sauron, watching us. And underneath is a newer sign. Black and yellow letters that say WARNING and alert us that the trail is closed and we are trespassing.

My pack shifts uncomfortably with each step. My shoes feel

stiff. My thighs burn. Ahead of me I can hear the conversations in bits and pieces that don't fully form in the quiet of nature and the tension of strangers being alone.

Every now and then Books points down to the trail and tells one of us to pick up trash. We carry it with us or shove it in our pockets, little collections of faded garbage and flattened empty cans of beer. The air finally begins to cool and the sweat on my body follows. King tells us to keep our trail eyes open and make note of things that look dangerous. Places that look like they might be compromised from weather or forest fires.

After what feels like a hundred hours, we stop in a clearing. The ground is level and perfect for our tents. There's a firepit dug out and surrounded by a stone ring. We clear the ground where we'll camp and check the trees nearby for damage so they don't fall on us in the middle of the night.

"Maps," King says. "Put up the tents."

And then he disappears into the trees.

I quickly learn the tents have no instructions. Just miles of vinyl fabric and fiberglass poles. No one is paying attention to me. Books is showing Junior how to start a fire, and Sugar is holding up a bag of rice and a pot like they're from an alien planet. It makes me feel a little better that everyone seems to be as confused as I am.

But eventually the sky above me breaks out into a riot of color and I know I don't have much time till the sun sets and I lose the light. The tent is still not a *tent*, and I'm beginning to realize it's actually a Rubik's Cube. King returns with more wood and everyone seems to be making progress but me.

The fire is roaring, something is heating on it, and I'm drowning in the fading light and collapsed shelter.

Junior gets up and moves to help me, but Books stops him. "Nope. This is hers to figure out." Junior makes a face that says, *I'm sorry,* but he doesn't argue with Books.

"You helped him with the fire," I remind Books.

"Fire is more complicated than a tent." Books leans back on a rock.

I'm struggling with the poles. Frustrated, I snap, "I think a tent takes more than one person to put up!"

I don't actually know how many people it takes, except I have laid everything out and I've crossed poles and put them into seams and it's still falling down. I'm going to scream.

"It doesn't," King replies, hunched over the fire.

"What happens if she doesn't get the tent up?" Sugar asks.

"Then we don't sleep in tents," Books answers.

I look at him, sure I've misheard. King leans back on his haunches and takes a deep breath before standing. With long slow strides, he moves over to me. I ignore him as I shove another pole into a slit. But this one is too short. "Mother fu—"

He sighs, leaning down, and does something to the corner of the tent and then motions for me to move off it. I do and then he lifts the pole and . . . magically, the tent is standing.

I feel my eyes go wide. "You did it!" I move over to the corner he's standing at and step closer to him so I can see what he sees. My shoulder presses against his chest. "How did you do that?"

He steps backward, out of the space I've just crowded, and frowns at me.

45

"Seriously," I say, looking up at him. "How?"

King takes another step back and motions down to the bottom of the tent. "Use the corners." And then he's walking away, our conversation clearly over.

I look down, trying to determine what *use the corners* could actually mean. As if I wasn't "using" them before.

"Next one," Books says to me, pointing at the other tent on the ground with his spoon. He's already eating with his back against a log and his feet crossed at the ankles.

"Another one?" I groan.

He holds his hand out like he's Yoda or some kind of enlightened leader. "This is how we learn."

The red tent doesn't work any better, and I struggle to get it to stand. "I want you to know you're shitty teachers," I grumble. "I rate this experience *no stars*."

I yank a pole into the upright position and the tent leans with one side completely collapsed. I glance over to King, who is sitting by the fire with a notebook and a pencil in his hands, and find his eyes already on me, but he looks away and scratches something onto the paper. Probably about my incompetence.

"*No* stars," I say through my teeth.

I eat. Hoping that will make me feel better but it doesn't. When black bleeds across the sky and we've made sure the fire is out, we head to bed.

Sugar rolls out her mat and sleeping bag.

"I was thinking we could sleep with our feet toward the . . ." I motion to the collapsed side of the tent.

She looks at me and simply says, "Maps, I think we could be

great friends, but you better figure this tent shit out tomorrow because I'm not sleeping like this again."

I crawl into my bag, seething. I can feel every rock and pebble and divot in the ground under me. "You could help me," I tell her.

"Actually, they said I can't. It's your job, apparently."

"Right." I pull my sleeping bag up to my chin. "This is how we *learn*."

7

WHEN MY EYES OPEN, it's to the red roof of the tent.

The fabric lays mostly on top of me and it must have rained because what's covering my face is damp. It's also bright. I pull my arm out from the warm down sleeping bag and try to move it off me. My skin against the tent makes a loud scraping sound in the quiet. Next to me, Sugar groans.

"What the hell?" she mumbles, sleep thickening her words.

I don't speak, only sit up, letting the walls fall over my head like a veil.

Somewhere outside, I hear a groan. A boy's groan. And then a tent unzips.

I reach for my phone but realize I don't have it here.

"What time is it?" I ask.

"Do I look like a sundial?" Sugar replies. She pulls something out of the pocket of her pack. Eyeliner. It takes her less than thirty seconds to apply it.

"It's six twenty-two." Junior doesn't yell when he says it. He doesn't even sound like he's sitting up.

It makes me realize how close we are, and how quiet it really is.

Sugar opens our tent, and we both sit in the door as we put our shoes on. It's something so normal on this completely not normal morning. I wonder what my mom is doing right now. Is she still asleep? Is she trying to work the coffeepot? It was never her job but was always my dad's, and since he died she's been trying to discover the alchemy of a perfect pot of coffee like my father made.

Junior leans down by the firepit even though there isn't a fire. His face is puffy from sleep and one of his eyes is still squinting shut. Books is rubbing at his stomach and yawning. And King watches us with a toothbrush in his hand. He's not wearing a shirt and I tell myself not to stare at the hard planes of his skin, which are a complete contrast to the soft way his hair looks as it sticks up at odd angles and the crumple of his shorts.

Sugar takes the eco-friendly toilet paper and unravels some in her hand. "Don't pee near me. If you even think you can see me, you're too close."

"Don't girls pee together all the time?" Junior asks as he stands.

"Don't guys use those urinals as a cover to check out each other's dicks?" Sugar launches back at him.

Junior only laughs. "So, *not* a morning person. Got it."

Sugar walks in one direction and I stalk off in the opposite.

When I get back, the boys' tent is completely packed and sitting on the ground.

Books looks at me and points to ours. "Take down your lean-to."

I hate feeling like everything I do is wrong, like I'm failing at something I don't even want to be good at. "You could help me figure out why it won't stand up," I say as I pull a tent pole out.

"User error," Books says without even glancing up from his pack.

"So you won't help me?"

He sighs and gives me a patient face. "This is—"

But I cut him off. "How we learn." I yank out another one. "I got it."

I'm struggling, trying to collapse the last pole, when King walks over to me. He takes it from my hands and I watch as he deftly twists and folds it. When he hands it back to me it's without explanation.

Books makes a questioning face but King only shrugs and says, "We'd be here forever."

Breakfast is protein bars and water.

Sugar starts to talk about coffee but Junior stops her. "Please. I can't think about coffee right now. I miss her so much."

Everyone seems to be in a better mood after eating something and the gnawing in my stomach subsides until Junior says, "So where is everyone from?"

I start counting my steps as we hike uphill. The sun hasn't even fully crested over the mountains, and the air is just beginning to heat up. My shoes feel stiff. My thighs burn. And I do not want to answer Junior's question.

"Why?" Sugar asks him. "You plan on stalking me after this?"

Junior looks back at her and rolls his eyes. "I didn't ask for your address and blood type. Just the city you grew up in."

Sugar takes five steps before she answers. I know because I'm counting. "The Bay."

The Bay Area is enormous. She could be from the city and get coffee every morning on her way to school at some third wave shop, or from Marin County and live with the redwoods, or from a neighborhood where everyone is struggling to get by.

"I live outside the Bay," Books says. "Vallejo."

Sugar nods. "Six Flags. I got my name airbrushed on a shirt there in sixth grade."

Books smiles. "I have a couple of those too." He ties red yarn onto overgrowth and felled trees that the forestry service will need to take care of. Books looks at Junior. "What about you?"

"I'm from outside Redding."

Books smiles like he's just said something funny. "Cult or marijuana farm?"

"What?" I laugh.

"All that's up there are weird religious cults or growers. Either way, everyone has guns." Books laughs like he's made a joke, but Junior's frowning.

"What about you, King?" Sugar asks.

"A little bit of everywhere."

"What little bit are you from right now?"

"Tahoe."

Somehow it seems to fit.

"Maps? Let me guess, Southern California?"

I frown.

"Yes," Junior agrees. "But not LA. The Valley or San Diego."

"The Valley *is* LA."

"That's exactly what people from the Valley say." Junior looks like he's just proven his point.

"You caught me." I mean it as a joke. I plan to tell him I'm from just outside Sacramento. That I'm close enough to these mountains to come here on weekends. That they have it wrong. But Junior's smiling and it feels like a relief to lie.

"I knew it. I can just see you in some kind of suburban utopia where everyone's houses are the same but slightly different. I bet you had a sweet sixteen party."

For my sixteenth birthday my dad had a chemo treatment so my mother and I went to the Applebee's next to the hospital and ate a sundae. "I got a car instead." That part is true, but it was my dad's old truck and it was so I could drive him to doctor's appointments.

Junior groans. "Of course you got a car."

"Lots of people get cars," Sugar argues.

Junior motions to Books and King. "Did either of you get cars?"

King sighs. "New rule, no talking on the trail."

"You can't keep us from talking." But after that Junior falls silent.

We cut back brush and pick up trash or move fallen trees from the path. The gloves I've been given are stiff and a little large and awkward, but they keep thorns and sharp sticks from poking into my palms.

Sweat rolls down my back and I reach for my water more times than I know I should. At one point King hands me a shovel and tells me I need to dig out the side of the trail for water runoff.

"When does it ever rain in California?" I complain. "Aren't we in a drought?"

"It rains here." That's all King says.

None of this is like the videos we watched, and this is nothing like the hikes I did with my dad. It's hard labor that has my throat burning from the heat and deep breaths and pollen and dust from the dried and dead plants we pull out.

But the biggest problem is the ground. Solid and hard and baked from the sun, it's like trying to dig into concrete. King watches as I drive a shovel into the dirt. He doesn't tell me what I'm doing wrong, just moves me from my spot and begins digging out the ground at the roots of a bush. His arms flex every time he impales the earth and sweat is collecting on his brow.

I don't offer to take back over, instead I put on the pair of thick gloves and begin to rip out a plant. I yank and yank and yank. Finally it comes free, and I feel a little victorious.

It must be close to lunch, so I ask Junior what time it is. He looks at his watch, an analog thing with actual hands. "Ten seventeen."

I tilt my head back and look at the sky above me. Maybe it will fall on me and I can die instead of doing this.

The only noise is the crunch and break and bust of our work paired with grunts and deep breaths. I feel it rub against me like a pebble wearing grooves in my patience.

"So," I ask, "if you could only eat one kind of chips for the rest of your life, what would it be?"

No one even bothers to look up as they ignore my question. Finally Junior takes pity on me. "Takis."

"I don't want to know what your insides look like." I pull at a thick branch from a bush. "What is the most overrated band in history?"

"The Beatles," Sugar answers without a pause.

"The fucking Beatles?" Books's shovel stops short of entering the dirt.

"Fine," Sugar tells him and points to his shirt. "Metallica."

"The Beatles are revolutionary," Junior argues. "They changed music."

"They just took a bunch of shit people were already doing and made it mainstream. *Overrated.*"

The look on Books's face tells me I need to move on, so I ask, "If you could have any superpower what would it be?"

I assume they're still ignoring me until Junior looks up to the sky so bright it's almost white and says, "I would fly."

"You can have any superpower and you pick flying?" Books says to Junior. "That's . . . an absolute waste of a gift."

"Yeah. Well, it's what I want." Junior shrugs.

Books stares at Junior like he can't believe what he's hearing.

"What would you pick?" I ask Books.

He looks like he's considering it seriously, despite just teasing Junior. "Invisibility." Books looks down at the ground when he says it.

"So you could spy on people?" Sugar asks with a laugh.

Books's teeth worry into his lip, but he doesn't answer her.

"I'd pick mind reading," she tells me. "Always knowing what people are really thinking . . ." Her words fade and I wonder whose mind she's thinking about.

"What about you?" I ask King.

"Immortality." He ties a red string onto a tree branch.

"You would live forever?" Sugar asks. "Longer than everyone you know and love? Just live right past them?"

"Yeah." It's simple. "Past everyone."

Sugar nods and takes a sip of her water. "What about you?"

I pick time travel.

"What moment would you go back to first? You want to go back and relive the time you were homecoming queen?" Junior asks with a laugh.

I never went to homecoming. I was too busy watching my dad die.

"My dress was amazing," I lie with a smile.

I think about the last day my father could talk. I know he told a story, but was I really listening? Did I hear it? Was I paying attention or was my mind wandering?

"We took a limo and my parents took a million pictures." I swallow. "My dad threatened my date and it was so embarrassing."

"Oh my god," Sugar says. "My mother did that. I wanted to kill her. She called all my friends' moms so none of us could go to any parties after."

No one seems to have noticed my lie. They are all telling their own high school dance stories. King's eyes are on mine and for a second it feels like he knows. I wait to feel embarrassed, but it never comes.

And I realize that I don't care if he believes my lie, because I do.

8

THE HOTTEST PART OF the day isn't noon. It's around three p.m. The sun beats down in oppressive rays that burn through my clothing and make everything I carry feel a hundred pounds heavier. My hair is tied up off my neck and the light is so bright I wish I had packed sunglasses. I squint as sweat drips into my eyes, stinging them. King is frowning at me when I lean my head back and let out a groan.

"Let's call it until the world cools off." He says it as if every other place on the globe is burning like the Sierras, but we're finally underneath the shade of an ancient pine tree. The ground is littered with needles that have dried into sharp points, but none of us care as we fall onto our packs. My legs dangle and I set my feet down to keep myself from rolling off my bag.

Junior leans against the trunk of a tree and takes a gulp of water. He makes a face as he swallows. "I would kill any of you right now in exchange for an ice cube."

This gets a laugh from Books. It tracks that he would find the threat of murder funny.

"I wish I could be transported to the North Pole for like five minutes," Books says. "That's it."

Sugar shifts on her pack, and it scratches against the needles in the dirt. Her eyes are closed as if she doesn't have the energy to even look at the world around her. "You would cause a polar ice cap to melt and then Florida would fall into the ocean or a hurricane would take out the Gulf."

"But . . . I would be *cold*."

I imagine a smiling Books standing in a hurricane.

My feet ache and there are several blisters forming on them. I can feel the skin being rubbed raw, but I just need to lie here. Until I'm dead and I don't have to walk back. And then my body will be someone else's problem. We didn't even have a full day of hiking and I feel like all my muscles are going to give out.

I'm broken.

Books tells Sugar to pull out everything for dinner. I watch as he gives her directions and she complains about gender stereotypes and how fucked she thinks this is.

Books smiles. "We get it. You're not like other girls."

"And you're so cool with your vintage concert tee," Sugar snaps. "Do lots of people come up to you and ask about your favorite metal band?"

Junior sits up and puts a hand on Sugar. "She's just hungry. She doesn't mean—"

But Sugar cuts him off and looks directly at Books. "I absolutely mean it."

King drops three empty water bottles in front of me and they clank on the ground. Empty like my energy levels. Empty like my will to live.

"Let's go." He holds four more in his hand. "Grab yours too. It's probably empty."

It is. Almost.

We walk through the brush and the quiet hum from the river grows louder and louder until it's almost consuming. Sun reflects off the surface as it moves downstream and even the trees here can't seem to provide anything with shade. King doesn't even pause as he wades into it from the shallow bank with his boots on. I make a face at him, but he looks down at my shoes, which still appear brand new. Despite my hike into hell.

"Those are waterproof." He says it with such confidence that I don't ask how he knows. Maybe he has a friend with these same ones. Or a girlfriend.

I don't say anything as I step in after him and we lean down together, filling up the plastic Nalgene bottles. I rub at my ankle, wishing I could take my boots off, but knowing it will just hurt worse when I have to put them back on.

"How're your feet?" King asks.

"They hurt." My words are plain but it feels like they're more.

"Books has some salve. Put it on tonight before you go to bed and then put on your socks."

"Sounds gross." I make a face but I'm grateful for the advice and there's a small part of me that hates that I feel that way. I don't want to like King.

The corner of his mouth lifts and he nods like he agrees with me. "It is, but it's better than the blisters."

The almost-smile doesn't fade from his face as he caps one bottle and grabs another.

I'm staring.

I know I am, but the small expression has transformed his entire face. My stomach flips gently and I remind my traitorous feelings that King is our enemy. King doesn't help with tents and he takes our cigarettes and he smiles like sunshine—fuck.

Apparently *Maps* is just as stupid as Atlas when it comes to hot guys.

I pull the bottle out of the water and hold it out for King. He takes a dropper from his pocket and "cleans" it.

"So, how come you're here?" I ask as I tilt a water bottle back and forth.

King takes a deep breath and does the same. "Same as everyone else. I'm volunteering."

"But why?" I press. I know what he's going to say. Internship. But I want to hear him say it.

He looks at me and asks, "Why are *you* here?"

"We aren't supposed to talk about that, right?"

His head tilts. "We aren't?"

"Isn't that part of the whole thing here? Nicknames and no pasts?"

He nods, gently. "Then why did you ask *me*?"

I bite down on my bottom lip and look up at him. "I wondered if you would tell me your secret." Am I flirting? God, what is wrong with me?

But King smiles. "You tell me first."

I could tell him about Joe and my mom and my dead dad and

59

how badly I fucked up everything at home. He's a stranger and after this trail I will never see him again. Never ever.

"Looks good for college." *Coward.*

"College? Hasn't everyone already applied?"

"Yeah, but if I want to get into a sorority or . . ." I don't actually know what I'm talking about and I wonder if King is the kind of guy who knows how people get into sororities. "My dad is really pushing me to go to college. He thinks this is a good idea."

The bottle in King's hand stops and he picks up another. "Yeah?"

"Yeah, he's pretty strict. But I just, you know, wanna do what I want to do."

"And what's that?"

I want to see my dad again. I want closure. I want to do the things on his list because he didn't get the chance to. "I don't know. Backpack in Europe?" That's what normal, well-adjusted kids say. Right? "He said if I complete this program I can go."

"Go?"

"On a trip." Close to the truth. "My mom and dad think I need some discipline."

King nods.

"Your turn," I tell him.

He looks at me and leans forward. "If I tell you my secret, will you keep it?"

"Yeah." I take a breath.

His eyes look sincere when they meet mine. "I'm also trying to get into a sorority."

I lean back and press my lips into a thin line. "Okay, asshole. I told you my shit."

"Did you?" he asks.

I think back over all the things I said to him and know there was nothing for him to not believe. I don't know if we're telling stories or lying to each other. I can't decide which would be better.

"I'll tell you the truth when you tell me." King takes his bottles and stands. I watch his back as he leaves and wonder how he knew that my words were a lie. Did Joe tell him about me?

No. Joe wouldn't do that.

We all do our assigned tasks. I struggle with the tents. Sugar starts on dinner with King's help. Books and Junior make a fire. There is a full thirty seconds where Junior just watches Books blow on the flames before he realizes he's staring.

It takes me longer than it should, but I finally get the tent mostly up. I'm improving, not that anyone cares. Not that I care, really. But I take the moment to breathe in and out, inside the tent. The cuts on my wrists where my gloves stop feel sore and I run a finger over them.

A second later, Sugar yells that dinner is done. We all gather and eat warm beans and rice. Sugar even shares some of her hot sauce with us. After we're done, Books hands me two brick-red pills. Painkillers.

"Here you go, Homecoming Queen," Books tells me. "Watch your feet or you won't be dancing anymore."

I nod and swallow the pills. Swallow the lies.

Swallow down the girl I am and try to replace her with the girl I wish I was.

9

THE RHYTHM OF THE trail begins to embed itself into my expectations, and as the days pass each of us come to learn our place in the group. Who does what, when, how. All of us keeping our tasks separate. Never touching. Like food on a plate.

And we form things that take the shape of the word "always."

Taking a tent down is *always* easier than putting it up. Firewood is *always* heavier than I think it is. Sugar *always* hands us our breakfast. Junior *always* washes up. Books *always* has the first aid kit. And King *always* has a comment.

If you fold it like that, it will get a crease.

You're gonna bust a tent pole if you keep pushing them in like that.

You need to wear pants. You'll get poison oak.

I tell myself repeatedly not to let his words irritate me. I remind myself that his personality makes him at least 60 percent less hot.

But I am an idiot and I have the brain of a lizard.

One day, after King makes a comment about holding the shovel wrong, I stupidly ask him how I'm supposed to hold it and he comes over to show me.

His hands wrap around mine, and his body isn't pressed *against* me, but close enough that I can feel the heat from it. King's breath is warm on my neck and—

"Got it." I pull my hands away from his and flex them against the shovel. A blush is probably covering my face right now and I hope everyone will just assume it's from the heat.

When I look up, King's gone back to the place he's been working. There's no flush to his skin.

At lunch we sit against a rock eating and drinking in silence.

King bends his head toward Books telling him something and Books shakes his head. They almost look like two guys just talking, except they're filthy.

And then they laugh.

King with his head down and broad shoulders hunched over. And Books, his opposite, with dark hair falling in his eyes. Head back and long throat exposed.

Watching them laugh cracks something open in my chest and I can feel myself bleeding. It makes me miss *easy* things. I could go sit down with them, ask what they're laughing at. But I don't and Sugar does. I watch them welcome her because Sugar is water, flowing and forceful. She goes where she wants. But me? I'm sharp rocks that haven't been softened by time. I'm still fractured and exposed and I don't know how to be water.

Laughing is for people who feel like they have most of the pieces of themselves. Not for girls who can't remember the last time they heard their dad laugh.

I'm being tragic and it's annoying even to me, but I can't seem to push out of the dark and stormy mood I'm in.

We walk. Next to the river. Through fields. Against rocks.

Junior hums a song under his breath until Books stops abruptly and turns to him. With a single look, he says, "Stop."

Junior rolls his eyes. "My vocal cords will atrophy if I don't use them."

But the day wears on in the same way. Silence punctuated by labor intensive work.

I've lost count of how long we've been out here. One hundred days? Two? At the river, the water has opened wide and looks calm, almost like a pool. We're only supposed to be rinsing off and refilling our bottles but it's Junior who says, "King, please let us swim and wash the trail off."

He looks at us with greasy hair and dusty clothes and mottled skin from the dirt mixing with sweat. "Did Joe go over river safety with you?"

I hear myself mumble, "It's just water."

King clenches his jaw. "*Just water.*"

"It's fine," Books continues. "We can stay in the shallow part."

King frowns as he looks to where it bends and disappears. I've noticed King making decisions like this, always searching for the thing that could go wrong. Weighing and measuring everything. "Fine. But *no* floating down it."

Junior and Books both glance at each other with grins. They pull off their boots and then they're gone. The two of them run into the water and as soon as it hits their knees Junior dives for Books and they fall into it with their hiking clothes still on.

Then Books is out of the water and moving fast. He grabs King and drags him into the water. King laughs as he's pulled under. I watch the chaos as I strip off my boots and socks. I'm shimmying out of my shorts when King approaches me. I keep my eyes on his face as he shakes the water from his hair with a hand. Blond strands fling beads in every direction and catch the light.

His chest moves up and down as a smile still ghosts over his face. "Do you know how to swim in the river?" His eyes dance when he asks it.

I've been going to the river my whole life. I've spent so many years listening to my mother yell about not going too far out, or her worry of the undercurrent, or not drinking the water, and being here now I realize how much I haven't bothered to learn about it. How much I relied on someone else to do all the basic things that everyone else seems to know.

"I've swam before."

He looks like he doesn't believe me, so he stands in my path, explaining the river, how she must be respected, and I try not to focus on his lips and the water shining on them or that he's standing close to me. My mind seems to have forgotten that he's my trail lead and this is literally his responsibility as he tells me about the strength of the current and that I need to be able to see someone at all times. "Got it?"

I nod but decide to ask, "How old are you?"

"Twenty." He answers like a reflex and it looks like it surprises him too.

"You are way too young to be this worried about everything." A little laugh rides on the end of it because I want him to know I'm joking.

His brows push together. "I take it seriously. And I don't really care if you think that's funny."

"I'm not laughing at you." I am. Like an asshole. "It's just—it's okay to relax sometimes. Even enjoy yourself."

He shakes his head and it feels like he's a little disappointed in me. I hate it. "You can grab your soap and clean up if you want to."

King goes to his pack and fishes his bar out and I do the same. He pulls off his shirt and hangs it over a boulder. I wade into the water, barefoot. The rocks are smooth under my feet and the sand feels silty. Cold water stings at the blisters and scrapes on my body, but it's worth it to wash away the dirt. When it hits my waist, I suck in from the freezing feeling and I realize how ridiculous I'm being. I pull off my shirt and dunk it in the water before taking the bar of soap to it. A second later, Sugar is doing the same thing. I purposely don't look at King as I do it. Or Books. Junior catches my eye as he floats on his back and gives me a smug look.

He's shirtless too. "I bet you're glad you wore a black bra."

I look down at my black sports bra before looking at Sugar's beige one and try not to smile. I can see the rings of sweat on hers.

She groans. "I should burn it in the fire tonight and just wear my other bra. It's not like anyone here cares what my boobs look like anyway."

"I care," I tell her as I dunk my head underwater and take the soap to my hair.

"God this feels nice," Sugar says mostly to the air above her.

I'm not even sure this is doing anything, but it doesn't matter. My standard for clean seems to have shifted.

When we're all washed, I throw my shirt onto the shore and

float on my back, feeling weightless. The water around my arms and legs is warm, but the water underneath my body feels cool and fresh.

I close my eyes against the bright blue sky and keep my ears under the water, listening to all of it move around me.

The water reminds me of my dad. It was his favorite place. The stillness inside the constant movement. The way it collects and carries everything. How it brings you things. Like gifts and life and truths.

In here I feel little pieces of my father's memory being whispered to me. I see his hands casting his fishing pole. The way his fingers would move over rocks in the shallow part of the water, watching the color dance in the light. Him patiently watching me throw hundreds of stones into the water trying to learn how to skip them. Tears collect in my eyes and I let them. I decide that it's all right to do that in this place. No one out here will know that I miss my dad. That I hear his voice in the current or feel him in the sunlight on my skin.

When I open my eyes, I stand up and feel a little lightheaded from floating. I look at the boy next to me. King.

The water hits his stomach and I force my eyes up his darkened body to his face that blocks out the sun. We look at each other and I see something the river has brought to me.

A gift?

I stand and pull my body from the water. "What happened to Sugar?"

He clears his throat. "She wanted to dry off . . . and you can't be out here alone."

I turn from the shore and look out toward the bend, but when I do, I trip and start to fall back in the water. King reaches out his hand on my arm to steady me and I fall into his space.

I spend less than a breath of time close to him with my shoulder against the skin of his chest. Looking up into his eyes. When I right myself, he's still holding my arm.

"These rocks," I grumble and run my feet over the bottom of the river like he can see it. "I rolled my ankle a lot when I was younger."

My lips press together as King stares back at me and I wonder if he'll realize I've just told him something true.

He drops his arm and takes a breath. "Did you spend a lot of time here?"

"Yeah. And no." This river is constantly changing. "The river is the same and never the same, all the time."

It was something my dad said, and I wait for King to tease me about it. It's unfair that I've given him something precious and he doesn't even realize. But he just stays silent.

"The river was my dad's thing." I can't swallow the words that are choking me. I don't talk about my dad. I don't know how to explain that this place feels so personal and so foreign to me all at the same time.

"Wanna talk about it?" King asks.

"About what?" But I know what he's asking.

"So, no." It doesn't sound like a judgment or like he's pressing me for something else. It just is. Like most things with King.

"Do *you* want to talk?" I ask.

He smiles when he hands my own words back to me. "About what?"

"Anything. Your life. Why you take all this so seriously." I have a thousand questions, but I pretend like this is just something to fill the silence.

He shifts. "Twenty questions again?"

"Nothing else to do," I tell him. "Lie to me. I won't know, anyway." I want to hear him talk. I'm not sure why the idea of him lying pulls at something inside my heart. "You have family?"

He drops his arms and runs his hands over the top of the water. When he looks up to the sky, his neck's exposed and his broad shoulders fall back, pushing his chest out. I have the urge to crawl up him and drag my mouth against his skin.

I can feel my face growing warm and I'm glad he can't read my thoughts.

He swallows. "I've got a brother. And a little sister who I don't—who my parents won't let me talk to. When they kicked me out, they said they would kick her out too if she spoke to me."

"What's she like? Your sister?"

King looks at me for a long beat. Eventually he says, "She's horrible. Leaves the lid to the peanut butter almost on, so when you pick it up, it falls. Listens to country music and bends the cover of paperback books all the way around. Fucking maniac." He smiles and I'm surprised at what a good liar he is. And a small part of me hopes he isn't.

"When was the last time you talked to her?"

"When I left."

"Why'd you get kicked out?"

He shakes his head once. "Same reason most people do. A series of poor decisions that my family decided were unforgivable."

69

"Give me an example."

He raises his eyebrows. "I smoked cigarettes."

My throat tightens. "Those weren't my cigarettes," I tell him again. My mouth opens and I'm going to tell him about my dad. About the pack I found and the secret that's just for him and me, but . . . "Is that why you're here?" I ask. "Cigarettes?"

"I'm here because this program saved my life and I owe Joe everything."

This is true. Even if the sister and family is a lie, I know *this* is true.

"And that's why you take this so seriously? Because of Joe?"

"Because Joe takes me seriously." And then he adds, "Because I'm hoping that this summer will give me enough experience so I can do an internship at a conservation."

His profile still looks downstream, staring at the water moving over rocks and rapids. I stay quiet because I'm hoping King will give me something else. Another truth.

"Joe is the person who'll recommend me for the job. If I do well."

"So, this summer is like your audition?"

He smiles at the word. "Something like that."

"And this internship is your passion? Your life's mission?"

His hand reaches into the water and scoops it up before it falls. "My dad worked construction his whole life and then one day he got hurt. But there wasn't anything else he could do. I don't want to do that."

"So the internship is like, your plan for the future." *Future* seems like such a big thing for someone who is only twenty.

"It's weird watching someone's whole life fall apart because life has only given them one skill and they have no idea how to learn something else. I'm supposed to leave for Alaska right after the hike. If everything goes well."

"Alaska." I pull out the word like a cotton ball. I examine each consonant for the thing that makes me dislike the word so much, until I realize what it is. "It's so *far*."

"Yeah," he says. "Kinda the point. What do you want to do after this?"

It's a straightforward and stupid question. What do *I* want to do?

What do I want to do . . .

Since my father died, I stopped talking about the future, as if all my dreams died when he stopped breathing. It's been about managing the chaos I've left in my wake since my father got sick. You don't do futures when your present is absolutely fucked.

What do I want to do?

"I don't know," I tell him. "College, I guess." It's something Maps would tell people she wants to do.

But Atlas wants to finish this hike. Atlas thinks about her dad's list full of dreams and wishes he never got to do. Atlas wants to finish his list and say goodbye to her dad once and for all.

It's such a weird thing to realize. With it in my back pocket. On this trail. When I'm pretending to be someone else.

King studies my face and I feel like he's seeing something more than just how confused I am. And then he says, "I thought we weren't supposed to be telling the truth."

10

"FUCK!"

The word seems to crack on the air as it breaks the silence. It sends panic between each one of my ribs as I wait for—

"*Fuck. Fuck. Fuck.*" Books's voice rings out from the trees that he and Junior disappeared into looking for firewood.

I look at King and Sugar, who stand by the fire. It only takes us a second to assume the worst. The three of us are running toward the sounds, our feet rushing over the uneven terrain of bramble and logs and sticks and rocks.

When we find them, Books isn't wearing a shirt because it's wrapped over Junior's arm. Blood seems to be everywhere. Junior has a scrape on his head and a rip through the knee of his pants.

"What happened?" King asks.

"I don't know," Books answers with clipped words.

"Is he okay?" Sugar presses.

"I don't know—"

"Is he hurt anywhere else?" she interrupts.

"I'm right here!" Junior practically roars. "*Fuck*."

King is on the other side of Junior a moment later. I feel helpless, not sure what to do with myself. And then my mind becomes clear. I run back to camp, find Books's pack, and grab the first aid kit. By the time I've got it, they've all made it back to camp.

I hold it out to Books, who nods at me. And then he's unraveling the shirt. Blood flows down Junior's arm all at once. Shit.

"How did this happen?" King says, grabbing the fabric back from Books and reapplying pressure.

"He fell down the hill."

"But like a man." Junior winces. "I fell like a man."

King laughs. "Do I even want to know why you fell?"

"I wasn't paying attention to where I was going," Junior replies. The words feel like they should be true, but something about the way he speaks sounds a little like a lie.

King takes the shirt from Junior's arm once more, and the bleeding seems to have slowed.

Books's face is pinched as he examines the jagged cut.

"Is it that bad?" Junior asks.

It's an odd moment of vulnerability from him, and Books looks like he's unsure of what exactly is happening.

King clears his throat and walks over to Books's pack. He fishes out a T-shirt that he tosses to him. Books pulls it over his head in a fluid motion.

He looks at the wound carefully with his head bent into Junior's space. I can't tell if the pain on his face is from the cut or from Books being so close. But Books's fingers are light and gentle as he rotates Junior's hand back and forth and presses on it. "Does this hurt?"

"Yes," Junior says through his teeth.

"It's mostly a shallow cut and some scrapes. You're lucky." But when he says it, it doesn't seem like he believes it.

"Does he need to go back down the trail to see a doctor?" King asks.

Books shakes his head and reaches for the antiseptic. "I don't think he needs stitches. Might have a scar though."

"Girls like scars," Sugar tells Junior, trying to be helpful.

I wonder if boys in anime tees like scars.

"Sorry," Books says as he positions the bottle. "This . . . isn't gonna feel good."

"It's fine. Falling didn't feel great either." Junior winces as the liquid hits his cut. "Fuuuuuuuuck."

Then Books is struggling with the gauze against Junior's skin.

"Here." Sugar seems to know what she's supposed to do without being told. She takes a cotton pad and places it on the wound before starting to wrap it. Her fingers press it to Junior's arm gently, and then she asks if he can move his hands. He nods. She asks if the wrap is too tight but he shakes his head.

"I'll go look for wood," King tells us. "Maps, finish the tents, and Sugar . . ." He gestures to Books and Junior. "Make sure they don't die getting cleaned up at the river."

Her face contorts. "Why do I have the hard job?"

The hard job is putting up the stupid tents. By the time King's back with wood and Sugar's already started dinner, the blue one is up. I try not to feel victorious, even if it's unwarranted and I

74

still have a red monster to assemble. The red tent is laid out and I want to cry thinking about putting it up.

But Sugar calls dinner, and we eat. Junior complains about being sleepy and asks me and Sugar to help him get undressed and into his bag.

"Don't want Books to help you?" she whispers, and all three of us look over to the tree line where King and Books are standing.

King is gesturing wildly, talking about something, and Books is shaking his head.

"King's probably complaining about his internship and how my injury has ruined everything, so, no. Sharing a tent with them is like a medieval torture test where I'm constantly annoyed and also a little turned on."

"Weird," I say.

"Yeah," Sugar tells us with thick sarcasm. "A real sacrifice sleeping in the same tent with the hot guys." She looks at Junior. "How hard did you hit your head?"

"You have no idea how hard my life is. King goes to bed without a shirt and Books mumbles in his sleep. I spend the whole night terrified I'm gonna burp or fart or be gross and never know it because I'm passed out."

Sugar gives him an unbelieving look. "But if you don't know—"

His voice is a stage whisper. "But *they* would know. *They* would."

I look over at Junior, with his defined jaw and his darkened skin that makes his eyes shine. "I feel like a hot guy with so many piercings shouldn't be worried about that."

"Hot, huh?" He gives me a lopsided smile with his perfect lips. "You're not my type."

There's no malice in his words. "Yeah, I know. Your type is wearing a One Piece shirt."

We all grow quiet as we stare out at King and Books. And finally Junior asks, "But are hot piercings *his* type? That's the real question."

"I don't recommend thinking too hard about that question," Sugar tells him.

"Thinking about what?" he asks.

Sugar turns to Junior with a serious expression. "If someone tells Joe, you're off the trail."

"For thinking about hot guys?"

"For hooking up. Last year ten people were sent home from different trails."

I give her a skeptical look. "For kissing?"

"Fraternization. It was in the contract we all signed."

I almost roll my eyes. "But do people take it seriously?"

She lifts a shoulder. "Joe does."

Junior's eyes light up. "But Joe isn't here."

I give her a smile. "Joe *isn't* here."

She pushes at Junior and me, but he winces, and I can tell she feels bad.

Inside the tent we help Junior out of his shirt and into another one and then settle him into his bag. While I'm making sure his arm is elevated, Sugar makes a face and shifts.

A second later she's holding up a bottle of brown liquid.

"What is . . ." Junior starts.

"Oh my god, it's whiskey!" Sugar practically yells.

A moment later Books bursts into the tent and is pulling it from Sugar's hands. "I found this!"

The bottle *does* look like it's been out in the elements, dirty and dusty. The label is peeling and faded.

"Why is it under your sleeping bag and not . . . inside your pack?" Sugar asks.

"I was going to throw it away," Books tells us. He looks to King for help, but King only shakes his head as he inches his way into the tent.

"Why would you throw it away?" I ask.

"Because . . ." But it takes Books too long to remember why. "No alcohol on the trail."

"Right," Sugar tells him seriously.

"I—I don't want to make everything about me, but I've had a bad day." Junior's face is serious as he looks at Books. "I could use that. For medicinal purposes."

Sugar can't keep the shock off her face. "You're going to drink whiskey you found in the woods?"

Junior shrugs. "It's sealed." And then he looks at me. "And Joe isn't here."

"Who knows how old your forest whiskey is. What if it's bad or whatever?" Sugar looks at me for help.

"You mean like *fermented*?" Books's question isn't a question. He's pointing out the obvious. "And turned to *alcohol*?"

King's arms are folded over his chest and he still hasn't said anything. Books looks at him, waiting for some kind of permission because we all seem to be at an impasse. We know we're not allowed to have this. But.

But.

"I have a solution," Junior says. "If we drink it, then it's *gone*, and then there will be no alcohol on the trail." He makes a poof sound with his cheeks, like he's suggested magic.

"Such a problem solver." I nod seriously.

He pats my leg with his good arm. "I've always been one."

"I hate you all," Sugar tells us.

"Well, no forest whiskey for you then," Junior says, taking the bottle and cracking the twist-off seal. We all watch as he takes a swig and makes a face. "Yeah, tastes like whiskey." He coughs after he says it, but Sugar is already taking the bottle from him.

"What?" I yell at Sugar. "Two seconds ago you were like *contracts* and *I hate you all*. But now . . ."

"Junior's right. If it's gone, it's not on the trail. And you can't tell me that Green didn't pack alcohol and I know Yellow probably has edibles marked down as essential items."

But we aren't Green or Yellow. We're Blue. And we have King.

Books looks to him for some kind of response but he only shrugs. "It's already done."

And that's all the permission we need.

We don't drink a lot, just enough that the places we normally keep fences seem to blur and bleed together in the small space. We settle and become a tangle of limbs and legs. Sugar leans against Junior, whose legs are pressed against Books. Books is crowding over into my space. My feet are under King. He adjusts them and ends up inclining his head toward my lap while his legs are behind Sugar. We are a human version of a Celtic knot.

The alcohol keeps us from acknowledging how we're lying

with the heat of our skin against each other or how it's the closest that most of us have ever been.

I don't know who brings it up, maybe Sugar, maybe because we all realize that we're breaking a rule and this could get us sent home, but she starts talking about why she's here. "I just needed to get away." Her hands gesture to the top of the tent. "See the sky. The stars. The . . . I just wanted to breathe."

"So this isn't mandatory community service?" I ask. "You volunteered for this?"

"Did you?" King asks. His eyes are on mine.

"Community service isn't always court ordered, you hooligan." Sugar fiddles with the zipper on the sleeping bag under her. Back and forth. Back and forth. "Some of us volunteer because it's our civic responsibility."

"And the sky," Junior reminds her.

"Obviously the sky."

Junior tips his head back. "I'm here because I'm trying to join Greenpeace and save the whales."

"I've been volunteering because I plan on running for president," Books adds, playing the game.

"There has to be an easier way to earn public office," I tell him.

We all look at King. "Internship."

We wait for something more, a joke or something sarcastic.

"On a space station?" Sugar asks. She's asking more than just a silly question. She's asking him to play with us. I can see him thinking, calculating the cost. I wonder if everyone can read King so easily.

79

And then he says, "How do you know about that? Are you applying for the same one?"

I don't know why, but this makes all of us laugh. The kind of belly laugh that has you falling over onto the person next to you. What he said wasn't funny. It was barely silly, but King's eyes find mine and my blood feels electric in my veins.

"So it looks like you're the only one with mandatory community service." Sugar nudges me with her foot. "Did you murder someone? Rob a liquor store?"

"Smuggled a truck full of heroin across the US/Canada border?" Books guesses.

Junior makes a noise. "She broke into a lab and let all the animals out."

"Why is my thing a crime?"

"You have criminal energy," Sugar tells me.

I can feel King looking at me.

"My parents went to Europe for the summer and I didn't want to wander around Italy with them."

"You expect us to believe that you didn't want to go to Europe with your family?"

"My parents are . . ." I make an explosion sound. "My mom nags and my dad is . . . a dad. All facts about old buildings and . . . you know. I just wanted to do something by myself before college."

"College. Of course," Junior says. "You're probably going to a fancy private school."

"And joining a sorority," Books says.

"How can I have criminal energy *and* sorority energy?"

"You obviously don't know any sorority girls," Sugar says.

"So, Maps is a college girl going to a fancy private school and entering the Greek cults after the trail," Junior says. "What about you, Sugar?"

"Gap year."

Junior laughs. "Only rich kids take gap years."

"That's not true!" Sugar exclaims.

Books shakes his head. "Poor kids don't say gap year. They say, *working*."

"And what are *you* doing?" Sugar asks.

"*Working!*" Books laughs.

I'm not going to college. I didn't even graduate from high school, but somehow I've let these people believe I'm the furthest thing from what I really am. An ache settles in my chest and I excuse myself to go to the bathroom.

"Make sure the fire is out," King tells me.

Outside the tent, I see the red one is still laying flat on the ground and the fire has now died. I head out to the woods to pee and marvel at how I've become an expert at the squat. When I get back I find my place on the sleeping bags.

We laugh until our eyes are heavy and Junior tells me and Sugar to stay. Books and King share a look before Books nods. I lean back and my fingers land on the spot where King's are. It's almost as if we're holding hands, and I can't tell if it's the alcohol burning through me or being close to King, but I notice everything.

The way he leans a centimeter closer into my space. The way he lifts his hand, just to put it back in the same place next to mine. The way his eyes move to my mouth when I speak.

When we finally lie down and give in to the sleep that has been hunting us, we look like sardines in a tin. Our bodies crowded in the space, and the distance we normally give each other is gone. Junior is sandwiched between Sugar and Books. Books and King have their backs to each other, and I'm between King and the wall.

Our breathing, in and out, feels heavy and comforting.

I try not to stare at the way the moonlight carves over King. The light breaks against his cheekbones and the stubble on his face makes me want to reach out and touch it. I want to run my fingers against the places that shadow and light blend together. But I don't do any of that, because this King is only for this moment.

I match my breath with his as our chests rise and fall at the same time. It feels intimate. It feels like something I can use to pretend. Maps is the kind of girl who gets to lie down next to cute boys. Maps might even be the kind of girl who can kiss boys like King.

But Atlas is still here, and the shards of her poke through the pretend.

Because when I wake up, I know this moment will be gone.

11

EVERY BIRD IN CALIFORNIA is right outside our tent.

They chirp and flutter while insects buzz and something rustles in the brush. I can't tell if it's my head, or if the noise is actually louder than normal. Only one of my eyes opens to the bright light filtering through the vinyl walls of the tent.

Everything is shaded in blue, someone snores softly . . .

And King.

His face is relaxed and the line between his brows is gone. He shifts, still asleep, and moves closer to me.

I can almost imagine him reaching out. Which, now in the morning light, is a ridiculous thought. I take a breath. And another.

But something about this moment unfurls the tension I carry. The way he looks calm and quiet here makes me think I can be those things too. My heart can be those things.

King stirs and I tell myself to look away, but I don't. His eyes open and he stares up at the tent and blinks twice before slowly they move over to me.

"Hey," I say, almost a whisper.

He stares at me and I wonder if his thoughts are still tangled in the memories of last night. We stay like that, our gazes focused on each other until King breaks the moment and looks around the tent. Everyone else is still asleep.

And then he smiles. King presses his index finger to his lips, telling me to be quiet before he sits up and stretches his hands over his head. The T-shirt he wears rides up and I can see the place where his back dimples right above the waistband of his shorts.

He unzips the tent and Books stirs slightly as King steps outside.

I let out a deep breath and look up at the ceiling trying to keep my heart from beating out of my chest.

But it only lasts a moment because I hear rustling. It's aggressive and a bit frantic. Even from inside I know it's wrong. Something's upset King, I just can't imagine what until I hear him say, "What the fuck?"

The zipper on the tent that was never fully closed is yanked open and King stands on the other side, furious. "What the *fuck*, Maps?"

My head pounds as I realize that I need water. I sit up and my stomach roils. "What?"

He breaths out his nose, heavy. "The *fire*."

I can't seem to understand what he's talking about, and everyone else is up now all looking back and forth between me and King.

"Get up. Now." It's an order.

"King." Books's voice is ragged from sleep. "What are you talking about?"

But I'm getting up and so is everyone else.

As we file out of the tent, I see what King sees. An abandoned tent flat on the ground. Granola bars and food wrappers scattered across the ground next to dirty pans. And our packs pulled apart by something in the night. But he's just as responsible for this as I am. I look at him, ready to tell him as much, until . . .

King kicks at the charred remains of the fire. When his boot pulls away, I see the red embers still alight.

Next to me Books closes his eyes tightly.

Fuck.

"You said the fire was out," King says.

"It was."

. . . It was.

"Really?" King challenges.

"There were no flames, no smoke—"

"Maps." It's Junior who stops me.

But I don't listen. "It was out. The fire was out."

"Obviously it wasn't, Maps." He circles the stones looking down. "You could have burned down the whole fucking forest."

None of us speak. I wait for someone to defend me. Someone to tell King, to tell me, I didn't fuck up. That this was an honest mistake.

Finally Sugar says, "But she didn't."

"Don't," King says, holding up a hand. "Don't try to defend her when half our granola bars are scattered all over this camp because *you* didn't put your pack away."

"You don't get to talk to me like that because you're worried that Joe might be mad at you and say you can't go to Alaska!" Sugar yells back.

King's eyes darken as he takes a step away from us. "This isn't about me!"

"Yes it is! You're the leader!"

"Whoa." Books stands in between Sugar and King.

"Who forgot to wash out the pans from dinner?" King asks her.

"Junior got hurt!" Sugar's voice becomes incredulous. "Why are you acting like you weren't there flirting with fucking Maps the whole time?"

It's a grenade tossed into the air. King looks at me. Books looks at me. Junior looks at me.

I didn't mean to leave the fire burning and I know I should say sorry. Diffuse this bomb that I seem to have at my feet. But instead I yell.

"Fuck you, Sugar!"

"Hey!" Books stands with his arms out as if we are all seconds from lunging at each other, and maybe we are. "This is ridiculous. You're making me be the voice of reason and I do not want to be the voice of reason. Sugar, Junior, and Maps, clean this shit up and make sure the fire is *out*. King, come with me."

And, surprisingly, we do. I'm pouring water onto the embers that sizzle and Sugar and Junior start collecting wrappers.

Books reaches out and grabs Junior's arm gently. "How is it?" Books turns the bandage over as if he can see through the gauze.

"It's . . ." Junior seems to realize how close they are standing and he takes a step backward and clears his throat, but he doesn't move his arm from Books's grip. "It doesn't hurt."

Books nods and runs his thumb over the bandage before dropping it. "Go slow today."

Junior gives him a salute and then goes back to collecting trash, but I see his hands shake.

Once we've picked up the camp and put away the tents, we head farther down the trail in the quiet and strain. We work and then at lunch we stop under a tree.

The noon light pokes through the tree branches above me. I close my eyes and see my dad sitting under the tree in our backyard. He would do the same thing, sometimes—close his eyes and end up somewhere else. Watching a flock of birds take off and paint the sky with their wings as sunlight peaked through the sky.

I bite at my lip and think about my dad saying, *Watching something leave feels like a gift.* He was talking about the birds, and the same tightness is back in my chest. Right above *Hiking the trail with Atlas* on my dad's list is *Watch the birds migrate south.*

He'd told the story of proposing to my mother at dusk on a tiny island off the coast of Florida. And as the birds migrated south for the winter, my father got down on one knee and asked her for forever.

Forever turns out to not be very long.

I don't even know what day it is. I don't know if we're making good time or taking too long or—

This is why I hate the silence. My stomach is like those branches. Tangled and knotted from my own thoughts.

We hike and work. I can't tell if we're working harder because we're angry, or if it just feels harder because we feel like shit. King hasn't spoken to me since he wandered off into the woods with Books and came back frowning. It's such a contrast to the person I woke up next to this morning.

As soon as I can talk to King alone, I do.

"Hey." He's in front of me and I watch his feet falter a step when I say it. When he doesn't answer, I just continue, "I know you're mad at me."

More silence.

"I'm really sorry, King. I swear."

One. Two. Three. Ten steps.

"I didn't know the fire wasn't out. I know the internship is important to you and I feel . . . if we need to tell Joe—"

He turns around and puts a hand on my arm, stopping me at the back of the line so the others keep walking. "Don't say anything about it to Joe. You'll just make it worse."

He takes three steps.

"Because . . . because Sugar was right. I should have checked."

"It was an accident."

His jaw ticks. "It wasn't. I'm in charge of the fire and I asked you to check after . . ."

"So you're saying I can't be trusted with fire?"

"I'm saying I can't be trusted."

My heart speeds up when he meets my eyes. "With fire?"

His chest rises and falls, and I feel the way the seconds pull around us. "With you."

The air feels heavy and buzzes, or maybe that's in my blood. "What does that mean?"

But King is back on the trail, walking, and not looking back to me.

Not paying attention.

The next section of the trail is overgrown with plants and bushes and debris. The river has been cutting into the side of the site and at least three of the trees have suspicious-looking branches hanging down. We work all day to make sure the trees that are still standing won't fall on us when we make camp. It's silent and mind-numbing.

The next day is the same.

My head hurts.

Not in a way that makes me feel sick or unable to hike. In the annoying way where everything is a little too bright and the ground a little too close to my feet. We all seem to feel it more than normal. Our guards are down and tempers are shorter.

Junior goes slower because of his arm, and I try not to think about what King said.

I'm saying I can't be trusted.

With you.

We're clearing a felled log, hauling it off the trail and taking out a spring pole. It's tedious and dangerous and makes the heat feel even hotter. I sit on the ground, my body aching. Books tells me to pace myself because he doesn't want to listen to Sugar complain that she has to do everything.

No one is talking about what happened with the fire. Sugar doesn't speak to King and pouts when asked to do anything. Junior makes sure his pack is always put away and Books still looks nervous all the time and is always asking Junior about his arm. As if an argument will break out at any moment. And I . . .

I am not paying attention to King.

Not thinking about his words.

King and Books are dealing with overhead branches that could become fall hazards. Junior and Sugar are moving blow-downs, and I'm digging out plants that have grown onto the side of the trail. It's still quiet, but it's embedded itself into our psyche now.

That's why I don't recognize the sound of boots on the dirt.

Or the low breath that someone lets out.

It's not till I hear someone speak that I look up.

"What the hell is this?" A girl with dark hair in braids stands in front of a group of people all staring at us.

I'm not sure what I'm supposed to do, so I go still, like I've been caught doing something wrong and if I'm still for long enough I will disappear into the background.

"Can we help you?" Books asks as he stands up.

The girl, who I recognize but can't place, only shrugs.

"Probably not, but we heard the audible sound of misery and decided to come check it out."

King smiles at her, something I haven't seen him do in days. "Does Yellow wanna help with that?"

She shakes her head vigorously and makes a face. "Absolutely not. But I would take a hug from the trail leads of Blue."

"Yellow?" Sugar asks.

But the rest of us are looking at Books and King, who are smiling at each other.

And then Books says, "Good to see you, Pidgeon."

12

YELLOW HAS SEVEN HIKERS.

It's only two more than us, but it feels like a hundred. I recognize most of them from before when they wore yellow dots on their name tags and ate frozen pops. It seems like that happened in another life.

Their presence immediately shifts the dynamic of our group.

Pidgeon and Ivy are the trail leads for yellow, and apparently they're King's and Books's best friends. Pidgeon wraps her beautifully sun-kissed arms around him and pulls Books in for a hug.

"Missed you." She squeezes his neck.

"It's been a week." But he smiles into her shoulder as he says it.

"Almost two." She hugs King. "Get up to anything interesting without me?"

I wait for him to tell Pidgeon about the whiskey or the fire. He doesn't. "You remember Junior, Sugar, and Maps?"

Pidgeon looks at me and repeats my name, "Maps."

"Hi." My greeting comes out flat.

"This is Rocky, Stuffy, Willow, Bucket, and Tiger." She

points down a line. Their names are even more ridiculous than ours.

"Yellow's going to camp with us tonight," King tells us. He doesn't smile when he says it, but I can tell he wants to. I hate how jealous that makes me.

We decide who will make the fire and who will help with the cooking. Everyone in Yellow takes turns putting up the tents and when Stuffy sees me struggling with ours she comes over to help me. Her dark hair is pulled into a high bun and she has on a wide fabric headband that covers her ears. "Here," she tells me in a beautifully raspy voice. "The long ones always go this way. And it's easier if you connect these two and stand them up first."

My eyes are wide. "You can just . . . put up a tent? All on your own?"

Her face is wary. "Yeah. Ivy showed me . . ."

I don't cry, but when I hug her, it's with tears in my eyes.

During dinner, King and Books sit with Ivy and Pidgeon. They laugh and Ivy tells the kinds of stories that require hand gestures and reactions from the audience. An ache settles in my chest that I recognize as envy. But I don't know if it's because of King or because everything about the four of them is easy and I can't remember the last time I had friends who were that way.

The three of us are sitting off to the side when Stuffy plops down right between me and Sugar. "Hi." She smiles at Sugar, who looks confused by her sudden appearance. "So, you guys don't have any more vodka?" Her eyes dance when she asks, and I decide I like Stuffy.

"I don't know what you're talking about," Sugar says, and there's a little pride in her voice. "But if I did I would tell you that it wasn't vodka. It was whiskey."

Rocky sits down next to me with an enormous stack of playing cards in his hands. "You know how to play Bullshit?"

"Bullshit?" I ask.

"It's all about who can lie the best. Want in?"

"Oh," Stuffy says and turns to Sugar. "You'll love this game."

"I'm an expert liar," Rocky tells us and then explains the rules. We go in a circle and have to discard at least one card. We discard in order. Ace, one, two, three, etc. "If you don't believe someone, you call bullshit. If they lied, they pick up the whole discard pile; if they told the truth, you do."

We play a round and Junior gets caught lying every time.

"*Bullshit!*" Tiger, a small brown-haired boy, yells. "You do not have *seven* Jacks."

Junior picks up the whole pile. "I am *injured* . . ."

After the first round the trail leads are dealt in. It's weird watching King and Books be casual with other people. It's like they're completely different humans tonight, and I try to not let myself think about how I won't be able to forget it.

I'm down to my second-to-last card and King is on his last. We've let the discard pile grow so when I set down one card and say it's a ten, everyone looks carefully at me. If I'm lying, I have to pick up all those cards.

"She's lying," Junior says.

"Am I?" I bluff. Obviously I'm lying. But Junior's face doesn't look so sure anymore.

"Is she?" Ivy asks Books.

He frowns. "I can't tell."

I can feel King's eyes on me and when I look at him, I wish I hadn't. His gaze is steady and his face passive. "Bullshit." He says it soft but confident.

"Are you sure?" I ask, but the air around me buzzes as he watches me.

"Bullshit," King repeats simply.

Rocky pulls my top card from the deck and reveals the queen of clubs.

The group erupts into cries of injustice. I pick up the entire pile and fan out the cards with a smile, but I don't look at King again. I don't trust myself.

When it gets to King's turn I think about calling bullshit, but I can't seem to say it.

We play three more rounds before Books and Ivy tell us it's time to turn in.

I'm down at the river when Rocky finds me. We wash our faces and arms in the shallow part of the river and we brush our teeth next to each other quietly. King and Pidgeon are only a few feet away talking to each other in hushed voices.

"What's the deal with your team?" Rocky finally asks.

"Deal?"

"The mean blond one keeps giving me dirty looks."

"King?" I smile.

He grins back at me.

"You know his name."

But Rocky just shrugs. "Mean blond one is funnier. What's his deal?"

"That's just his face." I'm still smiling but there's an edge to the way I say it making it clear he can't mock King. I like Rocky, but he's not on the trail with us, he's not Blue. And only Blue can tease Blue.

"You guys have bonded," he surmises. "Yeah, I get it. I wouldn't let anyone tease Ivy or Pidge either."

Him saying it out loud makes all the words feel heavy. I don't want his words to be true because that means the people here are important to me. "He's doing some internship after this if he does well here, so he takes it seriously."

Rocky nods, but it's clear he doesn't really care.

When I'm done, I lean back on the river rocks and watch the sky get darker above us. Stars begin to poke out of the bruised blue. Another reminder of a hundred evenings and thousands of constellations I had looked up at with my dad.

Everything seems to remind me of him now that I'm not distracting myself with a thousand other things. For a second, I wish we could just stay here. On this shore, staring at stars, eating granola bars in the silence.

I know any second King is going to come over and tell me to get up. To stand and go back to our tiny tent and sleep and get up and be exhausted again, but he surprises me by walking over and sitting with us. Pidgeon sits on his other side and no one speaks as we listen to the animals and the river and our breathing.

I point to the Big Dipper and tell everyone, "That one is Orion."

I wait for someone—*King*—to tell me I'm wrong, but I'm answered with silence, so I add, "That one is Capricorn." It's the Little Dipper.

When I turn, the rocks under me shift and make a tinkling noise, but I catch the smile fading from King's face as he says, "We should head back."

I stand and brush off my pants. "You're just mad I know more constellations than you."

He turns on the lantern and looks at me. "You have . . . stuff on your back." His palm is up like he wants to brush it off.

"Oh." I say and turn to let him, but then Rocky is there and doing it. His hands are brisk against my back and the sensation is almost jarring.

"You're good," Rocky says with a thumbs-up when he's done.

I hold up my hand, offering silently to return the favor. He shakes his head.

And when I look up, King is already walking back to the tents.

13

THE NEXT MORNING, JUST before dawn, I'm awoken by the cold.

It shivers against my skin and promises me that I won't find sleep again. So I push out from my sleeping bag and put on the only long-sleeved shirt I have.

Sneaking between the tents so I don't wake anyone up, I walk to the water. The rocks underneath me slide as I try to balance my steps and I marvel at how different the river looks in the promise of light.

When the sun starts to peek over the mountains, I forget about being cold and just stand in awe of the sky. The sun changes everything into pinks and yellows and purples and blues. And.

It makes me miss coffee.

The smell of it. The way the mug would warm my hands. The way my dad would smile down at me on those mornings that he would drag me fishing with him at four a.m.

His soft smile from under his green bucket hat with a fishing license pinned to it and his tattered blue down jacket that smelled like the back of the closet and tobacco and something that was just him.

Coffee.

The sunrise makes me miss *coffee*. I take the feelings about my father and I put them into a lockbox and toss the keys into the bottom of my heart.

To be dealt with later is written on the top.

When I make my way back to the tents, King is sitting on a rock and has his notebook open. He's writing something with his pencil, and I wonder if he does that every morning.

"Hey," I say.

He looks at me with a frown, one I'm growing used to.

"Where were you?" he asks.

"I went to the water." I point behind me as if that will prove something.

Everyone else is still asleep. Yellow hasn't even started to stir in their tents, and maybe that's why I feel brave enough to ask, "Are we good?"

He looks down at the paper, running his fingers against something written there, and presses his lips together. "I'm not really . . . good at this."

"This?"

The pencil in his hand taps at the journal nervously. "I have a hard time with . . . this."

I want to ask if *I* am this, but it feels too presumptuous and I'm worried that he'll say I am not.

He clears his throat. "Yeah, Maps. We're good."

It's what I wanted to hear so I'm not sure why the words feel like thorns against my skin.

I push a smile to my face. "So, friends?"

This time when King studies me it feels like he's deciding something about himself and not me. "How about trail lead and trail . . ."

"Friend?" I offer, still the same big smile that hurts.

"I'm not really interested in friends."

I hate the way he keeps putting distance between us. Each time I step closer to him, he takes two steps backward until there is nothing but a valley. It stings my pride and I wonder if he can see it on my face.

King only sighs. "We need to pack up."

"You in a rush to get out of here?" I ask. I hope my voice sounds light, but I know it doesn't.

And King doesn't answer me.

Blue is up and eating breakfast before a single person from Yellow is awake. I have the red tent completely packed away when Pidgeon emerges from hers.

She frowns at Books and King. "God, you guys are dictators." Then she turns to Sugar. "Blink twice if you don't feel safe."

Ivy climbs out of the tent and stands next to Pidgeon, both of them still brushing off sleep.

Books asks, "Where're you headed after this?"

Pidgeon shrugs and looks to Ivy. "Maybe up to the lookout? Not sure yet."

"Don't you have to follow the trail you were assigned?" Junior asks her as he pulls on his pack.

"Who says we aren't?"

Ivy puts a hand on Junior's shoulder. "There's more than one way to do a hike."

King smiles but says, "Not really. It's one trail." He moves his hand back and forth.

"Hey," Pidgeon says. "You do it your way, we'll do it ours."

Books and King say goodbye to Ivy and Pidgeon with promises of seeing them again at the end of the trail.

"If you make it there on time." Ivy laughs and adds, "With the way you're going you'll be here till fall."

King shakes his head, but I can't stop thinking about what she said. *Till fall.*

Are we behind?

I ask Books as we hike in single file.

"No," he says. And then adds, "Not really."

"What does that mean?"

He doesn't answer and we keep moving forward, rehabbing as we go. Without Yellow to distract us, the distance between all of us is back. Physically and metaphorically.

I decide to go back to the question game. "If you could only eat food from one continent for the rest of your life, what would it be?"

"What?" Junior asks.

"One continent," I repeat.

"Why?"

"Because I'm going to cut down a tree branch and use it to bash in my skull if I have to be silent another second." I hold up a log in my gloved hand.

"Like they would let you hold the saw," he teases. "Fine. Asia." He doesn't even have to think about it. "Indian, Thai, Vietnamese, Japanese—"

"You don't need to list every country in Asia," Books says, rolling his eyes. "We understand what Asia means."

I didn't even know he was listening.

"You could give up Mexican?" I ask. "All the food in South America? Pasta?"

"I'd forgotten about Mexican." Junior looks torn. "Never having another burrito . . ."

"In-N-Out?" Sugar adds. "Barbecue?"

"What about you?" I ask her.

"Europe." She shoves leaves onto the pile of brush for disposal. "I love French food. A good moule frites is indescribable."

I'm not sure I even know what moule frites is.

"You still pick Asia?" I ask Junior.

"Yes."

"Hmm, brave. I can't give up Mediterranean and middle eastern food. I refuse," I tell him. "What about you, King?"

"Same. Mediterranean."

There's a thrumming in my chest hearing that King and I like something the same and I try to ignore it. "What about you?" I ask Books.

"North America. I would die without a taco. Anything goes into a corn tortilla. Literally anything."

"Cereal?" Junior asks.

"Yeah. I'd eat that." Books pushes a tree branch farther into the pile. "What about a region of Asia?"

"Oh, that's good." Honestly, I'm just happy that Books is playing along.

Junior groans. "Southern."

"You've just willingly given up sushi, Wagyu beef, Korean barbecue—"

Junior stops me. "Is it willing if you made me choose?"

I smile. "Tteokbokki, udon, wasabi, *all* Chinese food, Korean *fried chicken*." I say the last one like he's decided to murder puppies.

"Do you just like telling people all the things they don't have?" Books asks.

"I want you to understand the impact of your choices."

King lets out a little scoff, but Sugar is talking before I can ask about it.

"I'd pick the south of Europe. And before you start, I don't care about meat pies or under salted food."

Books puts his hands on his hips and looks at her. "Fish and chips?"

I groan. "I'm so hungry."

From there, we're silent again. The quiet feels safer than a silly game about food.

The day wears on with instructions and sweaty tasks and everyone mostly still avoiding each other.

We camp on a vista that overlooks the river and set up our tents by a ring of stones that looks like it survived years of storms and fires. If the trail were open, this would be a very popular place. I take a deep breath as I stare out at the incredible view.

Junior asks me to go with him to get firewood because he's still taking it easy with his arm. We don't have to go very far to find kindling, and the trees open up to a cliff that overlooks the valley from a different angle.

"It's pretty, huh?" Junior says.

"Yeah," I agree.

And I feel the urge to explain *why* it's pretty to me.

"It feels kinda weird." He picks up a branch but throws it back down because it's too green still, and his piercing catches the light when he tilts his head.

"How so?"

Junior chews on the next thing he says. "It's weird that we're here, doing this super hard thing, right? And it sucks, but . . . it's also kinda great."

I look back out over the vista and think of my dad's ghost that seems to be hiking only a few feet ahead of us. Always. It's hard to see him in all these places and know he will never be here again. But it's also . . . it's also a place where he still exists. Because I can see him standing on the granite rocks that still glitter. Because inside the stones and trees and sky are threads of the past and threads of his memory. It sucks, but it's also kinda great.

"Yeah. It is."

Back at camp King and Books are arguing.

Sugar sits off to the side going through her pack and pretending to ignore them.

"You're being weird about this." Books pushes at King. They haven't noticed us yet and Junior and I slow our steps unconsciously.

"No, I'm not," King fires back. "You don't—"

"Just say it. The more you make a big deal out of it the weirder it's going to be."

"Let it go, Books." King starts to walk away from him, but Books follows.

"I know you like—"

He turns around and gives Books an incredulous face. "You're kidding, right?"

"The more you pretend like this isn't happening the weirder it's going to be. Just tell her the truth and—"

Junior clears his throat and King's and Books's heads whip around to see us holding the logs. They look like they've been caught.

"So," Junior says. "Whatcha talking about?"

Books looks at King and for a second, their guilt is so heavy I think they're going to throw it at us. Instead, King curses and walks over to me, taking the firewood from my hands.

"Maps. Today is the day you learn to make a fire," Books declares. "Everyone can do it but you."

King gives Books a withering look and I wait for their argument to continue. But Books doesn't back down.

I look back at Junior like he'll save me, but his eyebrows are raised.

"I do *tents*," I remind him.

"Yes. Badly. And it's time we teach you another skill."

Junior moves over to Sugar to help her unpack the food. "But she does so much already," he teases. "Complaining—"

"Arguing," Sugar adds.

"Complaining about arguing."

"See," I tell Books. "I've already learned a lot."

Books looks like he's going to argue, and I don't even mind that they're teasing me because everyone is smiling, but then Books smiles and says, "King will show you."

I look over to King, who is already kneeling by the fire, and try to ignore the way my heartbeat becomes a wild thing. Everything about this moment feels heavier because I can't stop turning his words over in my mind. Who is *her*? "I have to put up the tents."

"Sugar and Junior can do that," Books tells me. "You can build a fire. With King. It's not that hard, Maps."

I'm not worried about how hard it's going to be. In fact, I'm not worried at all. I'm nervous. King makes me nervous. "Fine." I stand with him in front of the firepit and wait for instructions.

"What are you doing?" King asks.

I look around as if I'm missing something. "Waiting for you to teach me how to make fire."

His brows come together. "No one's ever tried to teach you to build a fire?"

One year my father did, and I got frustrated and cried. Every year after he was in charge. Just one of the many things he left unfinished when he died. Now I'm frustrated thinking about how it shouldn't be King teaching me, it should be my dad. But I don't say that because Maps doesn't have a dead dad. I snap at him. "Have you seen me build a fire at any point on this hike?"

Now King looks annoyed. As he should be, I'm being a brat. "You didn't pay attention when everyone else was learning?"

My mouth hangs open as I point at the tent. As if he completely missed all the times I tried to build *shelter*. "I was busy trying not to be smothered by nylon."

He shakes his head and takes a deep breath. "You need tinder. The thing that's gonna start the fire. Small sticks and—"

"I know what tinder is." I grab what Junior and I brought over and suddenly realize I don't actually know what to do with it.

King's jaw clenches.

It does that through the entire instruction.

Finally, I have all my logs laid and a lighter in my hand. I hold it to the kindling and watch it catch and die. Catch and die. Catch and die.

"You might need to help it."

I glare at King, waiting for him to elaborate.

"Blow on it."

I strike the lighter again and hold the flame to the branches. Once it finally catches, I lean down and blow.

"Gently," he tells me.

I lean forward farther, pursing my lips, and release a breath softly. But the flame goes out.

I look at King, but he only motions for me to try again.

I swallow, lick my lips, and blow again. This time the flame picks up and moves across the kindling. I can see King watching me from the corner of my eye and I try not to let it make me nervous as I take a deep breath.

He leans forward and reaches into the fire. On instinct I grab his wrist to stop him. "Whoa!"

King's eyes go to my hand on his arm. I pull it off and we look at each other silently for a second too long to be comfortable. "The fire," I say as an explanation.

The side of his mouth rises, and he reaches back into the fire and adjusts a log. "It won't catch the way you built it."

He blows on the kindling, his lips pursed and his brows pulled down in concentration. It's gentle and intentional and confident. A moment later, flames lick up the side of the log.

"Finally," Sugar grumbles. "I thought we were gonna have to eat jerky and long glances."

Books barks out a laugh and I feel indignant.

"It'd be easier with lighter fluid," I tell them.

"Fluid is heavy, and it smells, and I don't like the way it makes food taste funny." Books walks past the tent Sugar had no problem putting up. "And it's unnecessary. Like your opinion." He gives me a smile.

The edges of Books seem to be a bit softer tonight, and I decide to do him a favor and drop it.

"Doesn't matter." I take a deep breath and hold my hands wide. "*I* started a fire."

King's eyebrows go up, but he doesn't contradict me.

"I'm going to change my review," I tease King. "Four stars."

"Only four?" Junior asks.

"Five is reserved for excellence and I have notes."

"Tell Joe," Sugar says. "He can add it to King's referral for the internship."

It's funny how one word can feel too big to climb. Every time I think I'm getting closer to closing the distance between us, I remember the mountain between us that makes me feel small.

King watches me and sometimes I'm so sure he can read the thoughts that attack me like arrows. But that's impossible. I don't know King and he doesn't know me.

After dinner, Sugar and Junior sit next to me like a sandwich. Junior leans over me and whispers to Sugar.

"What were Books and King talking about earlier?"

Sugar's eyes dart to me and then back to Junior. "I don't know. All of it was coded and annoying."

But she looks at me again and I frown, not sure if she's trying to tell me something.

"Hey." Junior hits me on the leg. "You made this." He points to the fire.

And even if I didn't *technically* do it on my own, I got close. "Yeah." I let my smile grow and push past the thoughts that gnaw at me.

Wrapping my arms around my legs, I sit in front of the flames and watch them after the sun fades, and after the food is gone, and after everyone has gone to bed.

I watch them dance until the last flame sputters and dies.

14

I CAN'T FIND MY gloves.

The morning is just like every other morning. When our routine has become so second nature that we don't even speak. Today we ate the last of our breakfast, and it was barely enough. Each day seems to be wearing at our resolve and I can't be sure, but they've felt hotter. Heat, exhaustion, and hunger have us all feeling worn down and fragile.

We take down tents, make sure everything has been collected, leaving no trace, and get ready for our hike. Tools, water bottles, and—

I search all my pockets. I unpack and repack everything. I even unroll my sleeping bag and mat.

I can't find my gloves.

"What are you doing?" King asks over my shoulder.

"My gloves are gone," I tell him.

"You lost them?"

I don't love his tone.

"No," I grind out. "I just don't know where they are."

King looks at all my things spread out over the dirt. He's frustrated, and he's not bothering to hide it. But to be fair, *no one* is more frustrated than me. "Well, where did you leave them?"

The question is stupid. "If I knew that, I wouldn't be looking for them."

Beside me, Sugar sighs, shrugging off her backpack, and leans against a tree.

Junior whispers something to Books and Books looks to King. They're all talking about me as if I can't *see* them. "Do you know how long we're going to be waiting on *Maps*?"

"We aren't," King shoots back at him.

He walks over to my bag and picks up my mat, but I snatch it from his hands. "I already checked there."

I look up at the four sets of eyes that are looking back at me. Impatiently. The longer we wait, the longer we work in the hottest part of the day. "Can you guys look in *your* packs? Maybe one of you accidentally grabbed them, thinking they were yours?"

Sugar shakes her head. "I'm not pulling apart my pack because you lost your gloves."

It takes me a second to realize she's just said no, because I can't understand why she's being like this.

Junior's already searching his own outside pockets, but he doesn't search inside his pack.

Books doesn't move. "I know what my gloves look like. I wouldn't have picked up yours."

King only shakes his head. "Maps, we have to work."

Anxiety claws its way through my nerves. "If Sugar—"

"No." She's annoyed, that's clear. As if I'm not also annoyed that I'm here looking for my gloves. "I already put away my stuff, Maps. I'm not unpacking."

I know going through her pack is an ordeal, but . . . "I've looked through everything already."

"And I know what's in *my* bag," she pushes back.

"*Sugar*," Junior warns her.

"No," she continues. "Just because Junior does whatever you say and King—"

"He *barely* looked!" I yell. "All of you are fucking—"

"Whoa!" Junior stops me. "I didn't lose *my* shit, Maps. Aim your sniper shots better."

"Sugar," I say stepping forward.

"Maps. No." King's words are final. "I'm not asking someone else to unpack because you were careless with your gloves."

I don't know why this bothers me, but it does. "I wasn't careless."

"You weren't? The same way you put out the fire?" he asks me. "We don't have time to stand around arguing."

My stomach tightens with embarrassment, and I swallow.

"How am I supposed to work without gloves?" I ask, but he's already walking away.

Books takes a deep breath. "We can walk back to Joe and get a new—"

"All of us?" I ask.

"Yeah." His face tells me this is the most obvious answer. "You can't go alone."

"No," I tell Books. I don't want to be here longer than I have to be.

"We can't go back," King says to Books.

"She can't work without gloves," Books tells him. "I know this will add days for you but maybe Joe can talk to someone—"

"I can't be late. If I am, I lose it."

Fuck. King's internship. I look at Sugar again. "Can't you just check?"

She lets out a groan and pulls out her pack. "I don't—" She unrolls it. "Have." She shakes it out. "Your shit." She takes out all her things one by one. Each item adding to the frustration. "Are you happy?"

I am not.

Books shakes his head in annoyed acceptance. "Well, I guess we can start back—"

"I don't want to go back."

Junior's brow furrows. "You don't want . . . Maps, what are you gonna do about your hands?"

"I'll figure something out." But that's a lie. The truth is, I don't know what I'll do.

I want to scream as we shove all our things back into the packs. I hate Sugar for being a bitch about this. *Shove.* I hate Junior for not just looking in his bag. *Shove.* I hate King for making me feel stupid. *Shove shove . . . shove.*

When all our things are packed, we take off back down the trail with angry steps.

He called me careless. About fucking gloves. It's so small and ridiculous, but it lodges itself between all my insecurities.

Even here where I don't have a past, it seems I still can't escape the mistakes I make. *Atlas doesn't care about anything. Atlas can't be counted on. Atlas is a troubled kid.* There is no magic number of apologies that will make someone forget the things you've done or stop judging you by them.

I guess Maps is the kind of person who almost starts forest fires and loses her shit.

When we reach King, he's already started on the clearing. I know what my job is. We've been doing it enough days that no one asks for instructions, but when I wrap my hands around the stalk of a hemlock plant, I can already feel how rough it's going to be on my hands.

"Fuck." I curse and pull them back.

Junior looks at me with a question in his eyes. "I can give you one of mine? We can do halvsies?"

"It's fine," I say. I don't want anyone's sympathy. I want *my* gloves and I don't want to add extra days on to the hike.

My teeth press against each other and my hands are red, angry, and scratched. King offers me a shovel, but I don't take it. I know I'm being stubborn, but all I can hear is King calling me careless. Junior asks me to help him move logs, but they destroy my hands at the same rate as ripping out the plants.

It isn't till the end of the day I start bleeding. I take a sock from my pack and wrap it around my hand and wonder why I didn't do that earlier.

At the end of the day King doesn't ask me to put up the tents, and instead he sends me to fill up the water bottles. I let the water run over my hands and I feel tears in my eyes.

I'm hurt. I'm mad. My emotions are stretched and pulled thin. They unravel and fray and I hate that there isn't anywhere for me to let them go. But mostly I feel misunderstood and that's what makes me cry. No one assumed the best. No one jumped to say we *had to* find gloves even when I refused to go back. No one cared. I'm feeling sorry for myself. Feeling lonely. Feeling like if my dad were here, he would never let someone treat me this way.

I squeeze my hand, feeling it ache from the pain. Every time I move my fingers, the cut throbs and I'm sure I can feel my heartbeat in it. I press a raw hand down on the surface of the water and just hold it there.

"*Holding hands with the water?*" It's my dad's memory. I hear it the same way I hear the river. Little pieces of the two of them echoing each other.

I've finished crying. There's no reason to stay here and pout, so I head back to the clearing with the water bottles.

And standing next to the fire is Joe.

A large bag is at his feet, and he's got his hands on his hips as he talks to Sugar. "That well, huh?" he says with his trademark sarcasm.

I hadn't realized he was coming today. And for some reason, seeing him here makes tears prick at the corners of my eyes again.

Joe notices me and says, "Hey." His head tilts to the side when he takes in my face. "You okay?"

No. Everyone is mean to me and my hands hurt and I miss my dad and I'm never going to stop being a total fuckup and I want to go home. "Allergies. I've been sneezing."

Joe almost looks like he believes me. Or at least wants to.

"What are you doing here?" I ask.

"Resupply."

I nod.

His gaze roams over me, trying to figure out why I seem so tired. "How's it been?" Joe asks.

"Fine," I say even though my hands don't feel *fine*.

I toss down our bottles and I walk over to Books. "Can I have some Advil?"

Books nods and starts rooting through his bag for the first aid. He hands me two pills and I pull out my water bottle as I toss them into my mouth.

"What do you need Advil for?" Joe asks, coming to stand next to Books and me.

"For my fucking hands," I bite out.

"Hands?" Joe's eyes narrow on my hands, and he reaches out to my wrist to stop me. "Maps, you have to wear your gloves."

"I know."

"Why aren't you wearing your gloves?" And then something dawns on Joe. "*Where* are your gloves?"

I take a deep breath. And another. "I don't know."

"You *don't*— Maps. You can't work without gloves."

"Technically, that isn't true."

Joe does not find my joke funny. He twists my wrists and looks at my palms. "Your hands are shot. What the hell, Maps?"

Goddamn it. Why can't he just let me walk away? I'm too angry and too hurt to have this conversation. "I can't find them. They're . . . gone."

"So you just didn't say anything?"

I don't speak as I let Joe work out what happened in our silence.

His eyes dart between King and Books. "You knew and let her do her job anyway?" They're quiet and look down at the ground. Joe looks back at me. "Did you even look for them?"

Anger scorches my words. "I'm not an idiot."

Joe scoffs.

"I tore apart my bag looking for them."

"You lost them." And I can see it in his eyes. *Maps the fuckup.* It's what he's thinking. But before I can argue, Joe looks at King. "You didn't assign her something else? Have you seen her fucking hands? She has a gash on her palm, and they look like hamburger."

I wince at the visual.

Sugar comes out of the tent, her face looking pale.

"This is *not* taking care of your team." Joe is pointing at Books and King as he reprimands them, and I should feel smug or victorious about this, but I just feel tired.

"She never said anything about how bad it was," King tells Joe. "I didn't realize . . ."

"She doesn't have to. You're supposed to just know. And it's fucking basic knowledge that you can't work without gloves. Maps, you'll have to come back down the trail with me."

"Wait. What?" My heart stops.

"I know you wanted to finish, but—"

"No, Joe." My panic has sharp nails that scratch down my lungs. Books's and Junior's eyes have gone wide.

"Joe," King says. "You can't—"

116

"No, *you*," he says to King. "You fucked up and—"

"Um," Sugar says. She clears her throat and . . . "I found Maps's gloves."

Everyone is silent as we turn to Sugar. She stands, holding my gloves together in her left hand.

"*What?*" Joe asks.

She swallows and looks down at the ground. "They were rolled up in my sleeping bag." Her words are slow and deliberate.

Joe looks at her. Looks at me. Looks at King. But everyone is looking at the ground.

"I didn't know," Sugar continues. "Honestly, I have no idea how they got there. I swear I wasn't hiding them. I pulled out all my stuff and I just didn't think there was any chance that they would be *inside*—"

Joe is furious. "One of the most important tools and you don't tear apart every inch of your camp? You don't walk to a post and try to grab another pair?"

No one speaks and Joe looks at me, so I say, "I didn't want to walk to a post. I didn't want to waste the time. It wasn't anyone's fault."

Joe is silent. "If you want to make a complaint or—"

"No." I cut him off. "I don't."

King's eyes are on mine. The dark color swirls and changes and I feel . . . strange.

Joe looks *disappointed* and he points at me. "Take care of your hands." Then he points to King. "*Follow me.*"

As soon as King and Joe disappear down the path, tension is back in the air.

117

Books reaches into his bag and holds out the first aid kit. "You didn't have to do that," he tells me.

"I know."

"King's internship—"

I stop him. I don't want to be reminded. "I *know*."

Books reaches for my hand, but Sugar is there taking the kit from him. "Here. Let me help."

"No, it's fine," I tell her and reach for the box myself.

She pulls it away from me and motions for me to sit with authority.

"Sugar. It's fine."

"Okay." But she doesn't look at me when she says it and something about that word feels soft.

We sit down on a log. Our legs are pressed against each other. She takes my hand into her lap and pulls out the same clear liquid that Books used on Junior, but she doesn't warn me as she applies it to my skin with a cotton pad.

"Fuck!" It stings my palm and I try to yank it away, but she holds my wrist with a vise grip.

"You're fine," she grumbles. "Even Junior didn't complain this much." Sugar takes a deep breath as she relaxes her grip. "Sorry," she mumbles as she takes the ointment from the kit. "Maps. I . . ."

I wait as she meets my gaze.

"I'm not saying sorry for holding your hand. I'm sorry about the gloves. I didn't know they were in my stuff. I swear I didn't." She looks back down and dabs at my wounds with the clear jelly.

"It's okay," I say because *I forgive you* isn't right, and *I understand* isn't right either.

"I know you probably think I was being an asshole . . ." She takes a deep breath. I feel it scatter against my open hand. "And I was. But I wouldn't have—" She stops, and I can see she's struggling to find her words. "I was . . . annoyed and I just . . . kept going. Like, I could see that I was being unreasonable, but I just kept digging myself deeper. Back home, sometimes it feels like I'm expected to do something. To have the answer or . . . It's hard to explain. And I hate it. I hate that no one's really asking me to do something. They expect it. So I accidentally turned into a werewolf and tried to eat you."

I look at Sugar, who keeps her focus on my hand and never meets my eyes as she works. The trail is a weird place. Where your past doesn't really matter, but you drag it with you, anyway. Like your backpack, you're never really without it, despite how heavy it makes everything.

"Sometimes I'm a werewolf too," I tell her.

She gives me a look.

"I could have said we had to go get gloves. I was being stubborn and I chose to work without them. I can speak up for myself. We're good, Sugar."

"Okay, Maps." She looks over to me, a smile carving across her face. "Next time. Next time I won't turn into a werewolf."

"Me either." I hit her with my shoulder.

She smiles as she wraps my hand in a thin layer of gauze. "What do you think they're talking about?" she asks, inclining her head toward King and Joe . . . at the exact moment King looks away from us.

I give a little shrug. "Probably about his internship."

She makes a thoughtful noise.

When she's done, I hold up both my hands showing off the bandages. "Is this penance?" I ask with a smile.

She shakes her head. "No. Penance is for people who have given up."

"Then what's this?"

"Me trying to make it right." She stands before I can say anything else. "Better than an apology."

15

JOE DOESN'T LEAVE.

He watches me set up the tents. He leans over Junior as he builds a fire. He eats Sugar's meal like he's a food critic.

"It's beans and rice," Sugar tells him. "Stop looking at it like you wish it was a steak."

Joe simply looks up from his bowl and says, "I'm a vegetarian."

In the morning Joe is still there. Sugar checks the firepit and Joe watches. Books straps gear to his pack and Joe stares. Junior puts our food away, sealing it, and Joe shakes his head slowly. King comes back from brushing his teeth and looks at Joe, waiting for him to yell or admonish him.

He does nothing.

Joe's hands are on his hips. I put the tent back into my bag, the nylon sliding against nylon in a hiss that I've grown to find soothing. I'm ignoring him. If he wants to yell at me, he's going to do it whether I'm nervous or not.

"Is it always like this?" He stands over me as I pack the last few things into my bag.

My gloves are on the ground next to me. "Like what?" I ask.

Joe gestures to everyone else and frowns. "Like. Quiet and . . . whatever the fuck this is."

I stand and take a deep breath. "Yeah. How else is it supposed to be?"

Joe shakes his head. "Not like this."

"Well, you're not here normally, so if you don't like it . . . take off. I'm sure there's another team that can't wait for you to watch them do things."

His brow pulls together. "You know, this trail, it's important to me. I didn't put Yellow in charge of this because I wanted someone to take it seriously. I didn't ask Red because I wanted someone who would respect this hike. I didn't ask Green because . . . well they would probably get lost. But what I'm trying to say is I put you guys here because this trail *means* something."

He's talking to all of us, but he's looking at me when he says it.

Because I know what it means. I remember this was my dad's and his favorite hike.

"I know it feels like a punishment, but it's not. I trust you guys." Joe shakes his head.

I push against the feeling that we've somehow let him down. Joe doesn't have a right to be disappointed in me. Joe doesn't get to be another person I've failed.

We watch as he collects his things and pulls on his pack. "Just . . . just try *talking* to each other. Words go a long way."

Instead of goodbye or instructions on what to do next, he walks back the way we came on the trail and holds up a hand. Once he disappears under the crest of a hill we turn back to each other and return to stuffing things in our packs.

When I stand, Sugar is in front of me, reaching for my hands. "How do they feel?" she asks as she presses lightly on the bandage.

"Good." It's a lie. They're sore and I'd really like some pain medication, but Books and King have been standing together all morning with frowns on their faces and Junior's injury is worse, even though he says it's getting better.

"We're supposed to be using words." She drops my hands and turns back to King and yells, "King! Did you ask Maps about her hands?"

King doesn't say anything but looks at me. In his eyes I can see something that looks an awful lot like regret. I almost feel bad for him. Except I can't stop hearing him use the word *careless*.

"Maps," King says slowly. "How are your hands?"

I click my tongue. "Same as they were thirty seconds ago."

King gives Sugar a pointed look and I roll my eyes and pull my pack over my shoulders.

"Let's go," Books tells everyone. "Whatever is happening here can happen as we walk."

On our first break, King asks me about my hands again, but I ignore him. The second break he offers me water when he sees mine is low. I walk over to Junior and ask him to share. While I'm carving out a ditch, King offers to help me, and I snap.

"I don't need your help." I can hear how petulant I sound, but I can't seem to stop myself.

"It looks like you need my help," he tells me. But he stops

123

asking how my hands are. Instead, we swipe at each other all day. He complains about the place I put the trash pile. I complain about how long it takes him to saw through a branch.

And then we see the spring pole.

Not one, but three.

A large tree has fallen in a way that's trapped three smaller ones and holds them against the ground. They don't *look* dangerous, but from the safety videos we were forced to watch, we know they are.

"Fuck," Books grumbles. "We have to—" He pulls out a piece of paper. "We have to take care of this."

Something changes in the group dynamic, and it feels like all the tension from the spring poles are now in the air around us.

King talks about pull and snapback. He describes injuries he's seen before and suddenly everything looks like a bomb.

"You need to cut it from the bottom," Sugar tells them.

All three of the guys' heads turn toward her. "What?" Books asks.

"Cut it here." She points at the bend. "One small cut here at the top, not very deep, but enough to give it a place to bend, and then small cuts underneath. Do it at the same time so you don't mess with the felled tree."

Books frowns as he looks at Sugar. "How do you know that?"

She looks at them like they've just said something incredibly stupid. "It's physics."

Sugar stands to the side and directs them as they make their cuts, timing them perfectly. Junior's, Books's, and King's forearms flex as they work together. But King is moving a little slower than everyone else.

"King, you need to go faster," I tell him.

He doesn't look up. They lean back and watch the wood crack and splinter before taking the saw to it again. But he's still slower than everyone else and it's making the log that is lying on the trees pull up on one side.

"*King*," I warn.

"Shut up," King grunts without looking at me.

"Be caref—"

And then the spring pole Books is sawing through breaks with a snap of the wood. The two other trees groan as they lift the larger tree from the ground like a slow-moving catapult. Junior's tree falls with a deep thud and then—

Someone is shouting. Sugar? Books? King's tree is still cracking and splintering. And I know I'm in its path. I know if the tree shoots forward, it's going to hit me, but I can't seem to make myself move. King's eyes meet mine and a second later he has a foot on the wood and the saw against it.

The trees fall and bounce as the tension leaves them, and everyone jumps backward.

"*Fuck*," Junior says, but it's with relief.

Books shakes his head at King, whose chest is still moving up and down. "You put your foot on the tree?"

King drops his saw. "The fucking tree—I wasn't thinking." He runs a hand over his face. "And Maps kept shouting."

My mouth opens in frustration. "You weren't going fast enough and—"

"I'm not a robot, Maps! I can't perfectly time something."

"Maybe not, but you could have tried!"

And then he's walking toward me. "Try? Me? How about

you? The tree was coming right for you and you just . . . stood there?"

"It wasn't!" I bite down on my lie, because in that moment, when the tree was breaking and ready to fly forward, it felt like it was.

"Maps," Books tells me. "You should be saying thank you."

"*What?*"

"He could have hurt himself." And then, lower, Books grumbles, "Because he's a fucking idiot."

"I was trying to be helpful." But I can hear how childish I sound. I press my lips against each other and wonder how much longer my words will always be the wrong ones. How much longer people will continue to not understand me.

King's jaw tightens and he steps into my space as he growls at me, "The last thing you are is helpful."

And then Sugar is between us. "What the fuck is with you two?"

But King and I are like shrapnel going in opposite directions.

We hike farther but we don't get very far down the trail before we hit a small fork. It's clear that the narrower path is less traveled.

King points at the smaller trail. "This meets up with the other trail, so . . ." He looks at Junior. "You with me, and Sugar and Maps with Books."

I'm already stepping toward the other trail when Books stops me.

He takes a deep breath and looks at King. "I think you and Maps should do that trail."

126

"What?" I ask. "Why?"

"Because . . ." Books clears his throat. "You guys are either fighting or there's a weird vibe. And honestly the rest of us could use a goddamn break."

Junior nods. "I agree."

"Of course you agree," I say almost under my breath, but Junior's eyes narrow at me.

"Honestly, I agree too. A break would be nice," says Sugar.

"So you're gonna go with Books and Junior? For a break?" I ask, unbelieving.

She waves a hand at Books and Junior. "Their shit is better than your shit."

But she gives me a sympathetic look, Books whispers something to King, and Junior claps both of us on the shoulder before nodding once and following Books down the trail.

And then suddenly King and I are alone.

16

"HOW LONG DO YOU think this trail is?"

We've only been hiking for a few minutes, but it's been in silence. Mind-numbing and anxiety-inducing quiet. My nemesis. The quiet *and* King.

"You don't have to fill every moment with talking," he replies.

Yes, I do. "I'm trying to get to know you."

King looks at me, his face filled with the annoyance I can feel coming off him in waves. "I don't really want to answer any more of your weird questions."

He's being a jerk. Maybe this will finally convince my lizard brain that King isn't *that* hot. Or capable. Or smart. "Good, because your answers are weird."

King pulls out his notebook and pen. We don't talk after that unless it's pointing out something on the trail. A blowdown, or overgrowth, or fire damage.

Somewhere around lunch, the trail begins to feel different. The trees grow closer overhead and blot out the sky with dappled green leaves. It feels . . . like the whole world has disappeared and it's just King and me.

King makes a face that tells me he's chewing on his thoughts in our silence, and it makes the moments I wait for him to finally speak tighten around my chest.

It's not until he's walking in front of me, under tall pine trees, that he says, "Why did you tell Joe that you asked us to check our packs?"

I let his question roll around in the air between us. "I don't know. Why didn't you tell him I didn't put out the fire? Or about the cigarettes?"

"There was nothing to tell." He doesn't even look at me when he says it. "Was this just so we could be *even*?"

"Did *you* want to be even?" I ask.

King stops in front of me abruptly and I brace myself so I don't run into him as he turns to look at me. "I want to know why you didn't tell Joe."

My mouth opens but I don't know what to say. I'm not entirely sure why.

"You did the same thing and it wasn't a big deal. Why did *you* do it?"

He turns from me. "Good question."

We're hiking uphill toward what feels like the surface of the sun and King . . . he doesn't even appear to be winded. "I am *so* tired," I groan as I throw myself onto my pack and King pulls out his journal. "I will never understand why people work out on purpose."

"Endorphins." King doesn't look from the tree he's making note of.

"Well, I must be broken because I don't have any of those."

"Everyone has those." He looks at me finally. "Drink your water."

I want to argue, but even I'm growing tired of myself.

He pulls off his pack. Sweat has dampened the back of his shirt and I know mine looks the same as I follow his lead. We sit on our bags and rehydrate.

King lets the water fill his cheeks before swallowing. "You get used to the heat and walking."

"Are you?"

He takes another drink and I think he's going to ignore me, but he says, "Sometimes. Working construction is hot. Your body remembers."

"I don't ever want to work construction."

"You don't have to. You're going to college."

There's a feeling you get when someone reminds you of your lie. An electricity that shoots through your body. Panic made physical. You work as hard as you possibly can to keep that panic from your face and remind yourself of what people look like when they tell the truth. "Right." I say it in an even tone.

"You're gonna pledge a sorority." The way he says it is like I've said something offensive.

I stand and brush my pants off. "We should keep going."

We start walking again, but my mind keeps running.

"I don't want to go to college," I tell him. It's supposed to be a lie, but it doesn't feel that way. It feels like something I've plucked from the dark parts of my mind that I never bring to light.

He doesn't say anything. "I used to think when I was little

that my parents would drive me to college like in the movies and my mom would cry and my dad would steer her toward the car and remind me to call them. They would wave at me and I would pretend to be annoyed but secretly not want them to leave. And as they drove away my dad would look back at me one last time and he would have tears in his eyes . . . and I would be a grown-up." I realize I've accidentally let an edge creep into my voice.

But I don't clear my throat because I don't want him to know that this dream I've accidentally shared with him cost me something. I don't tell him that my dad can't come. That this dream is just a dream. "Fuck college."

If King can hear something in my voice, he doesn't say. He just replies, "That's not how we become grown-ups."

I wait for him to ask me what I plan on doing instead, but he doesn't, and we hike in silence as the trail hugs the side of the mountain. One side is sheer rock, and the other is sparse land where only a few plants grow that don't require a lot of light. The valley below us is mostly obstructed by other rocks and boulders, and the trail is only a narrow walkway.

And then the mountain closes in, and there's only a thin gap to walk through. I'm not sure we will even fit and I'm getting ready to tell King that we should turn around when he says, "We'll have to go in sideways." King's already pulling off his pack.

"We still have to go?" I ask.

"Yeah, it's how we meet up with everyone else," he says and shimmies into the space. King drags his pack with one hand, and I watch him yank on it when it gets to more narrow parts. When he's reached the other side, he looks back at me.

And motions for me to follow.

Fuck.

Pulling off my pack, I step into the space, walking sideways like a crab. My lungs feel heavy as my body hits the wall in front of me. I take another step and another and I turn my head to look at the bag behind me. I'm not sure when I realize that I can't turn my body, but for some reason, it makes my hands shake. I yank my pack but I can't seem to free it from whatever it's caught on and I can't . . . I can't, I can't.

I'm stuck.

And I can't breathe. There is no air inside this crack and my bag won't move. And I can't move and I can't.

"Hey. *Whoa*." King's voice sounds like it's underwater.

"I'm stuck."

I'm aware he's speaking to me, but I can barely make it out until he shouts. "Hey!" King swears. And I just keep saying *I can't*. Over and over. Fuck. I don't know if my eyes are closed or if my vision has gone dark.

I feel his hand on my shoulder. "Hey. Maps, hey. Look at me."

I'm not looking at King. And I can't. My eyes stay shut.

"Deep breaths. *Look* at me."

I shake my head no.

"Leave your bag. Fuck the pack." His hand is on top of my arm. "Follow me, okay. Listen to my voice."

My hand reaches out and tightens on his arm, terrified he's going to leave me. "No, no, no, no, no."

"Maps. I'm right here." The words are soft and . . .

I follow him.

We're walking and I can't think of anything other than the way his hand feels against my skin. It's the only thing that lets me shimmy against the rough rocks and ignore the way they scrape the fabric of my clothes.

And then everything that was holding me up disappears, and I fall forward. I don't open my eyes and my lungs still feel tight.

"Maps." King's arms are around me. I feel him take my hands in his and place them over his heart. "A deep breath like me. Just one."

Under my palms I feel his chest move up and down.

"Like me," he repeats and inhales.

I copy him and we hold the air in. The shirt under my fingers is warm from the heat of his skin and mine. He releases it, and so do I.

Again. And again. And again.

Finally, we're just breathing.

"When my brother went to college, he went by himself." I can feel the words in his chest. "No one came to help him move in or . . . He was in a dorm with five other people. One of his roommates had their whole family there. He FaceTimed me that night and I could tell that he was pretending like he didn't care, but . . ."

One of King's hands moves up and down my back and the other holds mine against his chest as he swipes a thumb over the back of it.

"College doesn't make you a grown-up, it just reminds you of how much you wish you weren't." He clears his throat.

His words sit on the surface of my skin and I want to brush them off, but I press them against myself and let them mean something to me. Maybe he's just trying to distract me. Maybe.

"It's okay not to want something even if you're supposed to." He's quiet again and then says, "I want the internship in Alaska. A lot of people have gone out of their way to make sure I have this opportunity and there's this expectation that I should be grateful. I am, but I'm also annoyed that I have to be grateful. That it feels like even though they're telling me it's a choice, it doesn't feel like one." He shakes his head. "And the wild thing is, I want it. Like, *really* want it. This trail is the first time I've felt like I'm good at something. But it's also this thing that other people have told me I'm good at and has to be *gifted* to me. I'm repeatedly told what an honor it is to have Joe recommend me."

I want to laugh, but I don't. "That's what life is. A series of things that you're told are choices but are really just expectations and obligations."

"What are your obligations?" he asks me simply.

My grief. My mother. This program being a fresh start when I don't want to move on. Even if that means I'm a problem kid. Even if that means going to college.

Because moving on means I'm moving further away from my father.

I open my eyes slowly and realize what this looks like. King and me sitting on the ground. Me practically in his lap, and him with his arm around me. One of his hands is on top of mine and my face is almost against his chest. I pull my arms back to my sides.

A look I don't understand crosses his face. "Here." He hands me his water and leans against the rocks. I follow him until we are sitting side by side, our legs stretched out in front of us and pressed against each other. The heat and weight of him next to me feels like an anchor.

"Better?" he asks, looking sincere as he waits for an answer.

I nod. "Yeah." It comes out on a breath.

"So, small spaces are not great?"

In the quiet, I realize that I want to tell him. "I guess not."

Joe telling us that this trail is important with an expectation on his face has niggled at my mind. I know it's important, but I'm failing. I'm failing my dad.

"I don't belong here," I admit. "I can't even hike this trail."

King laughs quietly. "That's not true."

"You don't have to say that to make me feel better. I should have gone back with Joe."

King pulls at his bottom lip with his teeth. "You wanna know what I thought when Joe said you had to go back with him? I thought . . ." His eyes look up to the sky, like he's a little embarrassed to admit it. "I thought, *She can't leave. She's supposed to be here.*"

I don't breathe because if I do, it might take this moment from me. And this. This is the closest I've been to believing there is something more here. To him acknowledging this thing that feels electric under my skin and in the dark colors of his eyes.

And if it isn't real . . . I don't want to know that either.

"I wasn't worried about my internship or your hands. I just thought . . ." He presses his lips together and shakes his head. "I think you belong on this trail, Maps."

I pick at a string coming from the bottom of my shirt as if it will keep me in this moment. One where the ground beneath King and me shifts.

He runs a tongue over his lip. "Close your eyes." It's not a question.

"What?"

He doesn't explain, only repeats himself. "*Close your eyes.*"

Instead I roll them, but King just stares at me till eventually my eyes shut. I wait, feeling self-conscious that King's sitting next to me doing god only knows what.

Eventually he speaks. "Take a deep breath."

I do. My chest rising and falling.

"Again."

I do it three more times. Eventually the unease I feel drifts away and I'm left with the quiet of myself, the quiet of the trees. The smell of dirt and pine and plants. The sounds of the birds from somewhere above. My own breathing pulling into my body and then releasing.

"My grandmother would make me close my eyes when I needed to tell the truth. She said that if you close your eyes, it's like you're talking to yourself. And then the only person you're lying to is you."

I almost open my eyes. Almost, but King speaks again. "Are you okay?"

I'm fine. It's what I want to say even to myself. To everyone. I want to tell that lie so many times that it becomes true. But the word that leaves my mouth is singular. "No."

And then I say, "My dad died." Out loud it feels heavier than I thought it would, but somehow less . . . sharp than I expected.

King doesn't react.

"I used to have these dreams of him in a coffin, which is stupid since he was cremated. I would wake up and tell myself it was ridiculous, but then I would imagine his body in one of those morgue drawers or in the cremation oven and it all sounds so gross but I couldn't keep my mind from going to those places like a psycho and I just . . . I hate small spaces. Where there's no air or . . ." I run a hand over my chest like I can feel my lungs and then I open my eyes.

I've given King plenty of opportunities to tell me I'm being ridiculous or to point out that I lied to him, to everyone, but he just keeps looking at me . . . and I wonder when that look will turn into a weapon or into pity. It always does when I talk about my dad.

"I know I told you that my dad and mom are in Europe but . . ." But what? "I lied and I'm sorry—"

Am I sorry? I can't even tell how I feel. I wait for his pity to kick in and save me from having to own up to my lies, but King just looks back at me patiently. Waiting.

"Lying just seemed easier. Fewer questions. And I'm fine. Most days, I don't even think about it." *Lie.* "And being claustrophobic is common, right? Like being afraid of heights?"

I'm back to not telling the truth. He's quiet, and I don't know if I'm imagining the look of chagrin in his eyes.

King shifts and his thigh presses against my leg. "It's okay to be sad."

"I'm not sad." I swallow. The emotion is thick in my throat and I feel like I might vomit it up. "I mean, I'm sad, but I'm not, like . . . I'm fine." I clear my throat. "I'm fine."

"You don't have to be fine." He says it in a matter-of-fact tone, and his face doesn't change. "You can be anything you want to be."

I don't know what to say. Since my dad got sick, I've never just been anything. My mother has always tried to manage my feelings, too afraid they will turn into something unmanageable or, worse, make *her* feel something.

But King has no expectation of my reaction. It's strange when so many other people are always telling me what I should or shouldn't feel or say or act.

"Is that why you told everyone that your parents are in Europe?"

"No one in my family has ever even been to Europe." I bite my lip. "I just didn't . . . people always ask the same things, like how did he die? As if that will make it better."

King doesn't look upset or angry. He looks like he's using the silence to think.

And then he says, "Tell me about him?"

There are pieces of my dad that I keep locked in a chest deep inside me and only take out and examine when I know it's safe. When I'm alone. But. A small part of me wants to share him with King, who didn't know my dad and will let me paint him in whatever colors I want.

So I do. I talk about the stories he would tell, about how he loved strangers, and the way he would ask people question after

138

question, trying to learn everything he could about a person. I talk about how he would sing his favorite songs on the radio with all the windows down and about the time he came to pick me up at school in his bathrobe as a punishment for cutting class.

And I talk about smaller things too. Like the way he read to me every night before bed, or how when he really laughed, it was almost silent.

I don't cry because I don't want to. Like telling King means I don't have to worry about being pitiful with him. These memories can just be what they are. Memories.

When I look up, King isn't smiling, but he's not frowning.

I run my sweaty palms against the tops of my jeans. "Sorry, I've been talking this whole time."

He nods and takes a deep breath. "We should probably keep going."

I lean my head on the rock behind us and I bite the inside of my cheek. How long have we been sitting here wasting time? Are we farther behind now? I hand him back his water bottle and realize I drank all of it.

Even though King's let me talk, I feel embarrassed. I overshared when he was just trying to distract me.

I nod. And then I say, "Are you going to tell Joe?"

"Tell him what?"

"About . . ." I wave at the rocks. "My breakdown."

He looks me in my eyes again. "You're allowed to have a breakdown."

"Easy for you to say." My voice is thin around the corners of my words.

"I mean, it's not. I think it's shitty for anyone to tell someone else what they can feel, and it sounds like you expect me to tell you what your grief should look like."

"What it should look like," I repeat. "Yeah, no one cares what I want as long as I do what is expected. And don't cause *trouble*."

"Sometimes all you can do is cause trouble to make people take you seriously." He doesn't say more, but I understand the words that he's not saying in between the words he is. Sometimes you have to scream for someone to finally listen.

"Are you trouble?" I ask. It feels like a question I should define. I should explain. The different kinds of trouble float in the air, and I want to tell him that he doesn't feel like trouble to me.

His brows come together and he looks like he's deciding something. "I'm not here by choice. Or. I wasn't last year. It was court ordered." King looks up at me and says, "So yeah. I'm trouble."

It's simple, like a moniker he's worn for long enough that the word is comfortable on his skin. A tattoo in slashes of black ink and other people's judgment. And I can't help but feel like King has given me something. When I take the words out and examine them, I realize they don't mean anything.

So I tell him, "Me too."

King and me.

Bad kids.

17

SOMETIMES, I THINK OF my mother.

I see her standing in front of the mirror in her bedroom, trying on all her clothes as if she was searching for something. A pirate looking for treasure. She would run her hands down the sides of her body or over her legs and I would watch her trying to change. "Clothes can make you anything," she would say. Like fabric could be a superpower. A bit of magic. A caterpillar trying to transform.

My father would come into the room, lean against the doorjamb with a smile that he seemed to have only for her. And when she looked at him, when her eyes met his, that's when she changed. A butterfly unfurling her wings.

I look down at the hem of my shorts where a tear has formed at the top of my thigh. It seems to be getting worse. My finger slips into the frayed area. Soon these shorts will tear too far for me to wear, and I will be down to only two pairs.

I wonder what these clothes make me?

A shadow passes over and when I look up, I see King.

Since we rejoined the others, we've been circling each other.

We've stopped fighting and bickering, but we haven't been *talking*. King has been doing something else entirely.

Paying attention.

He will quietly hand me the salve if he notices me limping. Or set aside food if I'm still putting up the tents. Or hand me a tool moments before I realize I'm going to need it.

Sometimes we just sit on opposite sides of the fire, not talking, and I try not to admit that those are my favorite parts of the night. Quiet ones where I can pretend we are the kind of worn in and comfortable that doesn't require words.

And now he stands over me with a box.

"What's that?" I ask. King's holding out a dusty blue box with yellow latches as his shoulders block the sun.

"A sewing kit."

"Sewing kit?" I repeat and he motions down at the place my finger is currently poking through my shorts.

It's thoughtful, something I'm learning is a truth about King. I decide to make a joke instead of being grateful. "Is this considered a weapon?"

"Absolutely." The corner of his mouth lifts. "This is sabotage, and definitely not me trying to keep your pants from falling apart."

I take the small blue plastic box from him and open it. Several needles and a few spools sit inside and I pull out a needle and black thread. Squinting one eye closed, I try to poke it through the eye of the needle.

"Here," King says, taking it from me. A second later, he has the thread looped and tied. "Have you never sewn before?" I think he's going to hand it to me, but it stays in his hand.

"I didn't take homesteading in school." My voice doesn't sound as nervous as I feel.

"Your ancestors must be horrified." He kneels in front of me as he grabs the hem of my shorts.

"What are you doing?"

He looks at me from under his lashes and my heart beats a little harder. "I'm helping you since you can't sew."

I clear my throat. "Maybe I want to look like Joe," I say, but it comes out quiet and soft, like this moment.

He smiles, a small and delicate thing against his strong features, and turns his focus back to my leg. "Don't move." I feel his breath on my thigh.

I watch as he gets close to my leg, pulling my shorts up gently as he moves the needle in and out of the fabric. His eyes are focused on the black string against my navy shorts, and I'm mesmerized by how delicate his hands can be.

I wonder if they're this gentle—

"Where did you learn how to do this?" I ask, trying to distract my own thoughts.

He lets out a sigh. "My mother was really into cross-stitching. It's not exactly the same, but close enough."

"Did she teach you?"

When he speaks, I feel his breath on my skin. The words are slow and deliberate, as if he's too busy concentrating on my shorts. "My mother taught me a lot of things and most of them I don't want to remember." The needle pokes a little more

143

aggressively through a thicker part of the fabric, and King pulls the hem upward so that he doesn't stab me.

I don't flinch, but my body tightens.

"You okay?" he asks.

"Yep." Except my voice sounds tight and I realize he thinks I'm scared.

His eyes study mine. "I'm almost done."

I swallow my feelings as I stare at the sky, wishing it would just fall on me and put me out of my misery. Sugar steps into my view and her eyebrows go up.

King doesn't even pause as Sugar leans over his shoulder. "You're giving her stitches?"

"Her shorts." He's still focused.

Junior comes over and looks at King's work, nodding. "That's a decent seam."

Sugar gives him a surprised look. "You can sew too?"

Junior shrugs. "Can't everyone?"

She makes an appalled face and I would match her if I weren't so focused on King. "No, everyone cannot *sew*."

"'Kay," King says to himself and then, slowly, he leans down and takes the thread into his mouth to bite it off. His head is in my lap, his mouth only centimeters from my skin. I feel his lips brush my leg for the quickest second. And then he leans back and looks down at his work. "Good." He nods once and runs a finger against the stitches. Back and forth. Back and forth. "It won't last forever but should last till the end of the trail."

He sits up and offers me his hand so I can stand.

"Are you gonna say anything?" he asks, still squatting on the ground.

"Like what?"

The corner of his mouth raises and I'm positive he can read my mind. "Like thank you?"

"Yeah." I clear my throat. "Like thank you."

Now he's smiling. I roll my eyes and brush my hands off on my shorts.

"Hey," he says and wraps his hands around my wrist. He looks up at me from his crouched position. "You're welcome."

You're welcome.

Something about the way he speaks makes me feel like maybe I don't know what he's talking about. The words have another meaning, one I can't hear.

His eyes are on my shorts. On my legs. On me. He's wearing a smile I've never seen before, and I understand. The magic was never the clothes.

It was always the way my father looked at my mother.

After dinner, the five of us sit like birds on a wire with our legs dangling off a rock as the light starts to fade. The sunlight is golden and soft. It makes us all look a little filtered. And we watch the world exhale. The sky is turning orange and pink, and I look behind us as the moon and two brave stars peek out of a denim sky.

"If you could do anything, what would it be?" I ask. "A job, a talent, anything."

I can see them considering and I try not to feel too victorious that they're finally playing my game without question.

Sugar leans back and closes her eyes. "When I was little, I wanted to be a banana cooker."

"Banana cooker?" Junior asks. "What are we even talking about?"

"People don't cook bananas," Books tells Sugar.

"You don't get to set my limits." She doesn't even open her eyes when she says it. "What if the world had told Steve Jobs not to spite-start a company that would revolutionize animation?"

"You're a big Steve Jobs fan?" Junior asks with a smirk.

"It's important to understand the visionaries that come before you."

Junior pulls at her ponytail gently and smiles at her when her head falls back.

Books leans forward and looks at Sugar. "We're still talking about cooking bananas, right?"

"I wanted to be a doctor when I was little," Junior tells us.

"A doctor?" Books sounds a little surprised.

"Doctors are helpful," Junior says. "I wanted to be helpful."

"And now what do you want?" Books asks.

He lets out a heavy breath and his voice is hushed when he says, "To be selfish." And that's how I know it's the truth.

Books searches Junior's face for something I'm not sure he'll find, then looks out at the horizon. "I just want to be rich. I want a plane. Maybe a yacht."

"And what will you do to earn that money?" I ask.

"Nothing. I will do nothing. I will be generationally wealthy and I will become obsessed with random causes while I eat food from my private chef that I fly with me everywhere because I've grown paranoid that people are going to poison me."

"Anything is possible," Sugar tells him.

I don't mention that it's literally impossible for him to have generational wealth since it comes from your parents, and instead I swing my legs in front of me.

"What would you do, Maps?" Books asks. A woman named Maeve sang "Danny Boy" at my father's funeral. I remember all the times I had seen my father tear up at that song when he was alive.

I'll be there in sunshine or in shadow.

If I could do anything. If I could do the impossible . . . I would sing that song for my dad.

"I would be a singer."

"A singer?" Junior laughs. "You want to be famous?"

I shake my head and hate the flush on my cheeks for being misunderstood. For being laughed at and caring enough to be embarrassed. I shouldn't have said it.

I shall sleep in peace until you come to me.

I can feel everyone watching me as they search my words for meaning. The desire to explain myself is heavy on my tongue.

"I just want this internship," King says, and everyone's eyes shift to him.

"You can do anything," Sugar repeats. "*Anything.* It's supposed to be a dream."

King lifts a shoulder and repeats. "The internship."

"Maybe that's what he wants," Books tells us.

His *want* stings at me like nettles. I know that his internship is important to him, but King getting what he wants means the trail coming to an *end*.

Somehow, that word is no longer associated with the end of

my suffering on this trail or an item to be checked off the end of a list.

Somehow the meaning changed without me realizing it.

It feels like the end of *this*.

The end of *us*.

18

TIME IS AN ODD thing. Sometimes it's slow and excruciating. Seconds being pulled into the infinite. And sometimes you can see it slipping through your fingers. Wasted.

I lie in my sleeping bag and think about all the wasted time I've been so careless with.

School was a waste.

I never finished. I might never finish.

When I close my eyes I can see the moment I decided to stop wasting time there.

My junior year, almost ten months before my father died, we sat in the school office. Side by side in front of a cheap desk pretending to be made out of mahogany. With shaky hands, he held the white piece of paper with our school district's logo on it. TRUANCY was stamped in large black letters at the top. My father wore a gray beanie, but it was clear from his lack of eyebrows that there was no hair underneath it. His skin was sallow and sagged against the bones of his face.

"Students have to come to school." Principal Bartlett nervously shuffled papers on his desk.

"I understand," my father said. Since he got sick he took long pauses in conversations just to find the right words. "Last year was rough, but she's committed to school now."

My principal cleared his throat. "She's behind in every class. She was combative with teachers last year. One class, she stood up and walked out."

I had. I didn't even try to justify it. My father had a doctor's appointment that morning and I just.

I didn't want to be in class. I could barely focus as Principal Bartlett went on and on about me to my father.

I wasn't a bad kid, I was troubled. I wasn't disrespectful, I was misguided. This wasn't a punishment, it was an opportunity.

"Atlas, are you listening?" Principal Bartlett asked and then looked at my father, as if I was proving his point.

My father reached over and grabbed my hand. "I agree that Atlas isn't a bad kid, but I'd like to focus on what we can do to get her back into school."

"There will be a hearing about which continuation school program has an opening for her."

Continuation school was for all the kids who had been kicked out of regular school or were too old or the teens who got pregnant. It had a terrifying air of mystery around it; talk of fights and kids doing drugs in the bathroom. They were the kids no one knew what to do with.

I had become one of those kids.

Principal Bartlett turned toward me. "Actions have consequences. The things we do and the choices we make can change our lives."

I bit the inside of my cheek and stared down at the red woven fabric of the chair underneath me.

And sometimes it doesn't matter. Sometimes things happen and you can't control them at all and you're stuck coming home to a dad lying in a dark room because the chemo is exhausting.

"Do you understand what I'm saying to you?"

The idea that kids who acted out were somehow dumber than other kids would always be baffling to me. And if, god forbid, you actually showed them you were intelligent, they used words like *potential* and *wasted talent*.

What they really meant was you were a *disappointment*.

Principal Bartlett gave my father a look like they were on the same side. Just trying to save me from my own lack of attendance. "If she stays in school and out of trouble, she will be eligible to return after two semesters."

"Two semesters?" my father clarified.

"Yes, but she has to enroll in the continuation program to be able to reenter any school in this district."

My father turned to me. "Atlas, do you want to go to school here?"

I looked at my father, emotion welling in my chest. He was reminding me that I still had a choice. That even here, when I was being told I didn't have one, I did. "No," I said simply.

"Okay." He stood, shaking arms lifting up his featherweight body. "Thank you for your time, Principal Bartlett."

Principal Bartlett just blinked. Once and then again. "She has to attend school."

"I'm aware," my father said. He looked to me. "Do you have all your things?"

I nodded and picked up my trash bag. They wouldn't let me

151

go back to my locker to clean it out, instead having the counselor collect all my things. The message was clear. I couldn't be trusted. My father's eyes hardened as he looked at the bag and he shook his head gently. I put my arm through my father's and walked out with him.

"Your mother is going to be angry," he told me as we walked through the parking lot.

"I know." I took a deep breath. She yelled more now than she ever had. Asked me to give reasons for my actions that I couldn't find words for. She made assumptions and threats and cried. I knew all those things were going to happen when I got home. "I can't wait."

As soon as we were in the car, he turned and looked at me. "I'm sorry."

I felt myself frown and my throat tighten. My brows pulled together, confused.

"I should have listened when you said you didn't want to go back to school. I should have—" He broke off and tried to take a deep breath that made his narrowed chest look even smaller than it was. "I wanted your life to stay normal. I didn't want any of this to affect you."

I swallowed and pressed my nails into the flesh of my palm. Crying wasn't an option. Not in front of my dad. Not when he had so many other hard things to deal with. He didn't need me to break down. It was unfair.

But he was the only person who had looked at me, looked at how I was acting and didn't think the worst. He thought *he* was to blame.

"You're still going to have to do schoolwork. And you can't tell people to fuck off. Jesus, Atlas."

"I didn't say it," I clarified. "I flipped her off as I walked out."

My dad rolled his eyes. "I thought your math teacher was an idiot anyway." He smiled at me and then his face grew serious. "Do you forgive me for not listening to you?"

Forgive him. As if he was the one I was angry at. Not the cancer, not the universe, not life being unbelievably unfair.

"Dad," I grumbled. "*I'm* sorry."

He smiled at me and gently hit my nose with his knuckle. "Fine, but we all can't be sorry, Outlaw. It leaves no time to do better."

19

KING SITS ON A rock, his journal in one hand and a pencil in the other as the morning light shines behind him. The way his hand moves tells me that he's not writing, he's drawing. He looks like a picture. I want to commit this moment to memory. It's just him and me and the stillness before the sun has risen and the sky is casting orange hues onto everything.

"You draw?"

King looks a little surprised. I watch him take in my appearance, one I can't really see. It's probably messy hair and puffy faced. I haven't worn makeup since I got here, and my clothes are covered in god only knows what.

But. I feel self-conscious under his eyes. Like I want to be pretty. Like I wish I was.

He shuts his book and smiles at me softly. The same one as before.

. . . It makes me think I *am* pretty.

"A little. Badly."

I laugh quietly as I sit down on the other side of the ashes from last night's fire. "I don't think anyone cares how you draw the trees."

He looks at me like I've said the wrong thing, but I don't know what the right thing could be. I wait for him to tell me, but he only says, "I guess you're right."

"What is it?" I ask, tilting my chin to the book. "Just notes of what we still need to do?"

"Some." He nods. "Some stuff that we have already done. A bunch of maps of the smaller trails we've already completed."

"A book of Maps." I say it because it's funny. It's my name.

But then he says, "Yeah. An Atlas if you will." He grins when he says it. *Atlas.*

I don't know when I breathe next because hearing King say . . . Atlas—

It feels.

It feels like a secret he's just uncovered. Like a lie that makes me feel embarrassed. I want it to feel good. Him knowing the truth should be freeing, but instead all I can feel is pressure in my chest that King might find out the real me.

The one who exists outside this trail.

The dull roar rattles in my chest.

It seems to shake the granite beneath us and even shake the air. As the trees grow sparse in front of us, we move closer down the slope to the river. It opens up into a wide pool with enormous boulders poking out around its mouth. A waterfall. The river spills over the edge of a rock wall and at the bottom, where the water pools, are several hikers standing on the banks. A

155

group of younger guys are climbing up to the top of the water-fall. Some people have laid clothes on the rocks like wash on a line; others sit next to piles of hiking boots and packs. The faces aren't any that I recognize, until I see one that is unmistakable.

Pidgeon.

All of Yellow seems to be sprawled out on the banks and boulders and in the water.

"That fucking . . ." Books is complaining. "Did she tell you she was going to change her trail?"

King shakes his head. "She doesn't listen anyway."

Books and King share a look before Books says, "We should probably go down there and check on her."

"Right," King replies. "Just to make sure Yellow is okay."

"Right."

"So," Sugar starts. "To be clear, we're going down to the waterfall."

Books gives her a look. "Just to check—"

But that's all it takes. Sugar and Junior start running at the same time. He's pulling his shirt over his head and she's pulling off her pants and miraculously not tripping. By the time they reach the water, she's in her underwear and he's in his shorts. Junior jumps in with a splash and when his head breaks the surface, he yelps.

"It's fucking cold!"

Sugar is screeching as she wades in, but the smile on her face isn't one I've seen recently. It's carefree. Happy. She launches herself at Junior.

"Come on!" Junior yells at us as he catches her. "Get in!"

"It's freezing! And there are probably leeches in the water!"

Books yells back, but it's all for show. We know he's going to get in.

But King shakes his head. "Leeches only live in warm water."

"Is that true?" Books asks me, like I'm Wikipedia.

I look at King. Our eyes crash together and I have to look away. "No idea," I tell Books, already bending down to unlace my boots.

I run to the waterfall, stripping off my shorts and shirt.

Junior was right. The water is the kind of cold that needles all over my body, causing my skin to rise in goose bumps. But the sweat and the dirt wash from me and I wait for my body to stop feeling freezing and grow numb.

King and Books join us, jumping into the water. I stay close to the rocks but find a patch of still water and float on my back in the sunlight. Blue stretches above me without a single cloud in the sky. Next to me, Sugar does the same. We lie silently in the water, like starfishes on the surface. It feels peaceful and the noise around us changes to a buzzing.

"What the . . ."

When Sugar and I sit up, Books is staring at the waterfall as Junior climbs up boulders.

A group of boys stands at the top and offers Junior a hand. The muscles in his back bunch and relax.

"God, he's hot," Sugar says next to me. Books cuts her a look and she follows with, "Objectively."

Books rolls his eyes and yells, "Jump, you coward."

"We get it! You're a badass. Just jump, asshole!" Sugar complains, but it's with love.

Junior shakes out his arms like he's psyching himself up and then he jumps. It's a front flip until he's feetfirst like a diver.

And I feel my heart speed inside my chest.

"It's obnoxious that he looks like that," Books says.

King's laughter filters through all the noise of the water and people from the boulder he sits on with Pidgeon and Ivy. Pidgeon leans forward, her hand on his leg, and Ivy's pushing at King. It's friendly and comfortable and—

And then Junior pops up in the water between Books and Sugar. I didn't see him get so close.

It scares Sugar but Books smiles as he pushes him back underwater.

I'm not laughing. I'm not jumping or playing. There seem to be rocks tied to my ankles that keep me here. Drowning inside my own thoughts. Maps . . . the coward who floats on the water, but doesn't dive in.

I realize what I'm going to do after I'm already swimming through the water. The temperature changes as the current pushes around me and then I'm at the boulders. Pulling myself up and carefully planting my feet on the slick rocks, I grip the places I just watched Junior climb.

"Maps!" I hear Books call my name, but I don't care. I don't look back or down. Only in front of me.

One hand over the other as the air cools my wet skin, and when I'm close to the top a beautiful boy with dark wet hair smiles down at me, offering me a hand. I let him help me and notice the three other boys who stand there. One of them is blond with a tattoo snaking up the side of his arm and he says to me, "Ladies first."

I stand, looking down at the water, which now looks farther than it had before.

Taking a deep breath, I settle into the moment.

In my mind, I can see my father standing at the edge of the pool, holding my tiny hand. He looks down at me and says, "*On the count of three let's be brave.*" He smiles and I start to shiver from the way my skin cools.

I don't want to be brave.

The blond stands behind me. "Have you jumped before?"

"No." I say it quietly as my feet shuffle on the wet spot where everyone else has jumped.

"Just make sure you keep your legs together and tuck your arms in. Don't let them slap the water, okay?"

I nod.

I can hear his smile more than see it. "It's all about just stepping off and letting go."

Stepping off and letting go.

I look over to King, who is standing on the boulder now. Even from here I can tell he doesn't want me to jump.

But I don't focus on him. I hold my hands out at my sides like I'm getting ready to fly. *On the count of three.* I'll be brave.

One.

"Fuck it."

It's more like pushing off than stepping off, and my arms flail around me like I'm flapping my wings. The seconds fall like I do, waiting for the water, waiting to hit it, waiting for this feeling of my stomach dropping and my body clenching around nothing to end. And then the water gets too close and I tuck my arms into myself and cross my legs.

My entire body jolts at the impact and I carve into the water, falling. Down, down, down. The water gets darker and the world changes colors into blacks and blues but I never hit the bottom. It's quiet and feels nice, right before I panic.

I can feel the river moving me downstream in the darkness. I'm trying to remember everything I've ever heard about undertow as I kick my way back to the top. When I push up and break the surface, I notice how far I've gone downstream and all I can think is, my mother would be so upset. The current has picked up momentum and as I try to swim to the shore, I move farther away from the group.

King jumps into the water but I can't understand why he's coming after me.

I don't focus on him, I only try to get to the other side of the water. And when I reach the bank, King is there.

His bare chest heaves and when he speaks, it sounds strained. "What the fuck was that?"

"I jumped," I tell him.

"Yeah, I saw." He sounds angry and a little worried. "What if something had happened to you?"

"Junior did it too," I try to say. No one yelled at Junior.

"*Junior* didn't end up halfway down the river."

He shakes his hair out of his eyes and water rivulets sprinkle everywhere, catching in the light. When his head leans back I watch his breathing slow.

"Fucking Christ, Maps. You didn't even tell anyone you were jumping."

"I don't have to tell you everything I do just because you're the trail lead." God. It sounds petty even to me.

"If something happened to you—"

"Nothing happened. Don't worry, no one's gonna tell Joe."

"You think I'm worried because of Joe?" He looks hurt when he asks it.

I want to tell him yes, but the way his face carries disappointment makes me feel like I'm missing something else and he thinks it should be clear. "Why else would you be worried?"

"Because . . ." His eyes are on my mouth and I'm waiting for the truth to leave his.

Say it. Say it. Say it.

But he doesn't. I hold on to a boulder and realize we are out of view of everyone else. He follows my gaze. Understanding crosses his face, and for a second, I think he looks worried, and I expect him to swim away.

Instead he stays where he is.

I shiver. Maybe from the cold, but also from him. Shirtless and me in my underwear.

"It's cold." A stupid thing to say. I'm just filling the silence, but I lean toward him.

"Maps . . ." His eyes darken and I can see myself reflected in them. The river. Me. Us.

I move closer until only a whisper separates us.

He looks down at my mouth. "I don't know what you want."

Yes he does.

I want him to kiss me. I want him to press his body against mine and I want to feel his skin touching all of my skin. I want to feel if I affect him or not. I want to know what he tastes like and what he sounds like when he's lost in another person.

"I want to know if you think about . . ." I say softly.

But I can't seem to say it either.

King goes still and looks into my eyes. "Maps. I—"

"Maps!" Sugar calls my name from somewhere above us and King pushes back from me.

A flush runs down his chest as it rises in heavy breaths. I imagine mine does too. The truth is on his lips, and even though I can hear Books calling King's name, I want to hear it.

"King." I say it like a plea.

And then he's pulling himself from the water.

I throw my head back and stare at the sky for ten excruciating seconds. This place I stay in, the one where King has me wondering about him, makes me more unsure than I've been about anything in a long time.

For the rest of the day, we lie on the rocks in the sun and let the warm light dry out our skin and undergarments. We are a tangle of goose bumps and bruises and scrapes.

Junior flirts with the blond boy with tattoos and Sugar makes a face each time she hears him laugh. Books is busy pretending like he doesn't notice any of it. I call Sugar to come lie out with me and try to get a tan.

"Fine, I'll help you get skin cancer," she says, even though her skin has already turned into a deep golden brown. We lie on the boulders together like reptiles, and neither of us think about the boys.

My eyes are closed when I say, "I love the way the sun feels after you've been in cold water. The way it warms you up, super slowly." It feels a little like a confession, so I open them.

"How it kinda tickles," Sugar adds as a bead of water falls down her side.

"You're so weird," Books breathes as he comes to lie down next to her.

She laughs. "All of this is so weird."

It was said like a joke, but Books's body tenses and Sugar's fingers run over the smooth stone at her sides.

"Yeah. I guess it doesn't matter," Books says.

"What doesn't matter?" I ask him, even though I know what he means. I'm just hoping that he doesn't feel brave enough to say it.

Everyone is quiet for a long time before Books answers. "What I think. What you think. None of this counts."

I hate that these words hurt. Salt in the open wound of our shared truth. This isn't permanent. We are the people who don't count. The names that aren't real. None of this counts because we will go back to our real lives and leave all this behind.

I've been thinking it, but it hurts to hear out loud.

I want this to count.

But just like when I jumped into the water, I keep my hands tucked into my sides and wait to fall.

20

"WE'LL SLEEP AT BASECAMP tonight."

King says it as if this is the most normal thing in the world. Junior looks at me, confused, as if I'll have the answers. But I'm confused too.

Except for the dark part of my mind that tells me King wants to go to Basecamp because of someone else. Someone he wants to smile at like he smiled at me.

Basecamp turns out to be a campground right next to the falls where several hikers have their tents and folding chairs and kitchen set-ups. The large open field has firepits with people around them as flames dance at their center. I can't remember the last time I saw someone sitting on something nature didn't provide.

Not everyone here is a volunteer for the state park, which is clear by the things they pack. We walk past a silver coffee maker sitting on a rock near the fire and I try not to let a whimper escape me. I haven't been doing this long but I'm already making judgments about the luxury items people have brought with them.

God. When did I become a person who thinks *chairs* are an indulgence?

Evergreens shoot up like a fence around the meadow everyone is camping in. A few buildings sit on the edges of the meadow. Weather-worn wooden A-frames with sagging roofs have signs with symbols for bathrooms or showers. A large community space with giant all-purpose tables sits next to them and is currently being used for food prep. Several tents litter the pasture like giant, colorful rocks shooting up from the ground.

And the chatter of people.

Civilization.

It sounds like a river. A dull and indistinct roar. Groups of people sit next to their huddles of tents. Older hikers with gray hair and long beards sit in a spot closer to the bathrooms. Younger hikers in dirty clothes scatter through the place. You can see the days of the trail clinging to their skin and shining back in their eyes. There's a worn energy about them that feels almost calm. Like the hike has been hard, but it's shifted something in them. I hope we look like this too. Lived in and settled.

Most of the hikers are older than us . . . except for one group.

They're camped off to the side in green tents that sit in a semicircle near the bigger firepit, all brand-new and still shiny. They look like REI ads for hikers. Smiles and sun-kissed faces. Hiking boots that look fashionable with heathered grey wool socks. Their outfits match.

Next to them, we look homeless. White tube socks, trashed boots, giant stained T-shirts, dirt that cannot be scrubbed from under our nails.

Instantly, I feel self-conscious.

And standing with them are Ivy and Pidgeon. Ivy bumps Pidgeon on the shoulder, and she looks up. Even I know she's beautiful, and something inside me shrinks. Pidgeon runs up to King wearing that same smile on her face.

"Hey! You made it!" she exclaims as she follows us to a clear spot farthest from the fire and close to the trees.

He tosses down his bag and smiles an easy smile at her.

I judge it against the ones he's given me.

"She's not even that pretty," Sugar says as she tosses me the tent spikes.

"Who?" I ask, trying to keep some of my dignity by playing dumb.

But Sugar's never been good at letting someone play dumb. "You know who I'm talking about."

I stomp a spike into the ground with my boot. "Yes, she is."

Sugar nods her head gently. "Yeah. She is."

Ivy demands we have dinner with everyone at the site. Most of the camp is sharing in some kind of *bring what you have* hiker's potluck and Books shakes his head.

"So that's how you've been getting out of rice and beans."

Ivy gives him a mischievous look. "You don't earn more volunteer hours if you suffer."

"I should," Books tells her, and they laugh.

Junior stalks off into the crowd.

The best part of the campground is the showers. We take turns bathing in the almost warm water. It feels like a treat, to use soap and have water fall off my body instead of sitting in a river. Warm water should be mandatory. A basic human right of survival, like air and food.

People have packages of hot dogs and sausages, bags of chips, and someone has an entire package of Oreo cookies.

It doesn't feel like dinner at a restaurant; this feels better. Junior and Sugar find me, and we eat our feast like it's the first time we've ever had food.

A large fire roars and I feel grateful that no one has asked me to look for wood. Something in the air has my bones relaxing as Junior and I chat with two hikers from Colorado. They tell us if we're ever in Boulder, we can crash on their couch, which feels so odd. I'm a stranger, but they explain that we have a good vibe.

"There's a code. Hikers respect nature and respect each other," he says with a shrug. "People that do this are good humans. You can tell who belongs here and who doesn't."

My throat tightens, and when I look at Junior, he's smiling, but his brow is furrowed.

These people have made assumptions about us, but they aren't the usual ones. They think we are like them. The code isn't that different from the one we've been following, but all these people willingly live by it, and because we live by it too, the assumption is that we're *good*.

It feels odd for someone to assume I'm a . . . good kid.

Someone offers Junior an alcoholic seltzer and he says yes, instantly. I give him a look that I hope reminds him of the last time we drank, but he only points over to the pretty hikers. "They have a whole thing of them. I'd probably have to drink ten of these to actually get drunk."

I take it from Junior's outstretched hand. His sparkly nail polish is chipped and almost gone. The drink tastes like artificial berries and is bitter on my tongue.

King stands over at the fire with Books while they eat hot dogs and talk to Pidgeon and Ivy. "What's the deal with you two?" I ask Junior, tilting the can in the direction of Books.

Junior gives me a long look. "Same question to you, but about the blond."

"Nothing is going on. King follows *all* the rules. Internship." There's an edge to my voice.

"No he doesn't. He drank that whiskey too." Junior motions his arms around us. "Also, I'm one hundred percent sure that this place isn't a part of our trail, so the rules don't apply here."

"Like a black hole of rules?"

"Exactly. A fold in the space-time continuum."

I laugh at him. "We absolutely do not understand space."

"No." He takes another drink. "But I do understand rules and all the ways they can be bent toward something you want."

I ignore him because I need to believe my own words so that the line between King and me stays black and thick. Not like the water earlier when I almost dove across it.

I bite my lip and think about the way King wouldn't meet my eyes when he got out of the water. Guilty. I had done the wrong thing again.

"Yeah, well, Alaska is far." I take a long drink from the can and hand it back to Junior. "It's not worth it, you know?"

He takes a sip of what's left and then crushes the can. "Do I know? You're not marrying him. It doesn't have to be forever. It can just be for *now*."

"Is that what you're doing?"

Junior splays a hand over his chest. "I am playing an advanced game of cat and mouse. But I have yet to determine if I'm the cat or the mouse."

"I think you're the cheese."

He rolls his eyes, pulling me toward him, and kisses the top of my head. "This is why you don't have friends."

Junior puts another can in my hand and the world grows darker. The firelight illuminates our faces and the air grows cooler. The older crowd has a guitar and someone else has a small drum. People sing old songs that I recognize my mother and father played during dinner as they sipped wine and stared at the stars, reminiscing about the past or dreaming about the future.

Pidgeon comes over and asks if we want to play a game with Yellow. I can see that King and Books are joining even before she tells us they are.

I can tell Junior is going to say yes, so I say, "No thanks." My smile is tight and my tone is rude even if the words aren't.

"Okay, if you change your mind—"

"We won't." I cut her off and she only nods.

Junior raises his brows and I see his question on his lips.

"Don't. I don't want to talk about it," I tell him and take the last drink of the seltzer. King does something to me, and when I leave my body and look down at the person I am, I'm embarrassed.

"Incredibly healthy. Not talking about things that turn you into a monster."

"I'm not a monster. I'm just . . ."

"*Jealous.* That's the word you're looking for."

I hold a finger up to my lips and make a shushing noise.

But for the first time on the trail, the night gets louder, not quieter.

People laugh and joke and tell stories. A red cup with clear alcohol is passed to me and then to Junior. I hear a girl's laughter, but I don't look up to see if it's because of King or if it comes from the direction he's in. I just drink.

"Whoa, okay." Junior takes the cup from me. "Manners, Maps. This isn't our gross cheap booze. Save some for the locals."

But it helps. It makes the world fuzzy and broken around the edges. Something to quiet my feelings. My stomach tightens.

Later, King walks over to us, asking if we're doing okay. He sees the cup in Junior's hands and tells us to slow down, but he's only looking at me when he says it.

"It's water." My words sound like they're *under*water.

King looks at Junior.

"She's fine, really."

I make a large circle with my hands. "This is a black hole." Junior tries to pull me away, but I push his hands from me.

"What?" King looks confused.

I decide to help him understand as Sugar walks up. "Don't worry. That internship?" I give him a serious look. "You're gonna . . ." I clap my hands together and make a smashing noise.

"What did I miss?" Her eyes are wide and Junior just shakes his head.

"Black holes and rules that are like bendy straws."

"Bendy—" King frowns.

"Okay. We are going to go dance off all . . . this." Junior waves a hand at me.

King stops Junior. "Don't go too—stay close?"

Junior looks at him with kind eyes when he nods in agreement.

The world sways as we do, and I think of my dad dancing with me to a Bob Dylan song.

"I was looking for the troublemakers from Blue!" Rocky says, smiling mostly at Sugar.

Rocky flirts with everything that walks near him. He calls Junior the most beautiful boy he's ever seen, and he tells me that I'm too good for the grouchy one.

"So, be honest," he asks. "Am I gonna get beat up?" Rocky motions to King and Books, who sit on the other side of the fire looking at us. "I recognize *that* look."

"Those are our trail leaders," Sugar tells him. "They're just making sure we don't get into trouble."

He laughs into his cup. "Into trouble or into someone else?"

I find King across the clearing and I try to smile. But our eyes meet for a moment too long. Too much. A muscle in his jaw tightens and desire weaves itself low in my belly. Like a hunger deep inside me.

It can be just for now.

And then Junior is standing in front of me. "There be dragons that way."

He's right, but I can't tell if King is the dragon or the treasure.

"I'm not . . ." I trail off.

"Good," Sugar tells me, her tone turning serious. "Because I don't want to be the only girl on the trail because you got sent home."

"What?" I look between her and Junior.

"Who's gonna say anything?" Junior asks. "Everyone else is breaking one of those rules."

"This also applies to you," she tells him. "We don't know Yellow and you guys are so obvious."

"They aren't gonna say anything," he tells me, but he sounds less sure now.

"I hope not."

"This is supposed to be a black hole," I whine at Junior.

"Shhhh." He covers my ears and says to Sugar, "You're upsetting the baby."

I make a pouty face at her. She rolls her eyes but doesn't bring it up again.

The night moves on and I follow Rocky to another group of hikers who are all trying to eat Oreos off their faces with no hands. I look back to where Books and Junior stand so close there's no space between them. Rocky and I laugh at the stars and for the first time in these woods, I can't feel my grief.

I stand and dance and laugh, and then someone sings "Landslide."

A second later, there is a hand around my wrist. "Come on." The words are a whisper, close to my ear. I feel them flutter against my neck and the fingers that circle against my pulse aren't tight, more like a question.

King. He stands holding my hand, almost as if he's pulling me from my mind back into the moment. I lean forward, gently.

"This is the water she's been drinking," Rocky, my new best friend, says to King, and he nods. "I think she's ready for bed."

"I'm not," I say, but I let King guide me toward our tents. My new best friend is a *traitor*. "I don't want to go to bed."

"Okay," King tells me. "How about we just lie down?"

"I'm not drunk." I stop walking but I don't miss the way he said *we*.

"Okay," he agrees. But it sounds like a parent agreeing with a child.

"I'm buzzed, but I'm not drunk."

"Me too," he says.

"Then why do I have to go to bed and you don't?" I'm whining like the child I don't want to be.

King runs his tongue over his teeth, something I notice he does when he's thinking. "You looked like you needed a—a break."

My fingernails dig into my palms and I say, "I *need* a cheeseburger." I hold up my index finger. "I might have drunk more than I should. It's this stupid trail. All I eat is beans and granola bars. I *can* handle my liquor."

"Sure." He almost smiles. "But since there isn't a Taco Bell or Jack in the Box, let's settle for water."

God, I'm pathetic. Being sent to bed early, even though everyone else is staying up. And King having to babysit me.

I take a step forward, but I stumble a bit and hair falls in front of my face. I try to brush it out, but I know I look like a mess. Blowing strands of hair and stumbling. "You don't have to babysit," I say even as he laughs and takes my arm to steady me.

King digs through our packs and offers me my toothbrush and toothpaste. I do the world's worst job of brushing my teeth and he stays with me. Wiping my mouth with the back of my hand, I give him back the toothbrush.

He brushes my hair from my face and walks me back to my tent. Inside, he hands me the shirt I always sleep in and doesn't turn away when I change. We're past that, anyway.

"Why are you being so nice to me?" I ask as I struggle to find the arm holes of the shirt with my head trapped inside the fabric.

King pulls my shirt so my head pops out. "Why shouldn't I be?" But he doesn't look at me when he says it.

Because I drank too much, even after you told me not to. Because I spent all night hoping you would see me flirting with other boys and get jealous.

"Because I hate Pidgeon. Her name is dumb," I tell him as I finally free my arms.

"Why do you hate her?" A little laugh fills the night air between us.

"Because of black holes."

His face crumples in confusion. "What?"

I don't answer him; instead I say something else equally stupid. "I'm sorry I ruined your flirting."

Now he smiles. "You didn't ruin my flirting. I'm doing just fine."

I hope he isn't. I hope Pidgeon hates him. I hope she thinks he's a weird, mouth-breathing creep. I crawl into my bag and lie down.

"Are you good?" he asks.

No. "Yeah."

King nods and moves to unzip the tent, but I reach out and grab his wrist. My fingers on him.

"Stay here?" I ask quietly.

"Stay?"

"Yeah. Just. Just until I fall asleep?"

King looks torn and I can see *no* on his face right before he falls back onto Sugar's sleeping bag. "Just till you fall asleep," he promises.

"Okay," I say. My hands tuck under the side of my face and I stare at King, who looks up at the roof of the tent. Outside are all the noises of people shouting and laughing and playing the guitar, but all I can hear is my heart.

"Are you gonna look at me or are you gonna go to sleep?" he asks with his hands folded on his chest.

"Do you like her?" I ask him.

"Who?"

"That girl. Pidgeon."

He lets out a heavy breath. "I'm leaving for Alaska."

The reminder is a stone in my stomach. "That's not what I asked."

I expect him to be frustrated or annoyed, but instead he asks me, "At the waterfall, what were you going to ask me?"

"The waterfall?"

"You asked if I thought about—something. And then you stopped."

I don't know how to answer or what to say, or even how to say it.

"Do you want to leave?" I ask.

He turns now and looks at me, his whole body angled toward me. "Do you want me to leave?"

"No."

It's honest and something I won't be brave enough to say tomorrow.

His eyes dance over my face. "Why?"

"I didn't get to ask you my question."

"About leaving?" His voice is low.

"About kissing me."

King goes still, his eyes unblinking as they stare back into mine.

It's already out there, so I say to him, "Do you think about kissing me?"

He doesn't look like he's breathing. His whole body is tense as it lies on top of Sugar's sleeping bag. King lets out a breath and I realize how close he is to me. "Do you want me to?"

It can just be for now.

"Yes," I whisper.

King's eyes are on my mouth. "Maps."

"Do it," I dare. "Kiss me."

But he only sits there, looking at me.

So I lean forward.

Just for now.

I press my lips to King's, soft and gentle. He lets out a soft breath and I realize he's not kissing me back.

I move to pull away, feeling shame burn on my face, but when I do, his eyes are studying me. A question reflects back in the dark of his irises and I want to ask him what it means.

But then King's mouth is on mine again. At first it's gentle, but then he leans over me—into me—and everything turns.

His body presses into mine and I try to pull him closer.

176

The sleeping bag is still between us, but it doesn't matter. His mouth is fevered, and I run my hands over him. His waist, under his shirt, over his shoulders. I touch all the places I've spent the entire time I've known him wondering what they feel like. My hands are on his hips and I pull them closer to my own until they're pressing against all the parts of me that ache.

Everything is so intense that I forget. He kisses my neck, my collarbone. I want his touch in different places. On more sensitive skin. All over me. I want *him*. I take his hand and move it under my shirt, making it clear what I'm asking of him.

The noises that leave me are groaned against his lips. His entire body tenses and then . . .

King is sitting back on his haunches. It's so sudden I feel like it's knocked the wind from me.

"I—" He runs a hand into his hair. "You've had a lot to drink. And I can't . . ."

"King." I say his name and hope that it's enough to bring him back.

But he barely hears me. "There are things— I need—"

"*King*." What does he need?

"No. Just. Go to sleep, Maps. We can talk in the morning."

But I'm not sure if I'll be brave in the morning.

Tomorrow we will leave the black hole and *just for now* will be gone.

21

I WAKE UP WITH Sugar snoring next to me and spend an undefinable amount of time staring at the top of the tent hoping that I will fall back asleep. But my head pounds and embarrassment scorches through me as I remember King.

No.

Bits and pieces of last night find me. His hands touching me. His kiss. The press of his body. It makes me feel hungry and humiliated. Because when I close my eyes, I can't stop seeing his face as he left.

When I crawl outside, it's still dark and the campground is quiet. Fires are out, and gear is packed away. One of the older hikers is asleep in a chair and I wonder if he spent all night there.

The blue tent is quiet, and I know only a piece of fabric separates me from King.

From our kiss.

From him telling me that we will talk in the morning. I run a hand down my face. I need to take stock of what I'm doing. Organize my thoughts into a straight line. Standing, I walk over toward the stone firepit a few yards from our tents. Far enough that the blue tent is swallowed by a sea of small nylon boulders.

All my thoughts are about King. Not just this morning, but so often I can't tell when it started. I am not that kind of person. I don't want to keep thinking about a boy. A boy who is going to Alaska. Our lives moving in separate directions.

That's not true. His life is moving and mine isn't at all. The only thing I can think about after this trail is going home. My dad's list sits in my back pocket still, and something about it nags at me. Like I'm missing the obvious.

I unscrew the cap of my Nalgene bottle and fill my mouth with water until my cheeks are wide and then convince myself to swallow.

"You're looking ill." Pidgeon walks out from the woods, her shirt crumpled and her hair falling out of its ponytail. She points at herself. "Walk of shame."

But there is no shame in her at all.

Behind, a dark-haired boy walks toward the REI hikers.

I give her a tight smile. It's good to know she's not with King, even though I didn't really think they were.

"So," she whispers. "What're you doing up so early?" It's conspiratorial, like we're going to trade secrets under the morning stars.

I'm not trading anything with this person. "Just trying to get my shit together," I tell her.

She makes a horrified face as she sits down. "*God,* whatever for?" Pidgeon lays back on the long log with her legs dangling off it. "My most redeeming quality is being messy. No one likes people with their shit together. It's the great thing about this program. Everyone's messy, so. Be messy."

I think about King and the ominous way he talks about the family that doesn't want him. The way Sugar seems to be running. Junior, who is always fighting something, and the way Books protects himself.

And me. A mess.

I think about how sometimes our scars aren't things you can see. Like the absence of a person.

"My dad died." I say it because it feels like something someone other than King and Joe should know. And because Pidgeon doesn't seem like someone who will matter. Her reaction, or pity or apathy, isn't something I have to care about because I don't care about her.

She looks over at me with her large brown eyes full of sincerity and I steel myself for the *I'm so sorry* and the *you'll see him again* I know is coming.

"Man, that *sucks*."

It takes me too long to really understand what she's just said. Seconds where her words are the only thing trying to find a place in my mind to settle, the place where they belong. Sympathy, pity, awkward encouragement. They don't file into any of those categories. Her words are confusing. I can't even believe what she's just said. *Man, that sucks?*

It does.

It does *suck*.

My laugh bubbles up from inside me and rides on my words

when I tell Pidgeon, "Yeah, it does. It totally *fucking* does."

Her face turns to me as I laugh harder than I have in a long time. And she keeps the smile on her face when my laughter mixes with my tears and turns into crying I can't control.

Pidgeon doesn't hush me or soothe me. She sits with me, listening to me do all the things in between.

I wipe at my eyes. "I'm sorry. I don't know . . ."

Honestly, I don't know anything. Maybe I'm so hungover that I can't even really understand what I'm doing here.

But Pidgeon doesn't look annoyed or shocked or confused. She looks like she understands my mess. "Grief is fucking weird, right?"

And I realize that's what this is. It's not just the sad, or the broken, it's all the moments where I don't get to control the way I miss someone.

Pidgeon takes a deep breath and smiles at me, like this emotional outburst is actually the right thing. For the first time since my dad got diagnosed, I've done the right thing. "Yeah." She pats my leg. "You're doing just fine. You know that?"

I don't. I feel like I'm drowning and failing and I'm scared and angry and I've lost myself somewhere along the way. But instead, I just say, "I don't know anything anymore."

"Well, then you're doing it right. If you knew what the fuck you were doing, you'd already be doing it wrong."

Pidgeon is a forest therapist on a walk of shame. She's made me feel better about the mess inside my heart in these past moments than anyone has in a counseling session or conversation. "I get why King likes you," I surprise myself by saying.

She laughs. "I get why he likes *you*."

"Ah, I'm not sure about that. I think he sees me as trouble."

"Yeah? *Lucky you*." The grin on Pidgeon's face is enormous. "I wouldn't worry about King. He's so worried about Alaska it's twisting him into knots. He thinks it will make someone else proud and hasn't figured out yet that someone else's *anything* is bullshit."

I want to ask about it, but the next moment, she has us up and digging around for *breakfast beers* and the rest of the Oreos.

I drink the cold lager fast and it helps with my head.

"Here you are." Junior walks over to us from the tents.

"Here we are," Pidgeon says, arms wide. "Breakfast beer?" she asks.

Junior shakes his head. "We thought you were eaten by bears," he says to me. "Turns out it was just a bird."

Pidgeon smiles. "Clever. You're the clever one?"

Junior ignores her. "We are getting ready to head out."

I turn to Pidgeon. "Thanks for . . ." There are too many things to thank her for and all of them are caught in my chest.

"You're welcome." She lifts her beer at me in a salute. As if everything was simply nothing.

Our tent is packed and my bag is already rolled when we return. "Found her," Junior announces, and everyone looks at me. Everyone.

King.

King is looking at me.

"She was drinking beer with that chaos monster Pidgeon," Junior adds.

Books groans. "No one is ever allowed to be alone with Pidge."

"How did she get to be a trail lead?" Sugar asks. "What was Joe thinking?"

"People love her." Books shrugs. "Means they do what she says."

"Oh, I saw." Sugar hands me a bar for my breakfast. "You missed it last night. She climbed to the top of a tree and dared one of the fancy hikers to follow her. He ended up falling out of the tree. Probably cracked a rib. Where did you go last night?" she asks me.

My eyes move to King even though I don't want them to. "I went to bed."

"Lightweight." Junior pushes at my shoulder.

We pack up and head out without saying goodbye to anyone in the camp. It feels like leaving Neverland. Some secret place. *Black hole.* And I tell myself what happened between King and me, at the waterfall and in the tent, happened because we were caught up in the energy. In the gravitational pull of the black hole.

King stands to the side and waits until I pass, walking behind me, but he doesn't speak until we can't see Basecamp.

"Maps." He says my name, soft, and it makes me think of last night.

I take a breath. And another. Trying to think of what to say, how to speak to him.

"Maps."

I know what he's going to say. *It was a mistake. I shouldn't have. We can't.*

But all those things really mean one thing. *You're not worth it.*

"We don't have to talk." I stop and so does King. "We can just— It's fine."

"You're fine," he repeats.

And I'm back to being fine. I try to smile, but I think it's probably all teeth and awkward gestures.

He looks like he's struggling to say something and the last thing I can handle is his kindness. Letting me down gently. I'm already rubbed raw from this morning.

"I crossed a line and pushed and I shouldn't have. It's okay. It doesn't mean . . . anything." My lie tastes like ash.

"Right. It doesn't mean anything." The group continues to walk and King seems to notice. He shakes his head. "Fine, but it can't happen again. You can't just—"

He doesn't want me to kiss him. Because I'm not worth it. I can't let him finish that sentence and shatter my feelings. "Because of Joe."

"Joe?"

"If he found out. No fraternization. The internship." I'm listing off things to tell him I understand. I know why he has to let me down easy. I'm trying to make him feel better about the stabbing rejection I feel between my ribs. As if it will help me retain an ounce of my pride.

His eyes search mine and I remember when they were dark with emotion just last night. "It's unfair," he tells me simply.

That we can agree on. "I understand. You don't have to, like, worry. Or whatever." I tell myself I don't want him to argue with me, or push it, but instead I say, "We're good, right?"

I need him to say *yes*.

But when he looks at me and says, "Sure, Maps," I can't help feeling disappointed.

And I know I'm just lying to myself again.

22

MORNINGS AT CAMP ALWAYS start the same.

With the sound of sunrise. As if the light has its own melody and it reaches fingers down between the trees to gently stir the daybreak awake. Most mornings I lie on my mat and listen to the world begin. Birds, animals, bugs, and rivers. Everything feels possible in those early moments. New and optimistic.

After Basecamp things shift, but not in the way I expect.

King and I are not good. We are worse. We're two people pretending we are good. There's no fighting, or arguing, or sitting at the fire together in silence. King avoids me with tight, polite smiles and I only speak to him when I have to.

But at night, when no one else is around, I think about our kiss. I remember all the stolen glances at his face during the day and all the moments when I remembered what his lips tasted like. I pretend like nothing is wrong.

Junior and Books are the opposite. They are two people who are trying to pretend that they aren't magnets constantly being drawn to each other.

And Sugar.

Directly in the middle like a rubber band pulled taut.

But hopeful mornings only last until I lift my head off my pillow. For the past few days, the tension in the air has felt unavoidable.

King and me. Books and Junior. Sugar and me. Sugar and Junior. Sugar and Books. Sugar and King.

Sugar. Sugar. Sugar.

So I shouldn't be surprised when the first thing I hear is the sound of Books and Sugar arguing.

My eyes crack open and I hear her say something about tea, but I know it's probably not about tea. It was probably about the camp.

I push myself out of the sleeping bag and slip my boots on, but the minute I unzip the tent door . . .

Something feels wrong.

The air is still and I can't hear the birds or insects.

I smell the smoke before I see it.

I always thought it would be black or gray, but this smoke is white.

White. And I hear the pops of twigs and leaves.

Fire moves over the grass faster than I think is possible. I don't know what happens next. Maybe I'm screaming. It's moving to the underbrush as it pops and sizzles.

My heart is in my throat as the flames drag farther and wider. I can feel my pulse as it punches through my chest in a fast rhythm.

King is yelling as he stomps at the brush, but his voice buzzes in my ear. I grab my sleeping bag and lay it over the fire. I'm stepping on it and then picking it up and moving it. Sugar is doing the same. Books has a heavy tarp he's throwing over a bush. Junior is pouring out water. King is shoveling dirt onto embers. We are all panicking and yelling. I feel the fire blistering my skin, but I don't stop. My mind goes blank.

I don't know when it happens, but eventually our panic subsides and we realize the fire is gone. The patch of charred earth we stand on still smolders, but none of us move. As if we're afraid the fire will come back.

Finally, King speaks, keeping his eyes on the black earth. "How—" His voice cracks. "How did that happen?"

None of us answer. But only one of us is crying.

Fat tears run down Sugar's face as she hangs her head low. She sniffs and Books curses. My hands shake and a small burn in the shape of a circle is beginning to welt on my wrist.

Books digs in his bag and pulls out a green jar. "Put this on and take something for the pain. Second-degree burns can be really painful."

Junior takes it. King grabs the sat phone and it looks like a bomb in his hand. "I'm gonna . . . call this in."

"Do you have to?" Junior asks, but he knows the answer is yes.

"Fuck." Books looks up to the sky. "Joe is gonna be pissed."

That is a massive understatement and the phone in King's hand trembles as he stalks away from the group. This phone call could be the end of Alaska. It could be the end of this trail.

Sugar wipes the tears from her eyes and takes my sleeping bag off the ground. She holds it up, and even though it's not burned through, it's still charred. It probably reeks of smoke.

"Am I gonna get arrested?" she asks, looking at Books.

His mouth opens like he could catch the right thing to say if he just stands like that for long enough. And then he says, "I don't know."

The words settle on all of us.

Her bottom lip quivers and she says, "My dad is going to be so disappointed."

Disappointed. Disappointment is always worse. I remember when I had a dad who could make me feel that way.

We look between each other, all four of us wondering what exactly we are supposed to do, as Sugar starts cleaning up. I recognize this. The act of staying busy so you don't deal with emotions. I watched my mother do it. I did it.

Junior jerks his head toward Books, who only frowns and gives Junior a small shake of his head. Boys are cowards.

"Sugar?" I say.

"Yeah?" Her voice sounds steady and practiced, but she's shaking. Her whole body.

"Hey, stop for a second."

She doesn't look at me as she shakes her head no. "I'm fine, Maps."

"Sugar."

"We need to clean up and then . . ." She looks around, a little lost. "We need to clean up."

"Sugar."

"Stop saying my name like that! Just help me. Help me clean this up."

"You have a burn . . ." I say it softly as I point toward her neck. "We can clean up later. Let's clean ourselves up first."

She reaches up to the place between her collarbone and her neck and winces. "Oh."

"Let's go to the river and put some cold water on it."

Her eyes look frantic. "Do you have burns?" she asks me.

Other than the one on my wrist, I can feel one on my leg. "Yeah," I say as gently as possible. "I think we all do."

"Oh." Her voice is small. Tight.

"Joe is on his way." King runs a hand over his head as he walks back toward us. I look for signs of what happened on the call, but King's eyes are still on the ground.

"King, can you grab the first aid and the Advil?" Books asks.

He nods and Books and King look at each other in the way they communicate without words. I focus solely on Sugar.

Junior moves to the other side of her and we escort her down the hill toward the river with King and Books following. It takes a bit to get there, and we stay silent as we move together.

Junior takes off his shirt and I notice all the places it has little holes in it. The skin under it is red. I hadn't even considered any burns underneath our clothing. "Can I take your shirt off?" I ask as I sit her down on a rock. She nods only once. A stiff movement.

Sugar hunches over in her sports bra, and I straighten her up. There aren't a lot of burns on her skin. I look down at her legs, but she's wearing pants. Before I can ask her to take those off, she looks at me from under her lashes. Tears have welled in the corners of her eyes. "I started the fire."

Snap. The sound of the cord holding Sugar together breaks with her quiet confession, but it's not for us, it's for herself. She didn't mean to start the fire, but intention isn't action.

"Okay," I whisper back to her.

"I almost burned down the whole—" She chokes back a sob. "If you hadn't been there . . ."

"But we were. We were there." My words are delicate and I hope that's what they feel like against her heart.

"I wasn't thinking and I could have started a whole fire in the middle of the fucking forest." Her head goes into her palms and the sound that escapes her causes something inside of my chest to fracture.

"Sugar."

"I'm being such a brat. Why am I like this? I almost— Fuck." She's talking nonsense. It doesn't matter. I wrap my arms around her neck and let her cry into my shoulder. All I want to do in this moment is comfort her. Let her know I care. Stop the way she cracks and breaks. I feel her head lift and she says, "I'm sorry. Really, I'm so sorry. I didn't—"

"It's okay," Books whispers to her as he runs a hand over the back of hers.

"I've never been in trouble. Ever. I've never even gotten detention." She looks at Junior. "I'm a good kid."

Junior gives her a little smile and brushes hair off her forehead. "So are the kids that get into trouble."

"Maps." King stands beside me. "Let's go treat your burns."

"I'm—" But his hand is under my arm and he's moving me away from Sugar.

I look back at her, ready to protest, but Books and Junior crouch in the spot I just left.

Sugar is okay. Or she will be. Or maybe she won't, but I can't do anything about it right now.

We walk down the riverbank and King takes off his shirt, dipping it into the water. "Where are you burned?"

"Um." I look down at my wrist and the side of my finger. My leg.

"Pull up your shirt. I'll check your back."

It's not a question, but my emotions feel rubbed raw and I don't have the energy to pretend to be mad at King.

So I do it. And I tell myself the nerves I feel are just because Sugar almost set fire to the forest, and she is in the middle of a breakdown. Not because I'm keenly aware this could be some of my last moments with King. We could all be going home and . . .

King runs his fingers over the skin on my back, and I tense. A certain spot holds his attention, and he says behind me, "Does this hurt?" He presses on the small of my back.

I shake my head, before I remember I have a voice. "No."

His fingers move lower down my back to the waistband of my pants. He runs a finger against it and I close my eyes for a second, just feeling the sensation of him touching me. I don't lean back, but I want to.

Then his hands are off my waist, and he runs a finger against the edges of my sports bra.

He lets out a breath I feel on my skin and then King drops down on his haunches and I feel his hands on my legs.

"I think you're good."

"Good." I sound like a parrot.

192

"Let's take care of this." He takes my wrist and smears an antibiotic ointment onto it.

"Shouldn't we use the stuff Books had?"

"This is better," he tells me with complete confidence. "I burned myself a lot as a kid." He covers my arm with a bandage and takes medical tape and gently presses it on the edges. And then his hands move over my palms gently, as if he's remembering the cuts that were there. It feels like an apology for something that happened in another lifetime.

"We're almost done." I don't know if he means with the burns or with the trail. Maybe it's one of those things that means both.

"Your turn," I tell him and he stands up.

Without me asking, he pulls off his shirt and I spend more time than I should running my fingers against the soft skin. He has two small burns on his back and without asking, I copy what he did to me to treat the burns.

"Do they hurt?" I ask as he flinches when I treat the one against his side.

"No. I just . . . wasn't ready."

I hum my response as I focus on the second one.

King clears his throat and says, "You ran toward the fire."

"Hmm?" I ask.

"The fire. You saw it and you . . . I heard you scream, but by the time I processed what was happening, you were already moving toward it with your sleeping bag."

I let out a little laugh. "Stop, drop, and roll in school must have really made an impression."

"No," he tells me. "That was . . ."

"It just *was*," I finish for him. "I didn't even think about it." I swallow as I cut the tape. "But I was scared. The whole time."

"Everyone is afraid. It's not the same as someone who runs toward danger when there's a crisis."

"I think my therapist would call it an unhealthy disregard for personal safety."

"Is that what you were doing? Not thinking about your safety?" His tone is challenging, as if I will eventually realize I'm wrong.

"I was . . ." I think about the flames. Sugar's face as she stood in horror as the ground turned orange and red. The truth settles on my tongue. "I was afraid, and I knew the only way to stop being afraid was to put out the fire. I just saw something that needed to be done and did it."

"Not everyone can do that."

"You did."

"Maps. Stop." He turns to me. "You—you yelled. You moved. You— Junior tried to stop it with our *water bottles*." King laughs, but it's a pitiful thing. "You did the right thing. It was brave."

"I'm not brave."

King looks at me, his eyes looking into mine. "Yes, you are." His words are firm. They aren't full of lyrical prose and poetry. They're factual.

It's not a compliment. It's different. King's words are a truth about me that he can see. I fold them up like a love letter and hide them in my heart.

He turns to me, and I take the ointment and dab it on a burn on his jaw. I remember my hand on it when I was kissing him.

He takes the jar from me and finishes the minor burns on his legs and on his arms as if he can read my thoughts and wants to put distance between us.

Maybe he can.

We walk back to the camp. The dark patches of burned earth don't look terrible. In my mind the fire was bigger. Sugar stands in front of the black spot. Her hands bunch into the fabric of her shorts and her jaw tightens.

And then Sugar's crying. A heaving sob.

"I fucking hate it here. I hate it!" She screams it into the universe.

I wrap an arm around her waist, but I don't speak as she cries. I don't know when we became the kind of friends who hold each other, who try to stop the pain, but we are. There's nothing any of us can do to make it better and that knowledge bleeds onto me and stings worse than any burn.

And then she says, "I don't want to go home."

"Sugar, you're not going to jail. We won't let you," Junior tells her.

"No. When Joe comes. I don't want him to send me home. I want to stay here."

It's such a contradiction. She hates it here, but she doesn't want to leave. I try to imagine what would keep someone like Sugar here. What could keep a girl like her from wanting to go home, a girl who's never even had detention.

But maybe all of us have something that's worse than clearing trails. Maybe the four other people here are what we need even when we hate it.

I hold her as she cries. Until my arms are stiff and my shirt has a wet spot. It's worth it. We don't do anything for the rest of the day. Joe will be here tomorrow and that makes the minutes feel like they are burning up in the sunshine.

We all wonder what this fire will cost. Will Sugar get into trouble? Will King lose Alaska?

Will we be sent home and lose each other?

At night when the five of us crawl into our tents, and Sugar and I are lying on top of our bags, I wrap my arms around her and run my fingers through her faded green hair.

"I'm sorry, Maps." Her voice is thick as she turns to lay her head in the crook of my shoulder.

"It's okay," I tell her, and I don't even know if it's a lie. "You can talk to me. About anything. Even if it's off the trail."

She takes in a shaky breath. "I'm just so fucking angry. I can't seem to stop. It's like all my feelings are too much."

I think I know how she feels. Sometimes my emotions feel like something so big they're trying to break out of my chest. "You're allowed to feel any way you want as intensely as you want." My hand runs through her hair as I say the words to the top of her head, and I hear the echo of the words my dad told me the day I broke the mirror in my room. My mother was furious, but my dad just asked if it helped. It had. I repeat his words to Sugar. "You don't ever have to apologize for feeling deeply."

Her head tilts back up to me. "Who told you that?"

"Just someone."

She doesn't press, and I don't keep talking. Eventually we end up tucked into our own sleeping bags and I notice that my burned one is gone. In its spot is King's. I know because it smells like him.

I tell myself not to press my face against it, but I do anyway, and say *thank you* a hundred times in my heart. Because King is full of contradictions. He compliments me and touches me softly, but then puts distance between us. He gives me his sleeping bag, but he doesn't give any part of himself to me.

So I fall asleep telling my heart not to care that King gave me this.

And I tell myself not to apologize for feeling deeply.

23

"I DID SOMETHING WRONG."

Joe stands in front of us and stares out at the burned land. His hands grip the straps of his pack and he frowns.

Joe isn't yelling, and it's the calmness in his voice that feels scary.

"In all the years I've been doing this, no one has ever tried to burn down the whole fucking Sierras."

Junior tries to reason with him. "Joe, it wasn't—"

"Don't you dare say it wasn't a big deal. Not here. Not when you know there is a whole goddamn season dedicated to fire in California." He shakes his head sadly. "It spreads so fast, and we would have been on the fucking news talking about how you five dipshits couldn't figure out how the fire *started*?"

None of us look at Sugar as Joe talks. We all agreed not to tell him who was responsible and just take the blame as a group.

"They can't send us all to jail," Books had said. Sugar had looked guilty as she focused on the ground, but Junior looked at Books like he had just saved humanity.

"I just thought—" Joe shakes his head, confused. "I thought you all knew better than this. I thought you understood how important this is."

He uses words like *silly* and *harmless* when he tells us about the last five major fires in California. An education on how easy it is to destroy one of the most beautiful places on earth. All with a hefty serving of guilt.

"You have no idea how lucky you were. *No idea.*"

"We do," I say, but immediately know it's wrong when Books's eyes cut to me.

Joe takes three wide steps over to where I stand and levels his face with mine. "You absolutely do *not* know. If you did you would be sobbing. The whole fucking forest, Out—" He stops and straightens. "*This trail.* You could have burned down *this* trail and no one would hike it again for years."

He says *this trail* like the others care about the Western Sierra Trail the same way. Like their dad's legacy hangs in the balance.

Joe walks over to the blackened dirt and toes at it with his boot. "So, we're gonna hike off the trail. It's gonna add three days to—"

"No, Joe," King interrupts. "I don't have three days."

Joe shakes his head. "King, the list of things I care about right now is very fucking short and I cannot begin to stress how far down that list your internship is."

King's jaw tenses and my stomach turns as I think about how one thing, one stupid thing, could keep him from what he wants.

I don't think about why that bothers me so much.

Sugar's gone white and she opens her mouth to say something.

But it's done. There's no argument left to be made with Joe. We follow him as we leave the trail and head farther away from the river. I know the moment I stop being able to hear it because my mind tells me something is missing. Something is wrong.

When the sun is starting to fall in the sky, we finally see it.

The underworld.

Beautiful pine trees and green shrubs give way almost instantly to blackened poles of wood and empty ground. Trees, some still with needles and leaves that have dried to a rust color, stand like shadows against the dirt and large rocks. The burned ground looks like a wave meeting the shore.

"What is this hellscape?" Junior asks. "The upside down? Did you really walk us all the way to this nightmare?"

"This is the forest after a fire." Joe keeps moving. Amongst the dirt and rocks are small green plants and shrubs just starting to fight for life.

Every kid in California knows what the destruction from a fire looks like, but most of the time it's seen from a car or the safety of your television. It's something that turns your skies orange and the air gray. It's the dusting of ash on everything outside, but it's never . . . this.

Something about standing in the carcass of the forest feels all-consuming. It feels hotter here in the sun without any shade and the earth smells burned and dusty.

"Fuck." Junior breathes it out as we look around.

"The Campbell Fire burned out this section," Joe explains as he toes at an ashy log that crumbles under his boot. "Third largest forest fire in California's history. Started with a small spark that was *no big deal*."

"What do we do here?" I ask.

Joe shakes his head. "Erosion is the biggest concern. The forestry service will come in and straw and seed all this and take down all these trees. Just keep your eyes open for ones that look like they could fall."

"But everything looks like it's gonna fall," Books says. "It's an apocalyptic wasteland."

"We do what we can," Joe says as he picks up a log with his bare hands and tosses it down from the path. His palms come away blackened, and he wipes them against his pants. "Some things just need to heal."

"Fucking hiking Yoda," I complain as I dig in a pocket for my gloves. "I don't even know where to put down my pack."

"Here." King holds out his hand for my backpack.

He's being kind, or at least that's what it looks like. How can he be kind right now? When Alaska might be fading from the map of his choices.

"Are you okay?" I ask as I hand him my bag.

His shoulders stiffen. "I don't wanna talk. Not right now."

I nod and tell him okay, because I don't really want to talk either. Not about this. Not about another thing King might not get because someone else is always in charge of the things we want.

Being this close to King, every day, and realizing he's the thing *I* want, feels like the worst kind of torture. The slow ache that burrows deeper and deeper into me, until I feel the pain breaking and buckling underneath me.

And I'm afraid of what happens when I fall.

I'm digging into the side of the path when Sugar asks me, "What's your favorite movie?"

I shrug. "I don't know."

But that doesn't stop Sugar. "What? I can't ask a question? You're the only one? You don't like movies?"

"I do," I clarify.

"So what's your *favorite*?"

She's playing my game and I realize maybe she doesn't want to sit in the silence either. Maybe the quiet is also whispering her pain back at her like it did to me. But there's a tattered edge to all her words after the fire, so I tell her, "I like *Your Name.*"

She makes a noise. "I love that one. But why didn't he just write his *name*?"

I dig the shovel into the earth. "Because it wasn't about his name or remembering *him*. It was about her remembering that she's loved. It's the whole point of the film."

"That's . . . kinda beautiful." Sugar looks a little impressed.

"I'm pretty sure the entire point is that we are all seconds away from the world being destroyed," Books tells us.

I hit my shovel against Books's. "You're not an expert on anime because you've seen every episode of *Demon Slayer.*"

"Then how does one become an expert?" Books asks.

"My favorite anime is *Spirited Away.*" Sugar shoves the hoe into the dirt.

I stop and turn to her. "The one where the parents are pigs?"

Sugar looks up from her work, surprised. "Yeah." She wipes sweat from her brow. "Is it weird I thought the dragon was hot?"

A beat passes.

And then another before I tell Sugar, "Yeah. Yeah, it's really weird."

She keeps shoveling. "Honestly, I don't have to explain myself to any of you."

King pulls out his water bottle. His fingers unscrew the cap and his throat work as he swallows.

Books shovels dirt out of the ditch and puts it on the top of my boot. I give him a dirty look and shake off my foot, but his point was made. I'm staring.

He rolls his eyes. "Don't you think it's kinda weird that Joe is basically Yubaba?"

"What?" I ask and look over to Joe, who is busy marking a tree with spray paint up the hill from us.

"He takes our names," Books explains. "Like Yubaba, the lady with the big head who ran the bathhouse."

"I know who she is," I tell him.

"Do you think if we forget our names, we'll be trapped on this trail forever?" Junior asks.

"Clearing trails and eating beans for eternity," Sugar says ominously.

We all grow silent, thinking about our names and what it would mean to forget them. If no one ever called me Atlas again . . .

Or Outlaw.

For a second I try to remember what my names sounded like in my dad's voice. My throat begins to close as I struggle.

I can't remember.

"Maps?" Sugar calls me.

And I wonder when hearing that name became normal for me.

I move a shovel of dirt out of the ditch. "I feel more like Maps than I ever did my name," I hear myself say. I don't know where it comes from, but it's true. Something about the heat, the mountains, and the ash pulls things from me that I don't realize I've given up.

I wonder if they'll ask me my name finally. If they're even curious. And then I realize they won't.

For the same reason I don't ask them theirs.

It doesn't matter.

"Yeah." Books digs his shovel into the ground. "Me too. I like being Books."

We make our way through the burned-out sections. King making notes of things in his journal and Joe marking trees with string or spray paint. We move, remove, and dig out parts of the trail. Something about being here, amongst the nothingness the fire has left, makes even our silence feel emptier.

"What about you, Junior? What's your favorite movie?" I ask, letting my mind walk away from my task.

He bites at his lip. "I don't know. There're just so many."

I frown at him because something is weird about his answer. "Top five."

Junior turns away from me and continues to dig out a ditch. "I don't . . . I don't know. King, what's yours?"

"*Howl's Moving Castle.*"

Junior just makes a noise.

"Really?" I ask.

King smiles, but it's confused. "What?"

"Do you really like it or are you just saying it because we all said movies like that?" It sounds aggressive when I ask, like I'm accusing him of something.

"Why would I lie?" King asks. He stabs his shovel into the dirt again. "If I was gonna lie, I would say *Avengers* or something like that."

"I like the Avengers movies," Books adds. "Nothing wrong with liking something because it's popular."

"*Howl's Moving Castle* is my favorite movie," King repeats. "I like the door that changes and how each time Howl walks through it, he's a different person."

Howl. The boy whose heart is a star.

Books says, "I like that Sophie saves herself. She doesn't need Howl."

"I like that he always sees exactly who she is the whole time." King digs his shovel into the ground. "I like when he says her hair looks like starlight, because it's what's left of the curse. It's changed her, but Howl thinks it's cool."

Sugar smiles. "He ate a star."

I bite my lip. "Do you think Howl could always see her like that because she told him to find her?"

"I think once you start looking at a person, it's impossible not to see them." King throws a smaller log from the trail.

I pretend like King is talking about me and let his words fall like a stone into the river, sinking to the bottom of my heart.

Junior's gone quiet as he drives his shovel into the earth. Like he's trying to make himself invisible.

I ask Junior, "You don't like *Howl's Moving Castle*?"

His tongue darts out and wets his lips, and he sets his water bottle down with a deep breath. "If I tell you something, you can't make a big deal about it."

I smile and laugh as I hit his shoulder. "Okay."

He doesn't smile back. "Seriously."

"Fine," I say and look at everyone else.

He swallows and I watch his eyes calculate a risk in each of us. But what risk can he have when the truth doesn't matter here anyway? We don't matter.

"I don't watch movies," he tells us.

Books cocks his head to the side. "You don't like them?" We all feel like we're missing something.

"No," Junior says and presses his lips together before he continues. "I just. I've never really seen one."

I smile. I can't help it. It's absurd.

"Maps," Sugar whispers. "Don't."

My grin slips because his words might not be true, but the look on his face is. And he's . . . hurt. "Okay, Junior. *Why* haven't you seen a movie?"

His jaw ticks. "I wasn't allowed."

"So, you just *never* saw one?" Sugar clarifies.

"But school or a friend's house—" I press.

"I didn't go to school, and I never talked to anyone who didn't go to my church."

"Your church?" Sugar leans against her shovel.

He looks at Books. "Cults and pot farms, right? That's all there is in Northern California. Well, I didn't grow up on a farm."

Sugar's brows come together. "Were you . . . were you raised in a cult?"

"They don't call sects of Christianity cults, they call them *churches*. My parents are the kind of religious people who have

206

all kinds of conspiracy theories. End of days and God's fucking chosen people." He throws out the curse word like it's a bomb that he can aim at his parents. Like he's hoping it does the damage to them that it has done to his heart.

"You curse a lot for a religious person," I tell him. It's the first thing I think of.

Junior shakes his head, but it's with some other emotion that I can't decipher. He looks almost scared, but how could he feel that way? With us? Junior looks like he's searching for the right words. "No. It's not—" And then suddenly everything shifts, and Junior looks right at Books. His face a mask of passivity. "Never mind. I'm joking."

I look to King out of habit. I'm not sure why, and he only shakes his head once, telling me *no*. Don't get involved. Don't say anything.

Junior stabs the shovel into the ground again. "My favorite movie is the *Avengers* one. I like Captain USA. He was my favorite."

A breaking is happening. I can see the cracks in Junior widen and grow. He can feel it too because I can see him panic. He's trying to hold all the parts of himself that he can feel beginning to shatter.

Junior tried to show us his wound and instead of helping him heal, we pressed against it to make sure it was there.

Why do people always have to bleed for someone to know they are hurting? "Junior."

"Ah," he groans and takes a step backward. "Don't do that. Do you know how it feels to have someone look at you like . . ."

Poor Atlas. Lost her dad. Wasted potential. Trouble.

Kissed a boy who doesn't want her.

"You're right and I'm sorry—"

King cuts me off and takes a step to Junior. "Fuck them."

He looks at King. "Fuck them? My *family*?"

"Yeah. Fuck your family. People don't get to hurt you just because you share genetics."

King's words are like all the other ones he speaks. Plain and honest. There's beauty in the truth he directs at Junior, and I feel my heart shape itself around this gift that isn't even for me. It's for Junior, but I feel grateful all the same.

Junior's eyes stay on the ground and the air feels heavy and tense, so I tell him, "The Marvel Cinematic Universe *is* a cultural phenomenon. You are a *victim*."

A painful reality wrapped in humor. Like when you feed an animal their medication in a treat.

Junior gives me a smile and wraps a sweaty, filthy arm around me. I pretend not to notice the tears in the corners of his eyes.

He doesn't wear his tragedy on his chest like a badge.

And I don't have to either.

"Well, I'm probably not gonna make it to heaven now, anyway. I guess I should watch it when I get out of here." Junior laughs.

"Them," Books says as he pushes past us to throw a charred log off the trail. It has Junior's arm slipping from me, which feels intentional. "There's more than one, and all of them are worth going to hell for." Junior is smiling at Books when Books tells him, "We'll watch them all. After this."

After this. We all pretend like those words don't feel fragile. Of life off this mountain. In the real world. When Yubaba has given us back our names and written them on our palms. When you can still see the curse of the trail, because it's changed us.

Like starlight.

24

WE ARE FILTHY.

Soot is smeared across our skin and ground into every surface of our bodies. A black mark across Sugar's face has been there for two days, and I can't seem to find the energy to tell her about it. No matter what we do, we never seem to get clean.

I've been digging out drainage for two days and listening to Joe tell us different fire statistics. My fingers have calluses despite my gloves.

We barely hike as we try to do our best to place a Band-Aid on the gaping wound that the Campbell Fire left. The earth here has scabbed over, but I can see signs of life still persisting. Plants starting to reclaim the ground in a riot of green and flowers. The tree that refuses to die despite its blackened trunk, the bird still searching as it perches on a branch.

"It's just so sad," Junior says, looking up at the almost white sky above us. Soot smears against his cheek and his brow. He's laid a T-shirt on his head, and he pulls out an extra to show Sugar how to wrap it on her head too. He steps back from her and walks to me. "It's all over social media. Everyone is doing it."

I pretend to be thoughtful. "I don't know if it will really match my look."

"Nothing matches 'grubby hiker,'" Sugar tells me as she takes my hands and pulls me up to stand.

I laugh and hold still while Junior and Sugar bicker about how best to keep the shirt on my hair like theirs. Their hands are gentle as they wind my hair away from my neck and twist it in the fabric of a T-shirt, carefully.

Once they're done, they stand in front of me and smile. Both of them check their work with pinched brows, fingers fluttering over me. But with each beat of my heart, I can only hear one thing.

Almost. Over. Almost. Over.

It rings in my ears, and I can't even decide why it feels like each beat is a knife being twisted.

I smile at them as they fuss and argue over me.

"Here." Junior takes his water and pours it over his head. Most of it absorbs into the fabric, but what doesn't falls down his face and leaves gray streaks that disappear into the collar of his shirt.

He doesn't ask as he holds the water over Sugar, who lets out a little yelp before finally smiling. And then he does it to me. At first I can't feel it, but then the water sinks down over the shirt and onto my neck. It feels cool and I can't help but laugh.

"This is a neat trick," I tell him.

"Spent an entire summer farming," Junior says like it's normal. "It's the little things."

Sugar touches the wet shirt on her head and laughs.

It's stupid. This moment where we all stand in the burnout

of a fire, under the oppressive heat, and the weight of our individual decisions that made a summer of manual labor our only real choice. Somehow this feels like the most important place in the whole world.

It feels like the center of the universe.

Junior's face falls as his eyes move over mine. Sugar's gaze follows his and they both give me a confused look.

"What's wrong?" Junior asks.

"Nothing." But my voice cracks over the word.

"Then why are you crying?" Sugar asks, but it's gentle. Another knife.

My hand reaches up to my cheek and comes away wet, and not from the water Junior poured on me. "I don't . . ."

There is a softness on both their faces as they stand in front of me. A realization that glows back at me and doesn't ask me to explain or define this emotion.

I am understood.

At the end of the day, Joe's eyes skitter over all of us. "You look like the chimney sweeps from *Mary Poppins*. I think we all could use a shower."

Sugar steps forward and Joe takes an unconscious step backward. "Like an actual shower? In a hotel?"

"Not a hotel," Joe clarifies. "Campground showers. And if you're nice, I'll let you get something at the gas station."

After Joe tells us about the shower and the gas station, we spend the next day and a half listing types of food at the store and ranking them according to what we want to eat first. We don't acknowledge that this is just one more way we're getting closer to the end.

"I want to eat everything that comes in chocolate," Junior says.

"I want Takis," Sugar says.

Junior groans.

"God, me too," I tell her. "I *need* them at this point."

"What about you, Books?" Junior asks, hitting his shoulder with his own.

"Trail mix." Books is predictably boring.

Sugar sighs. "That's unacceptable. At least get the kind with M&M's."

Junior has a faraway look when he says, "I want a Red Bull and those gross mini donuts that are made of wax and—"

"You're not getting an energy drink."

It goes on like this. One of us remembering something disgusting we would never eat on a normal day and acting like it's a five-star meal.

When they learn I love grape candy, I'm forced to walk in the back. "Some choices are unacceptable, Maps."

As soon as we leave the destruction from the fire, I feel like I can breathe again. Plants and trees and leaves reach up to the sky and cover us in shade. I run a hand over the healthy trunk of a tree as we pass it and notice the black under my nails. A reminder of what can happen. I've never felt more appreciative of nature until it was gone.

And then suddenly we are walking on the highway. The pavement is unforgiving and artificially flat under my feet as we walk single file on the side of the road.

"Is this the end of the trail?" Sugar asks Joe and I wonder if I'm imagining the anxiety in her voice.

"No. This isn't the trail. This is the way to the showers."

We walk around a bend in the road as vehicles speed past us. Loud and artificial and grating. The smell of the cars and the asphalt bothers my nose, as much as it's familiar. There's a sign for a campground and we follow Joe to a gas station.

A picnic table sits under a tree and Joe sets down his pack. "Before we head to camp, you can use the phone. To call home." He looks at me. "If you want to."

Joe holds out a charging cord and cell phone. It should be normal, like this gas station and the asphalt in the parking lot, but it makes me feel like an alien coming to a planet I don't know. It's been so long since I used a phone or saw a car that it feels strange.

A month. It's only been a month, I remind myself.

Books takes the phone and cord from Joe. An outlet is uncovered on the side of the convenience store and Books sits on the sidewalk as he waits for the phone to turn on.

We watch Books talk to someone on the other end as he smiles and laughs in an easy way. Sugar goes next, her face turned to the wall as she talks to someone in almost whispers. When she finishes, there are tears in her eyes.

Joe doesn't offer the phone to King or Junior and they head into the store.

I'm left with Joe. He holds out the phone and asks, "Ready?"

I'm not. But I press the ten digits I've known my whole life.

The name that comes up isn't one I expect.

Patrick's Wife Don't Answer

My hands are still on the call button, but I only stare down at my father's name.

"Oh," Joe says, pushing off the bench and walking over to

me. "Sorry, it's—it was a joke, and I never took it out. I—I obviously answer when your mom calls. I just—"

He thinks these are all the reasons I'm frozen. Not the millions of feelings that slam into me like fists over and over.

I look up at Joe.

I open my mouth to yell at him. To tell him to fuck off or maybe ask him to let me go home.

Instead, I can't keep the words from my mouth. "I don't want to call her. I don't want to think about going home in a few days."

Confusion blooms on his face before it settles into understanding.

"Yeah," he tells me. "Yeah. I get that."

I'm grateful that he doesn't push because truthfully, I don't know why I feel like this all of the sudden. Like I'm being shoved to the edge of a cliff and left scrambling for traction.

My voice is small when I tell him, "I don't want to leave the trail."

Joe nods, his eyes on the woods behind the gas station. For a moment I think he's going to walk off into them, but then he says, "Did your dad ever tell you why I camp so much?"

Without thinking, I recite something my father had jokingly said about Joe to my mother when he thought I wasn't listening. "Because you're a crunchy granola freak who jerks off to nature?"

Joe laughs, a distant thing that floats away like my father's memory. "No, the real reason."

I shake my head.

"When I was young, I loved a boy who died in a boating

accident." Joe sounds like he's reciting facts. No emotion is attached to it, except his voice has gotten quieter. "I hate the way people look at you after someone dies."

I look at Joe now.

"Being in the mountains is like being a wounded animal looking for a safe place to hide. You think you're there to heal, but you're just trying to forget. It doesn't last long. Eventually, you have to deal with your shit. The trail, *this trail*, was the one your dad found me on. We hiked it every year until it closed. The trail isn't a place to hide from hurt, Atlas. It just makes it easier to pretend."

I start at my name. Something I haven't heard people use in what feels like forever. *Atlas.* Like she's a person I can't really remember.

"You wanna call your mom?" he asks.

I shake my head. "No."

I don't want to call her. I don't want to go home. I don't want to have to stop pretending.

He pulls the phone from my hand, and *Patrick's wife* disappears from the screen. "I'll tell her you're good and make up some excuse."

I nod, not able to say the thank-you that I really mean. Joe walks back toward the store and I call his name before he makes it around the corner. "Hey, Joe." He turns back and looks at me. "I'm sorry about your boy who died."

He gives me a small smile. "Hey, Maps, sorry about your dad who died."

It feels cathartic to joke about grief like this. I smile back at him. "Does it get easier?"

He takes a heavy breath and looks thoughtful. "No, but it gets quieter."

I sit there for longer than I should, waiting for things to get quieter, but they don't.

"Maps," King says my name and I feel foolish. He watches me, his head tilted to the side, and his voice is soft when he says, "Everyone is waiting."

A second later, Books, Junior, and Sugar walk around the corner without their packs.

"Let's eat gross food!" Junior says, bouncing on his heels, smiling.

They look like a picture. All golden light and warm tones. I'm reminded of a photograph of my parents that sat above our fireplace. The two of them standing in front of a ridge somewhere on the trail I've been calling home for the past month. I realize they kept it on the mantel because it was one of the many memories they collected, and eventually, that's all time leaves you with. Memories.

I collect this moment and stand.

Pushing through the glass doors of the gas station, I follow after them as the door chimes. Civilization feels exactly as I expected it to and yet completely different. Like I'm a trespasser here. I stand in an aisle of brightly colored chips in enormous bags and wonder where I would carry something so delicate. I guess that's the point. I don't have to pack any of this. Junior makes a noise and I see him standing next to a microwave as he unwraps three frozen burritos.

"You're gonna eat that?" I ask, surprised. "You have money?"

"No," Junior looks at me like I've said something ridiculous. "King does, though."

King. I look at him as he squeezes ketchup onto a hot dog. He doesn't even look up as he says, "Get what you want."

At that exact moment, Sugar comes up to me holding a paper tray of chips covered in golden goo.

"Nachos!" Her eyes are wide, like she's just discovered treasure. "There are *jalapeños*." King makes a face but doesn't say anything. Sugar and I slather our chips with cheese meticulously. We could get paid to be professional cheese distributors. "King is the best sugar daddy."

We sit on the picnic bench underneath a sad evergreen. Sap has dropped onto the weathered wood, but we are *sitting*. At a *table*. Just the five of us. Like young gods.

We watch people pump gas as they head up the mountain to camp or down it for a weekend in the city while digging into bags of chips and eating handfuls of peanut M&M's that we wash down with syrupy carbonated drinks. It feels like a feast. Trashy, gross gas station delicacies.

"My stomach is never going to forgive me," King mumbles as he shoves a Taki into his mouth.

"But it's so delicious." I say it around a chip with too many jalapeños.

"Is it Saturday?" Books asks.

Junior nods his head yes. "That's what the calendar inside said."

King makes a noise and leans back on his hands, looking up at the sky. "That's so weird."

And it is. The concept of *days*. On the trail, they don't really matter. All of them feel the same. At first, the way time moved felt disconnected and made me feel like I was floating in space. Waiting to be rescued or waiting to die. I couldn't tell.

"Saturday." He repeats it.

It's weird.

We sit there for so long that I get hungry again. "We should get ice cream." I stand up and everyone looks at me a little funny.

"I couldn't eat another thing." Books rubs at his stomach.

That doesn't discourage me. "There is always room for sweets. I'm getting ice cream."

"Fine, but we'll be at the campsite." Books points to the small path behind the gas station.

I stand and practically skip inside. It's not till my hand is inside the freezer that I realize I don't have money. But when I look up, King is already at the counter, his card out. He has a large bag of sunflower seeds on it and two water bottles.

He looks back at me. "Is that it?"

For a second I let myself imagine what it would be like if King and I were on a road trip. Just the two of us stopping for snacks before we drove through the mountains so we could hike at the lake. Would I roll down the window? Listen to my favorite song too loud? Would King sing along? Reach over and hold my hand just so he could be touching me?

Would he kiss me?

In another timeline, are we in love? Are we happy? Has our hurt dulled to an ache?

King asked me a question. *Right.* I nod. "That's it. Joe would not be happy about your bottled water."

King sighs. "Yeah, well."

He pays and takes the water while I take the ice cream in my hand. I hear the door open and when I look up, I see him.

Not King, but someone I didn't expect.

Conner Washington stands in the doorway of the store with his eyes wide and his mouth open in surprise.

25

CONNER.

A memory of the last time I saw him flashes in my mind. His hands fumbling with my bra as the steering wheel of his car dug into my back.

It's odd, but at this moment, I can't remember if I liked them there or not. He seems just as surprised as I am and I think he might stand there forever gaping at me, until he says, "What are you doing here?"

The way his voice sounds makes me feel like I don't have a right to be wherever *here* is.

"Hiking," I answer simply.

Conner looks shocked and angry. But I can't figure out why Conner Washington would be angry with me. "Did you move?"

"Move?" I clear my throat. "Like to the mountains?"

He nods. "Yeah."

I don't answer him, mostly because I can't figure out what's happening in this conversation. "What are you doing here?" I ask.

Conner ignores my question. "I heard you dropped out."

"What?" I step toward him like I can silence his words with proximity. King is still standing by the register, and I look over at him. His expression is blank, like he hasn't heard what Conner just said, but I know he did.

"That's what everyone said. You dropped out. Got caught with drugs or something."

I laugh and hope it sounds light. "No."

The door opens again and Joshua Yoon comes inside. When he sees us, he smiles at me. "Hey, Batty Atty." The nickname erodes my pride and makes me feel like shit. Batty. Crazy. Maybe the girl they knew was, but even I barely knew that girl.

"Hey." I stand there with my ice cream melting in my hand. I can't even look at King anymore.

"I haven't seen you in forever." Joshua wraps me in a hug that I don't return because my hands are full of ice cream. "Wanna come to the river with us?" Joshua asks. I don't want to go anywhere with them.

"She's got plans." King stands next to me chewing sunflower seeds casually, as if he couldn't care less about these boys talking to me.

Joshua looks him up and down and lets out a small *whoa*.

King is impressive. He's filthy like I am, but he's also taller and broader in a way these boys are still waiting to grow into.

"This is your new guy?" Conner asks. As if there is always a guy. I don't want to tell Conner he has it wrong, that he was the only guy, because that might make him feel like he was important to me. And he wasn't. He was a way to forget. A way to cover a wound without bleeding. Conner looks at King. "Right."

I think they're gonna leave, but Conner takes a deep breath and looks back at me. "I heard about your dad."

My stomach tightens.

"I'm sorry. That—"

"It's fine." I stop him and I wonder how far the others are. Can they hear Conner?

"Is that why you didn't call?" Conner asks.

His voice is filled with hope, and I want to scream. He's using my tragedy to make his pride feel better. As if the reason I didn't call him back was because my dad died and not because I can't even remember if I liked kissing him.

"Hey. I have to go, but it's good seeing you." It's not. I don't even know why I said that.

I hear someone yell "Atty!" behind me but I keep walking. I throw my ice cream in a trash can outside and I start down the road.

It's only a few feet before King falls into step next to me. I wait for him to demand an explanation or tell me to stop or ask me where the fuck I think I'm going.

But seconds fade into minutes and transform into the sounds of our breathing and the occasional car passing. Until I say, "You don't have to babysit me."

It's six steps before he asks, "Are you okay?"

I bite the inside of my cheek. King moves to walk in front of me, puts a hand out until I stop.

And then King asks again, "Are you okay?"

I'm gonna tell him yes. I'm gonna say everything is fine and I'll take all my feelings and I will shove them so far down that even I won't be able to find them.

But then my eyes meet King's. I say, "No."

He lets out a deep breath and takes my wrist as he walks me back toward the gas station.

We sit next to each other on the bench, close enough that our fingers touch. Just the sides of our hands. It's so small that we can pretend it's not on purpose. That friends don't even notice things like this.

"Was that guy your boyfriend?" he asks me. His voice is even, like he doesn't care what the answer is, but it sounds like it's on purpose.

I make a laughing noise. "No. He was absolutely not my boyfriend. He was a guy that I hung out with sometimes." I look at King. "He was a bad choice, not a boyfriend." Now I take a deep breath.

He nods but doesn't say anything else.

King looks down at the bag with two bottles at his feet. "And college? You're not going."

I bite my lip. "No." It's a quiet shape more than a word. "You have to have a high school diploma to get in."

"And you don't?"

"I dropped out when my dad died. I just didn't go back. It seemed so stupid. A piece of paper saying I sat in a seat and memorized facts. What was the point?"

"So, the whole thing about college and homecoming was just . . ." I can see King grappling to understand why I lied. "It wasn't just the dad part?"

The more he gets to know me, the more lies he realizes I've told. "They assumed and I just . . . I didn't want to be sad. I wanted to be normal."

He looks at me. "You are the furthest thing from normal."

I know that he means it like a compliment, but it aches in my chest and separates me. I want to be exactly like everyone else. I want to be invisible.

King takes a breath, like he's deciding. "Being normal doesn't mean you're not fucked up. That's the most normal thing about you."

"*Everyone's messy.*" I repeat the words I can't stop thinking about.

King gives me a curious look.

"Something Pidgeon said. Everyone's messy, so be messy."

He laughs and says, "Don't take any advice from her."

Silence stretches as we stare at each other, but it must go on for too long because King's face looks nervous. Maybe he can tell that the gratitude I feel in this moment makes me want to kiss him. It makes me want to press my face into his neck despite the gray ash that covers his skin. Maybe he can tell that his kindness is something I can't seem to stop craving, like his touch.

He frowns and his eyes move to my lips.

"I know." I clear the emotions from my voice. "I know what this is . . ." I'm gonna tell him that I shouldn't have kissed him, that he's leaving for the internship, and we *can't* anyway, but my pride is getting the better of me.

"What is this?" King asks me. "Tell me."

"It's nothing," I whisper to him. I try to make myself sound like a girl who is fine with nothings.

I want him to repeat the word. To let it break my heart.

He has to, because out there is the pain I know will come at the end of this, and it's better to stop now. My teeth sink into my lip as I stare at King's hands. Hands that were on me. Pressing into my skin—

"Nothing."

26

THIS CAMPSITE IS NOTHING like Basecamp. It's more of a rest stop than anything else. Off a small logging road with cars passing every so often in the distance, it feels like the least hiking thing we've done. The forest here is dense and thick and I can't see the sky above me. At least when we were in the burnout, I could see the sky.

Joe has left us again after giving Books and King directions back to the trail. Our trail.

And I know King wants to talk.

So, like the avoider I am, I do everything in my power not to be alone with him. Because if we don't talk, he can't tell me he knows I'm getting too attached to him. He can't tell me he knows I think about kissing him more than I don't.

I'm putting up the red tent when I hear clapping.

It's Junior and Sugar with mockingly proud looks on their faces.

"You did it," Junior says. "You finally did it."

Sugar wipes away a fake tear. "I always knew you could."

Junior loops his arm through hers. "We are just so proud of you, baby."

"What the hell are you two talking about?" I ask.

"The. Tent." Sugar makes a wide gesture toward it like a gameshow host. "You fucking did it."

"I've been putting up the tent for weeks now."

"Overstatement," Junior corrects. "You've been spending hours assembling tents into almost tent-like structures. This—" He copies Sugar's arm motion. "This is an actual tent shape, put up in an actual reasonable amount of time."

"You didn't even use a curse word." Her eyes are wide. "Like, not *once*."

I roll my eyes and fold my arms over my chest. "I've put up . . . I've done . . ." Have I? "*No* curse words?"

"It's a big day for team Blue." She nods her head. "We should celebrate. Family dinner. We can have . . . beans and rice!"

"Oh my god, beans and rice?" Junior puts his hand over his mouth and fake gasps. "I always wanted to try that!"

Junior and Sugar are feeding off each other, each statement more ridiculous than the last.

"I love you guys." I say it softly, but they hear it and the bit they've been doing stops as they turn their attention back to me.

I watch the words I've spoken sink in, and they understand.

Junior moves first, but they both wrap their arms around me at the same time, and the three of us hug.

"God, it's gonna suck when we have to leave," Junior says against my hair.

"I almost don't want to go to college," Sugar jokes and my stomach turns.

"We can text and FaceTime and drive to meet up. No one's dying." Junior even laughs.

And I feel it. The thing that separates me from them. Lies and omission.

So, I shower. The gray water swirls around my feet, but it feels like the shower I had hoped for. Warm water and soap and clean clothes. I wash off my gloves, but the ash seems to be embedded into the cracks of the leather. Permanently stained.

Like me.

After dinner, I'm lying on top of my sleeping bag listening to the sounds outside. I can't wait to be away from the buzz of electricity and the hum of cars passing. I can't wait to be back on the trail and spend the little amount of time I have . . . pretending.

And then I hear someone giggle. I think it's Junior. A second later the door to my tent unzips and I'm flooded with a light. On instinct I shield my eyes, waiting for them to adjust.

"Maps." It's Books's voice. "Grab your shit. Let's go."

He's wearing a headlamp that is a blinding bluish LED monstrosity.

"Go *where*?" I ask.

"For a little climb." His lip pulls up into a grin.

Junior sticks his head around with both his hands on Books's shoulders. "Night hiking!" he whisper-yells.

"We hike all day," I complain, but I'm already sitting up. "I don't want to hike when it's *dark*."

"Yes, you do," Books says, handing me a headlamp. "Let's go." He stands up out of the tent and holds his hands out to help me up. Everyone is waiting for me, it seems.

King holds out my boots and I slip them on while Sugar plays with the strap of her headband. Junior's fingers fumble with the elastic as he struggles to tighten her strap. When Books leans over to help, he stands directly in front of Sugar. The three of them are so close to each other, it's almost like they've been piled together.

"Jesus Christ," she curses and pushes at both of them. "I got it!"

I think of the first day as a team when Sugar wanted help with her pack. Now she's fighting it off.

King points up. All of us turn on our headlamps and Books leads us up a steep incline. Junior is in front of me and King is behind. At a few parts we are climbing up large rocks and Junior reaches around to pull me up. King's hands find my waist as he helps steady me. His touch on me makes it hard to remember to breathe. As we walk, he stands at my back, and I can feel the heat of him, his presence heavy in the air.

We reach the top of the outcropping and I stay away from the edge of the cliff, not sure how far the drop is. We sit in a row, something we've gotten used to. Our places in an order. Books tells us to turn off our lamps. I do and look up at the stars and galaxy in the sky. I might never get used to the way they look when it's truly dark.

But it's not until King motions for me to look out in front of me that I see why we're here. In front of us stretches the most beautiful lights. Yellows and whites and reds and greens.

"My grandmother called it her jewelry box," Books says. "She lived on a hill, and I would sit up with her at night as she knit and told me stories about all the lovers who gave her jewelry."

"Really?" Sugar asks with a soft smile. "Like, what kind of stories?"

The corners of his lips pull upward. "She told me about a boyfriend who proposed with a giant ruby, and every time she looks out at the lights, she remembers the boy with the ruby."

"What happened to him?" Junior asks.

Books shrugs. "Life."

I wonder if I will be a story to these four people one day. A memory in lights.

Sugar speaks first. "I would have married a boy who gave me a giant ruby. Or a girl."

"Me too," Junior says. "The boy. Not the girl." He makes a face and we laugh.

"So there isn't a boy or a girl back home waiting for you, Sugar?" Junior asks and he bumps her shoulder.

"As if I'd tell you." She takes a rock from the ground and throws it into the dark.

Junior smiles.

"What about you, King?" Sugar asks.

"I'm going to Alaska."

It's not really an answer, but no one calls him on it, and I hate how curious it makes me.

"Do you have a boyfriend?" Sugar asks me.

I don't even have friends.

"She could have a girlfriend," Junior says, hitting Sugar's hip.

Sugar shakes her head thoughtfully. "She doesn't like girls."

"How do you know?" I ask.

Sugar smiles now. "I know it's not me you're checking out." She throws a wink at me.

"It's okay not to like girls," Junior tells me. He puts a hand to his chest and in the dark I can see his face grow serious as he leans over Sugar. "I personally think they're gross."

"We are not gross!" Sugar throws a small rock at him.

Next to me, King laughs. I look over at him and his eyes find me.

"I don't . . ."

"You don't have to explain yourself to anyone," King leans in and tells me.

"And do *you* know any girls you like, King?" Junior asks with a smile.

He takes a deep breath and I hate that I watch his chest expand and hope that somewhere inside it is my name. "I know a boy I *don't* like."

Junior leans forward toward us, eyes darkened. "I am very attractive."

"You are," he tells him. "Until you talk." King stands. "And stop asking people to define shit that some people never figure out."

"This is how you find shit out! Normalize talking about sexuality!" Junior yells after King.

Sugar grabs his septum piercing and he grunts. "Don't!"

Books says, "King's not really the relationship type. Too focused on Alaska."

"Are you the relationship type?" I ask him.

"I'm twenty years old," he tells me. "I'm not really any kind of type."

I don't want to be any kind of type either. "Be messy."

"Messy?" Sugar asks.

"Pidgeon said it."

Books groans. "God, that sounds like some bullshit Pidge would say to justify her absolute nonsense."

"It's pretty up here," I tell him just to fill the air.

"Still can't believe this is almost over," Junior says. "How is it almost the end?"

It's hard to sit here in the summer night heat and imagine fall weather—school and holidays and a whole world outside this place. King comes back and sits down at the end of our row, and I take a deep breath. I always know where he is.

"When I get home it's just gonna be constant," Sugar says. "Shopping for my dorm, picking classes, picking classes again because my mother doesn't like the ones I picked, meeting new roommates. The whole thing is out of my control."

"It just feels like that now," Books tells her. "When you're doing it . . ." He takes a breath. "It's hard to explain, but it's not going to be that bad."

"At least you're going somewhere." Junior tosses a rock in the same place Sugar did and we wait for the sound of it hitting the bottom. "We can't all be college-bound like you three."

"I'm not going to college." I blurt it out before I talk myself out of it.

Everyone looks confused, but no one speaks. They all wait for me to continue, but I don't, so Sugar clarifies, "Like, you're going to defer?"

"Like, I didn't even get in." I swallow. "Because I didn't finish school."

"You didn't . . ."

"I dropped out." I run my hands over the tops of my thighs and then grip my knees. "Because . . . my dad died. And . . . I didn't want to go."

Everyone is quiet. I can't even look at them as I wait in the silence for their response. The verdict they will cast about what I've admitted to. In those moments I make up a hundred scenarios. Only two of them involve them tossing me off this cliff.

"Your dad died?" Sugar asks.

I nod. "In March."

Junior lets out a deep breath. "Fuck, Maps."

"I'm sorry," I rush to explain. "I know I shouldn't have lied."

They look at me like they are waiting for more, but I don't have anything else. Nothing past what I've already said. Nothing that will justify *why*.

"I'm sorry," I whisper again.

King's eyes meet mine and he nods his head once.

Sugar stares out at the lights and Books is looking at his hands in his lap.

But Junior is watching me. "Damn, your dad died. That must have been fucking awful."

My laugh sounds thick in my throat. "*Is*," I correct. "It is fucking awful."

"Why didn't you just tell us?" Sugar asks. There's hurt in her voice.

"I don't know. Which is a shitty answer. I guess because it was easier than explaining to people I didn't really know that . . ."

"Yeah," Sugar says. "And you didn't really know us."

"I *am* sorry."

"Eh. You never lied about what was important," Junior whispers as he wraps an arm around me.

It's so gracious, more gracious than I deserve. I'm not sure I would feel the same way if the situation was reversed.

Books runs his hands over the top of his pants. "We all keep things—sometimes the truth is a hard thing to . . ."

"Do you have something to tell everyone?" Junior asks Books.

His mouth opens and he looks at me. "I just—" But something changes on his face. "I think you're really brave, Maps. It's hard to hold something in and I'm glad you felt like you could trust us now."

Sugar's arm comes around the other side and pulls me toward her and she shakes her head. "I don't love that you lied to us, but I think I get it. Kinda. I'm not going to waste the few days we have left being mad about it."

Books leans against her shoulder and puts his hand on the top of my head as it rests against Sugar's. Junior is still leaning into me and King reaches over to hold my hand.

The few days we have left. The words feel worse every time I hear them because I love it here. In the heat, with shitty food and calloused hands.

And at some point, a tear falls onto my hand that holds King's. He brushes it away with his thumb. Maybe it's something about these hills that makes my tears more acceptable to everyone, which only makes me cry harder.

My friends hold me together and tiny lights blink below us in the dark.

I hate that my dad isn't here. I hate that my mom never knew that this is what would have fixed me. I hate that I've been scared of my own feelings.

These four people know me better than anyone else at this moment, and I expect to hate that, but instead I love it.

That these four humans know I need to just cry.

27

WE HIKE BACK ONTO the Western Sierra Trail, but the real world has already bled into our lives here. Like a cancer spreading into our bones.

Our diagnosis? Terminal.

It starts during breakfast with Sugar talking about college. Not the way she did before, in the abstract. Now she talks about class supply lists, and she wonders if she's been assigned a roommate yet in between bites of mush and water that I've come to find comforting.

"They probably think I'm one of those weirdos who isn't on social media."

And then Books, talking about how his mom won't let him live in a dorm. "She'd be happy if I was at home till I was married. Actually, she would probably love it if I stayed home after that too."

Junior looks tense as we talk about the future.

"What about you, J?" King asks.

He's quiet till eventually he says, "Funny thing, I'm not leaving."

I'm confused. "Not leaving? The trail?"

"I'm staying after the summer and working at Bear Creek." He takes a bite of his food.

"When did that happen?" Sugar asks.

Junior clears his throat. "Joe offered before I even started the program."

None of us ask for clarification, because it dawns on us in that moment what Joe has done. We are the kids who needed a little something more. Something extra. And not only is he helping us, but he's stuck all of us together. Joe's charity cases. Except that's not how it feels. It feels like Joe has chosen us.

Sugar shakes her head. "Fucking Joe." But she smiles when she says it.

"He wants me to apply to colleges and try to go in the spring." Junior leans back. "I don't even know how to do that. Like, what the fuck is a FAFSA?"

King pats Junior's leg. "Joe will help you."

"Yeah, but he . . . he shouldn't have to. You know?" Junior looks down at the food in his bowl. "Parents are supposed to help their kids with that shit."

It's all real life. Growing up. Stress and responsibilities and decisions that you're told will define your entire future.

None of this is permanent. I whisper it to myself and catch King's gaze. He has his knife out and he's carving something into the leather of his notebook in short strokes. The blade catches in the firelight and I wonder what is worth permanently etching into the cover of his book.

It can just be for now.

One by one, everyone goes to sleep but King and me. We stay by the fire. It dances off his face, casting shadows in the angles of it. He reclines back on his elbows, and I notice that his shirt has risen up at his waist revealing a small patch of skin.

Even if it's subconscious, I remember the way his skin felt against mine. King motions for me to lean back with him. We watch the embers float up past the treetops and fall into the stars. He turns and looks at me. His gaze is so intense. I wonder if I look grubby and dirty. I worry that my hair is a mess. I worry because I see his eyes move over my face and evaluate what he sees.

In just a few days, King and I won't be safely tucked away in the hills of the Sierras. I don't want to ask about what will happen next.

Because I know what happens next. King disappears.

Maybe.

"Did Joe say anything about your internship?"

King takes a deep breath and turns away from me. "Yeah. He said that he'll still refer me, but I can't . . . I can't fuck up again or no Alaska."

"Oh." I say it softly. "That's good."

I'm pretty sure that's just another lie I've told. His head turns and we are looking at each other again. In quiet moments like this, I can feel the pull of King. The way he looks at me . . . down to the marrow of my bones. Looks that make me feel exposed but still safe.

"What are you thinking?" he whispers.

"That I wish I could time travel." I watch his throat work as he swallows. "What are you thinking?" I ask.

"You don't want to know," he tells me.

But I do. I want it so bad I feel like my skin will set fire to the forest around us.

"Close your eyes," he tells me.

"Why?"

He takes a breath. "Just do it. And I'll do it too." King's eyes shut and I know what he's doing. He wants me to copy him so we can tell the truth.

The night is warm but the fire is warmer, and King next to me feels like lightning. I hear him inhale and then, "I wanted to kiss you. From the moment I saw you."

The words feel different when they're all there is. When you can't see the way a person looks or if they're smiling. All you can do is hear the way their voice curls around the syllables and pray that it's hope wrapping itself into the words.

"You kissed me," he says. "But I wanted to kiss you before that."

I feel his words all over me, inside my chest, on my skin, in my core. "I want to kiss you." I wait for him to acknowledge that I didn't say it past tense like he did, but he's quiet.

"Maps."

"I know. We can't. If Joe found out." I swallow.

I hear his breath scratch out of his lungs. "There's something I need to tell you abo—"

I cut him off. "We don't have to think about that. We can just . . . we only have a few days left. I don't want to—" I don't want to think about what comes next. I'm sick of thinking about the future. "I won't tell. I just want to be here. Right now."

"Right now." He repeats it and I wonder if he still has his eyes closed, but I'm too much of a coward to open mine. "Okay," he whispers, so close I feel it on my lips. "I want to kiss you . . . right now."

And then he's kissing me. I sit up and move closer to him without breaking apart as I scoot onto his lap.

King's mouth is on mine when he says, "I always want to kiss you."

My hands wrap around his neck and I bunch them in his hair. He groans deep in his chest as he pulls me flush against him. A second later, King's hand slips down from my face and I open my eyes as he leans back. His chest rises and falls like he's trying to catch his breath.

I swallow heavily and King looks down at me. Something dark is there and it's not desire. It's . . . regret maybe? Because this is ending? Because he's leaving? Because when this is over, we go back to the people we were?

My hands are still in his hair when I say, "Don't do that. Don't look at me like . . . It's almost over. Just pretend with me."

His eyes still search mine and I wish . . . I wish I could read his mind. I wish I could just tell him whatever he's thinking doesn't matter because in a few days none of this will matter and we can all go on pretending that this past month didn't happen.

"I'm not pretending," he says.

"Yeah?" I run my mouth against his jaw until I reach his ear and whisper, "Then why do you tell me you want to kiss me? But look at me like you don't." I press my hips down onto him,

241

letting him know I can feel what his body wants. He groans softly as his head falls back.

"It's not pretend," he whispers. "I can want you *and* think it's not a good idea."

I don't move as I feel his eyes across my skin. They darken to almost black as he looks at my lips. His chest moves up and down and the look on his face is pain.

I take his hand in mine and I press it to my breast, squeezing it over me. "Stop thinking."

His lips are soft against mine, sweet. King leans forward but even that feels gentle. Like I'm fragile. "I wish I could stop thinking about you."

I wrap a leg around his waist and shift my weight on his lap. It changes something in him, and his hands trail down my sides, on my neck and face. King's kisses are back to the ones before, and our lips meet with intensity.

"God, Maps," he says against me. I love the way I can feel him losing himself.

I push each thought filled with doubt down as I kiss him harder and become more fevered. I take every feeling of desire I've had in the past month and I put it into the kiss.

I pull up his shirt and touch the hard plane of his stomach and drag my fingertips down his firm back and across his chest. My hips roll against the hardness between his, and I can feel him moving upward. When my hand moves to the elastic of his waistband, he stops.

"No." His voice is rough like it's being pulled from his throat.

It stings, but I nod. "Okay."

He presses his forehead against mine and takes deep breaths. The world has gone from the roaring of my pulse to utter silence that rings in my ears. King leans back and pulls down his shirt. It's not supposed to be rejection, but it feels like it.

I push off him, trying to give myself room to breathe, and for rational thought to come find me.

He looks at me with dark eyes that flash and swallows thickly. "I want to." He clears his throat. "I'm just not ready for . . ."

"Right," I say. My face burns as I stand.

King nods. "Are you . . . okay?" His eyes are wide, concerned as they look over my face. It feels . . . kind.

I hate that I can feel his concern pressing against the delicate parts of my heart. I'm afraid that if he keeps pressing, I will bleed. *No.* I want to ask him what this is. What are we doing? Does he feel the same things I do?

"Yeah." I take a deep breath.

He nods, believing my lie. But King doesn't look okay either. His lips are swollen and red and his hair is messy from my hands. He looks shaken. His hands shudder at his sides and he flexes them.

The smell of his sweat is on my skin, and all of it makes me greedy.

"I should—" He clears his throat. "I need to take care of the fire."

At the river I run water over my face and wonder to myself what happens next. King will shift and change, and I'll just be waiting to see what version of him I get.

28

WHEN MY DAD DIED, it happened slowly.

And also, all at once.

Like one day he just decided to give up.

That's how cancer is. It's long days of torture and then suddenly they're gone. And you're left wondering if you're a bad person because you feel relief at it finally being over. Left wondering if you wasted moments that could have been spent with that person. Wondering how the world keeps going on without them in it.

All while people sit around waiting for you to break.

It happened on a Wednesday. Right in the middle of the week. He had stopped talking the day before. Stopped opening his eyes. Stopped everything but breathing.

I didn't know if he could hear me, but I wasn't sure what he was waiting for. With my mother in the other room, I took his hand. Paper thin and sunken, with bruises that never healed from IVs. I could still feel the calluses on his palms. And for some reason those bumps made me incredibly sad. This man who had lived a life long enough to get calluses was going to die. His hard work, a footnote against his skin. All his scars and stories and laughter were going to disappear.

I leaned over and whispered, "It's okay, Daddy. I'll be okay."

I didn't know if it was for him or for me.

But after that he stopped breathing.

My mother spent days cleaning after my father's body was wheeled out of the house on the hospital bed he died in. She went through all his clothes and belongings and pictures as if he should've taken all those things with him when he left.

And next to the bedside was a list.

His messy handwriting, shaky from the drugs and chemo, spelled out all the things that he wanted to do before he died. There were big things, like *see the Grand Canyon* and *take my girls to New York*. Small things, like *talk to Henry. Tell Joe the truth. Reread* The Call of the Wild.

But it was the last two things that broke my heart.

See the birds fly south from the beach.

Open the WEST trail and hike it with Atlas.

I ran a finger over the last two. When my dad talked about places that defined him, it was that beach and that trail.

My father proposed to my mother on that beach, after the birds flew away and it was just them, the quiet, and their love. He had said, "If places have memories, that one is filled with beginnings."

And he always said the trail was a place for answers. I wonder if that's why he wanted to hike it again before he died.

I slipped the paper into my pocket, worried my mother would

throw it away. I wanted to keep it. I wanted to keep something that reminded me of all the things we don't get to do. That sometimes, you can't go back.

His funeral was on another Wednesday.

I crouched by the side of the house next to the bear-proof trash cans and a rusted bicycle. Tears ran down my face and my black dress was getting wrinkled, because sometimes you make coffee and it's fine. And then other times you make coffee and you have to stop yourself from throwing the pot across the house in a rage because your dad died and now you have to make your own fucking coffee.

I liked my anger. I understood it. It felt like something I could hold. I could feel my emotions clench and pull tight.

Unlike the sadness of grief. That pain felt like water falling from your hands. The slow drag of being pulled under. Your lungs filling up with your own tears. Drowning.

No. I wanted the fight. I would not submit.

"You okay?"

I cleared my throat and wiped at my tears.

Joe stood in the driveway, looking at me curiously.

No, I wasn't okay, but he didn't look okay either. "What're you doing out here?"

Joe chewed at his lip for a second before he lit a cigarette. "Your mother is trying to kill everyone with a build-your-own sandwich bar."

Trays of deli meats and cheeses sat on every surface of the house. A cheese ball and crackers were displayed on the coffee table where my father used to put his feet while he watched hockey. Casseroles filled the dining room table where we played dominos my entire life. The kitchen was full of deli platters, and I couldn't help but remember my father cooking his famous potatoes, making a mess as he went along.

"Also, all your dad's friends from the school are boring."

I laughed.

Joe leaned against the house with me. Our shoulders pressed into the wood siding. "Fuck. I hate that I'm here and he isn't."

"Yeah," I said, not because I would have traded Joe for my father, but because I had wished he was here too.

"Come on. If we go back in together, maybe no one will talk to us."

"I doubt it."

Joe rolled his shoulders. "I have to wear this fucking suit and . . . this is the most god-awful thing I've ever been to."

"It's . . ."

"Fucking awful," he finished for me.

I laughed because he was right.

"Promise me you won't let anyone do this shit for me," Joe said. "Blood oath swear."

"Who says you're getting one of these? We'll probably just dump your body in the river."

He sighed. "That actually doesn't sound bad. Better than making people eat a cheese ball."

I asked him, "Hey, did my dad ever talk to you? Tell you . . . the truth?"

Joe studied me. "The truth? It's a hundred different things."

"But did he tell you . . . something important?" I didn't know why I was pressing, maybe because I just wanted to know that my dad had done *something* on the list.

Joe shook his head and looked out at the street full of parked cars. "Your dad said everything he needed to say, Outlaw." His teeth scraped his bottom lip. "He wouldn't have given up if he hadn't."

On my last days on the Western Sierra Trail, I wonder if I've given up. My anger. My pride. Some of my grief.

We're almost at the end of the trail, but there are no cheers or sighs of relief or excitement. We are all silent, realizing what this actually means. That these moments are our last moments together like this.

After our kiss, King is cautious, but I don't let him pull away. We walk down to fill our water bottles and I kiss him. Against a tree. I let my hands find places on him that make him groan and breathe into me. And I tell myself it's okay to know this is something that I won't take from here, even if it hurts.

We stop counting the days until the trail ends, because—

The end comes slowly. And all at once.

29

AND JUST LIKE THAT, it's over. There's no fanfare or congratulations. Just a motel and a sad strip of stores next to a laundromat.

The end of the Western Sierra Trail is only a sign that reads TRAIL CLOSED. NO HIKING. I can't tell how I feel that soon the sign will be gone and it will be open again.

Other people will hike *our* trail.

Sugar and I are assigned room eight.

Inside are two beds, two nightstands, and a bathroom. All the paintings are of animals in human clothes against dark green walls.

There's no phone, or mini fridge, or fluffy towels. All the linens look threadbare but clean. I should be ecstatic to sleep in an actual bed, but . . .

We are the dirtiest thing in the room. My eyes catch on the mirror and I almost start. I barely recognize myself. Even with the occasional bath in the river and the shower a few days ago, my hair is flat. It's not as oily as I thought it would be. My face is tanner than when I left and I'm not wearing any makeup.

But I also look different. Stronger. My face doesn't look bloated or puffy. It's hard, and my eyes are clear. I reach up and touch the face of the stranger in the mirror.

"You wanna take the first shower?" I ask Sugar.

She comes to stand next to me and stares at her reflection. The one she doesn't recognize. I know that's what she's doing because I'm doing it too.

"Whoa," she says. "Have I looked like this the whole time?"

At some point she stopped wearing makeup and started wearing the sun. I give her a smile. "Yeah."

I hope she can see the confidence and strength that I do.

Her chest rises and falls, and then Sugar locks herself in the bathroom. I look around for somewhere to sit and decide on the floor, ending up staring at the popcorn ceiling.

When I was little, my dad took me to my grandmother's house, and I remember falling asleep making shapes in the patterns the light cast on the ceiling. But instead of reminding me of my dad, I just lie here thinking about how the ceiling isn't the sky.

Those aren't the stars.

When Sugar comes out already dressed, she looks at me and makes a face. "Didn't anyone ever tell you not to lie on a motel floor?"

"I think people like me lying on the floor is the reason people say that."

Her face changes like I've made a good point. "It's the worst shower I've ever had. The water pressure sucks and the shampoo and conditioner in there are trash, but it was warm water all over my body and actual soap and a washcloth. It was the best goddamn ten minutes of my life."

I wait a few minutes and watch Sugar brush her long hair and her teeth at the sink. It all feels so . . . normal, which makes it feel incredibly not normal.

When I get up, I pull out the least dirty things I own and head to the shower.

Sugar's right.

I make the water as hot as I possibly can and let it turn my skin red. The floor of the shower brownish gray beneath me, and for a second I just let my body do the very normal thing of standing under a shower.

I watch the dirt swirl around my feet and disappear into the drain and feel empty. The last of the mountains is being washed from my body, and the emotions that have been rubbed into my skin like the dirt and sweat of the trail.

This is an ending.

Eventually I get out, and Sugar tells me we should wash our clothes.

The laundry room looks like everything else. Floor to ceiling dark wood paneling, but instead of odd artwork of animals in clothing, it's pictures of hikers. Old and new, some framed on the wall and some taped. They cover almost all the space in a collage. Against the walls are ancient buttercream washers and dryers. There is laundry soap sitting on a long bar that says LAUNDRY.

Sugar stuffs all her clothes into one machine.

"You're not gonna separate your stuff?" I ask.

She looks at me patiently. "Should I be worried that they might get a stain?"

Her point has been made. These clothes are already trashed.

I can't seem to take a full breath. Being under a roof with walls and windows makes all the air feel stale and heavy in my lungs. I push out of the heavy glass door. The dollar in my pocket is supposed to be for drying my clothes, but I see a vending machine with sodas and one with snacks.

"Fuck it." I buy a Snickers and watch it fall from the machine into the tray.

"Candy?"

When I turn around, the candy bar in my hand, I see King standing with his arms folded. His hair is a little damp and his body looks scrubbed. Even his clothes are clean, and I can't say exactly why, but it makes me a bit sad.

"Did you spend your laundry money on a candy bar?" he asks.

"I found this." I clutch the bar to my chest. "And the laundry is free."

His lips turn up, a bit amused, and it makes his whole face look handsome. He's shaved, and I wonder if I got close enough would he smell like the same soap as I do. I can feel myself blush at the thought of us smelling the same.

He holds out his hand and then folds his fingers up rapidly in a gimmie motion. I sigh as I put the bar in his hand. He unwraps it and takes a bite before handing it to me.

"That was mine!"

He only smiles at my outrage.

Books orders dinner from the restaurant, but we eat it on the grass with our legs folded underneath us. We're all clean; the trail has been cleared from our skin. The noises of the forest have been replaced with the sounds of cars and the hum of electricity and people. And we aren't eating rice and beans.

I go back to my laundry and find King standing with one hip propped against a large industrial dryer. I ignore him and walk over to the machine that I started, but when I open it, it's empty. King is already looking at me when I close the lid. "I switched yours already."

"You did?"

He nods and I think about King grabbing all my clothes and underwear. The dryer behind him has a clear door and I watch the clothes tumble.

I run my tongue over my teeth. "I can't believe this is almost over."

"I know."

I clear my throat. "I . . . wish . . ."

"I know."

"I wish we could just . . ."

His arms are crossed over his body as he watches me. He practically whispers, "I know, Maps."

I pull myself up onto the table in the center of the room and sit on it. My legs dangle over, and I search for something to say. For the reason I don't leave. The sound of the machines is a low static that I can feel inside my chest. The air here feels humid and warm even as the air conditioner blows. And I run my thumb against a nick in the wooden table. Everything feels heavy. The noise, the air, us.

Tomorrow morning, we will be with our families. And King and Maps won't exist.

I look outside. "The weather is weird."

He makes a noise. "It almost looks like rain."

I laugh because rain in the summer in California would be an act of God. I jump down from the table and start to look at the hikers on the wall. Faces in faded sepia tones and high gloss and bright flashes. I wonder where all these people are. If they miss this trail. If they make lists and put hiking this trail at the bottom.

I wonder if my dad is on this wall.

I wonder if I belong on it now.

"Should we take a picture?" I ask King.

"I don't have a phone," he tells me.

And that's the moment I realize that King and I won't take anything off this trail that is *us*. Not a picture to prove even to ourselves that we were together. That we were an us.

"You don't have to wait," he tells me. "I'll bring your clothes to you."

I can hear something else in his voice, something I'm not entirely sure about. Everything about King right now feels like we are teetering on a wire. One move in any direction will send us falling. "Are you sure?" I ask him.

He looks at me for a long moment before he says, "Yeah. I'm sure."

So I just nod and go back to room eight.

Sugar is gone so I lie on my bed and watch the sky darken. The thunder cracks overhead, so I almost don't hear the knock at the door.

When I open it, King stands there.

With eyes as stormy as the clouds above.

30

MY CLOTHES ARE NEATLY folded in his hands and the look on his face makes the breath in my lungs catch.

"The weather is weird," King repeats my words from earlier to me.

We're talking about the weather now. "The air?"

"It feels weird, right?"

I don't know, so I just take my clothes from him. He steps in behind me as if I've invited him. This moment feels like electricity under my skin.

Or maybe it's the storm.

I set my clothes on top of my pack and wait for King to tell me what he wants, but I'm only met with more silence. God, I hate the quiet.

"What's happening right now?" I ask.

"I brought you your laundry." He's silent for so long I think he's going to ask what I'm talking about, but then he says, "I know that's not what you're asking, but I don't know how to answer you."

I turn toward him. "What . . . does that mean?"

His eyes move over my face. "What do you want it to mean?"

When I speak next, it's without regard for my pride. "I think you know what I want it to mean." I'm done playing games. "If you don't want—"

"Who said that?"

"King."

"There are things I . . . I need to—"

"Please don't." I stop him. I can't hear him list all the reasons why this is a bad idea. I don't want to be a bad thing anymore. "Please. Can we just not do that and—" I hear thunder again. The ground seems to shake with it and a second later I hear the sound of rain falling outside. My eyes shoot to his, which are also wide.

The sky brightens for a second—a flash—and then it's dark again.

King counts under his breath. "One. Two. Three."

Thunder shakes again.

"What are you doing?" I ask.

"Seeing how far the lightning is." He runs a hand down his face.

"It's raining," I say. How can it be raining?

The corner of his mouth lifts and his eyes trail down to the place my shirt rides up. "Yeah, I noticed."

We sink into the quiet as we listen to the rain fall heavily on the concrete. This time when the sky lights up, the thunder follows directly after.

It feels like a sign of the impossible being possible. If it can rain in a California summer, maybe King and I have hope.

"I don't really like lightning," I tell him. He nods as he sits

256

on the opposite bed. "Sugar should be back soon, so you don't have to wait with me."

"No, she's with Junior and Books tonight. They are . . . making themselves scarce." He waves his hand and the sky lights again. And King counts.

His eyes close and his mouth moves over numbers and then he speaks.

"You're like lightning." His words feel warm and soft, and not cheesy like they should. I tilt my face up to his and look into his eyes. "I feel like I'm always counting to see how far away you are."

Maybe it's the weather that's made everything feel electric and hot, but looking at King, all I can think about is how I'm always *too far* away from him.

I move over to the bed he sits on and his chest inflates. I know the shape of King. The way his broad shoulders frame his silhouette. The way his stomach contracts when he laughs and makes the muscles there stand out. The clench of his jaw, the furrow of his brow. Gently, I reach up a hand and trace his cheek. When I move to his mouth, he parts his lips for me. I run a finger over them and remember what it's like to have my own lips on them.

"I want to kiss you again," I whisper. "Is that okay?"

"Yes," King whispers with his brows drawn together.

"I might want something else too. If you do."

King licks his lips. "I want you, Maps. But I only want what you are willing to give."

"Are you going to push me away? Are you going to run?"

His mouth opens and I can see the truth waiting to be spoken, so instead, I kiss him softly with the sound of the rain beating down against the window. It makes it feel like we're in our own little world. Hidden.

"I want you. I want this," he tells me.

Every kiss before this with King has been asking a question, but when our lips meet this time, there's only answers. In the way his tongue finds its way into my mouth. The way he sounds a little like he's in pain when I bite gently at his bottom lip. His teeth scrape at my neck and he only pulls away when he tugs my shirt over my head. I fall back onto the bed and King's mouth is on the soft space between my breasts.

There is a hunger in his eyes when he looks at me. I take his hand again and place it on the waistband of my shorts. "I want this."

He groans and moves up to kiss me. I can feel him pressing against the soft parts of me. Right where I want him. We move against each other and every inch of me feels like it's building to a lightning strike.

King takes my shorts off and I'm lying there naked. Not perfect. I don't even know what I look like, but King takes a breath and I watch the dark outline of his chest move. "Maps, you're . . ."

His words are lost as his lips find the space right below my belly button. King's hands are on my breasts and I arch up to meet them. It causes the ache at the base of my spine to grow stronger and when I feel like I can't bear for him not to touch me other places, I take his hand and move it down between my legs.

His fingers press on the sensitive parts of me, but King doesn't ever take his mouth off my body.

He licks stripes up my skin and kisses my mouth. The ache grows stronger and more intense. I'm making noises and giving directions that probably don't even make any sense. I can't stop myself and then . . . My cry is lost in the sound of the rain as I fall off the edge of the world.

I throw a hand over my eyes and try to catch my breath. King moves to sit up, but I pull him forward.

"We don't . . ." He clears his throat. "I'm not assuming, I'm just telling you, we don't have anything." A condom. I smile. I move his hands back to my breasts and my own to his shorts. I could tease him. Run my hand across his length while it's still covered, just to listen to the noises he makes, but I can tell he's close. He presses his forehead against mine as I take him into my palm. Our breathing fills the silence as he sounds caught between agony and pleasure, but it's only moments before he falls off the edge after me. I find his shirt and wipe off my hand as he falls backward, trying to find solid ground again.

"Did you use my shirt?" he asks, still breathless.

"Yes," I tell him with confidence. "At least there's laundry here."

King laughs as he pulls me toward him. "You are something else."

With him.

With King I am something else.

31

THERE'S A LOUD BANGING outside.

King and I sit up at the same time, disoriented and naked. "Fuck," he says as he searches the floor for something to put on.

"Car's here!" It's Books shouting from the other side of the door as King slides on his boxer briefs.

He opens it and Books shakes his head with a groan. "Are you fucking kidding me? Joe is at the car. *Now.*" He hands King his pack.

King slams the door and the two of us dress as fast as we can.

"Fuck. Fuck. Fuck." I throw on my clothes and shoes and put all my stuff in my bag. King's fingers are wrapped around the knob, but he turns to me.

And suddenly time stops.

His hand goes to my face and he opens his mouth. There's something in his eyes. Dark and broken. I wait for what feels like a hundred years before I realize what he's going to say isn't something I want to hear.

The truth is an odd thing to tell someone.

Most of the time, we don't give it. And even when someone says they want it, they don't.

The truth makes you vulnerable.

King looks vulnerable.

He drops his hands and opens and closes them, trying to shake them out.

"King?" I say his name like a question.

"I need to—" He clears his throat. "I know this probably isn't a big deal or maybe it is or . . . fuck."

"You're making me nervous," I tell him.

"I wanted to explain last night but then you kissed me and—"

I laugh, like a Band-Aid over my fear. "You're not married, are you?"

His eyes meet mine and he goes still. "I want to show you something." He reaches into his pack and he pulls out his journal. The one he's been writing in on the trail. His hands shake slightly as he hands it to me.

"Okay." I breathe the word as I open it. Flipping through, I see dates and detailed maps of different sections of the trail, mixed with drawings of trees and descriptions of what needs to be done still. But I also see other things. My name written and traced over. The description of something I did. The date we kissed circled underneath it. A drawing of me. "King . . ."

He flips to the first page. "This is what you need to see."

King,

Sorry leaves no time to be better.

Be better.

Patrick.

261

I know this writing. I have a list that has the same shaky script. I have seen the signature all my life.

"Oh fuck." I whisper it, but each word feels like it's been yanked from me.

"I . . . I knew your dad."

My stomach churns. I frown. "I don't understand."

He takes a deep breath, but instead of exhaling, he speaks. "I know your name is Atlas and I knew that your dad just died because . . . I knew him. Patrick."

My pulse beats in my ears, and suddenly it's not silent anymore. My father's name has just come out of King's mouth. It's written in the journal King has been using. "How?"

"Last year Joe had us rehabilitating a part of the river that feeds into the lake."

I know the exact spot he's talking about. I don't even have to clarify because I spent a thousand mornings there with my father. Before.

"Joe's friend would come out and sit in a chair and talk with us sometimes."

"King." I want him to stop, but he doesn't.

"He would bring us lunches and coffee and bottles of water that Joe would complain about because of the plastic trash. One time this guy forgot a hat, and the next day Patrick brought a hat."

My stomach feels sick and I hold a hand over it. I remember this. The long mornings my dad was gone spending time with Joe while I slept most of the day away. I didn't realize I was losing hours with my dad. Hours he spent with *King*.

"He was just this sick guy who hung out with Joe. Except he was funny, and Joe was always easier to deal with when he was around. And he would talk about you sometimes. His daughter, Atlas."

I swallow a lump in my throat, hearing these precious pieces of my father being repeated by a stranger. Is King a stranger? I hug myself tighter and feel the world sway beneath my feet. I had always regretted those mornings, but assumed my dad spent them with Joe. Not talking with random kids at the river. Anger swells in my veins. No, not anger. Jealousy.

"He was good to us, and he made me feel like . . ." He shakes his head. "When your dad died, we heard about his service. I saw you there with Joe."

Oh god. My stomach churns from embarrassment. When they played his favorite song and I cried so hard that I had to be carried out of the building. That was the lowest moment of my life, and King witnessed it. It feels like he's always known a secret about me. "What a stupid fucking song."

King shifts on his feet. "I knew who you were the first time we met. You . . ." He bites his lip like he's trying to keep an emotion in check. "You had my cigarettes in your hand."

My dad's secret.

The cigarettes.

They weren't his. They were *King's*. "Fuck."

"Your dad had taken them from me one day at the river and yelled at me about cancer and being an idiot and disrespecting everyone I was working with. I felt like shit." Tears well in his eyes. "Here I am smoking while I'm literally watching this nice guy die of cancer. The next day I apologized and that's when he told me not to be sorry. To be better."

This can't be happening.

"And then you're holding my cigarettes. Like a fucking sign."

My mind swirls with all the things King's saying. And all the things he's not.

"I wanted to tell you, but it . . . goddamn it." He runs a hand over his face.

I don't even know what to say. I feel humiliated and lied to and violated and he's talking about a sign? I find my voice. "Does Books know?"

King looks down and nods his head once.

It all feels so unbalanced. King has always seen the girl I've tried to hide. He can see my heart. The shattered thing bleeding on the floor. He's been watching it gasp as it tries to pump blood.

And King? "I know nothing about you," I tell him. "And you're telling me you were at one of the worst days of my life?"

"I've never, ever lied to you." All his words are punctuated by his earnestness.

"You lied about knowing who I was."

"Everything else was always the truth, Atlas."

I reel back like he's slapped me. "*Don't* call me that. Don't you fucking dare."

"Maps," he corrects himself.

"You do not know me. Just because you hung out with my dad or whatever. Fuck you." I pull it out so each consonant and vowel sound is exaggerated. "Seriously, fuck you for saying my name like that. Like you know *Atlas*. You don't know anything about her."

It's all true. That girl at her dad's funeral and the one my father talked about. I haven't been able to find her since then.

"I'm sorry. I just." His hands are in his hair and he looks . . . scared? Broken? Worried? How could he be any of these things? How, when he lied to *me*?

I take a deep breath. "I knew this was never going to be something more. I have no idea why you decided to unburden your conscience on me. You're going to Alaska and you've made it clear we aren't going to be anything more."

I'm lost in all my feelings, so I stop talking. The image I've drawn of King at my father's funeral keeps playing in my mind. As hard as I search my memories, I can barely remember anything about that day. So many people hugged me, offered me stories of my dad that I could barely hear. Was he one of them?

I walk out and see Books, Sugar, and Junior all standing outside the door. With Joe. It's clear they heard every word. Their eyes are on the ground. Everyone's but Joe's.

"Maps," he says to me.

"No. Fuck you." I mean it to sound angry, but it comes out broken and full of my hurt. "Fuck all of you."

And I walk away from the Western Sierra Trail.

Because all my endings are destined to be brutal and tragic.

32

I SEE MY MOTHER before she sees me.

Sitting in the car as she scrolls through her phone. And I see the ghost that sits next to her. The space my dad is supposed to be in. I'm so angry that he's not here to come get me. I bite my cheek as hard as I can and try to focus on that pain and not the huge hole in my heart.

But I can't stop the tears. My feet hit pavement and, like stepping into another world, suddenly I'm back to the place I left. Like nothing has changed.

My mother is out of the car before I can get to her and she wraps her arms around me.

I cry.

She holds me. For so long, I should be embarrassed. She whispers things to me. Soft and sweet and reassuring. Exactly like a mother is supposed to. And I just fucking miss my dad. I can't help it. I just wish he was here, even though this moment doesn't even matter. I just miss him. I just miss him. I miss him.

"Hey sweetheart," she says against my hair. "Long time no see."

I dig my fingers into her sweater and count to ten before I let her go. She smells the same, and her hug feels exactly like it has my whole life. Just like the one she gave me when I left.

We get into the car and close the doors.

And we drive away from Bear Creek.

I can't shake the feeling that I've missed something.

When I was five, my father and I were driving down a windy back road. He liked sharing small facts with me as we passed different places. He would explain that the field next to us was full of strawberries, or that the big building on the side of the road was a fish hatchery and then explain how salmon swam upstream, or what kind of trees lined a creek. On this day, he told me that the state flower was a California poppy and that people weren't supposed to pick them because they were protected. Special.

But he stopped the car and got out. "Just one for your mom," he said with a wink. "Because she's special."

I cried as he plucked it from the dirt and got back into the truck. My father had done something illegal and now he would have to pay for breaking the law.

"What's wrong?" he asked, surprised.

"I don't want you to go to jail," I cried as I held on to his shirt, pressing my wet nose against him.

"Oh," he whispered, pulling tighter into the hug. He smelled like leather and the tobacco from his cigars. "I'm not going anywhere, sweetheart. I promise."

I promise.

I don't believe in promises.

It's a two-hour drive back home. My mother doesn't even ask

as she stops at In-N-Out. I eat my Double-Double so fast I don't know if I really even taste it. She orders me a Neapolitan milk shake and makes a face when I end up mixing all the flavors together. "Your dad ruined you."

She means it as a joke, but the words are something that my mind keeps tracing over and over again until they are pressed into my thoughts.

My dad did ruin me. His cancer and his death *ruined* me.

I stare out the window at the sun in the sky and wonder if it can reach me behind all this glass and metal speeding down the freeway.

And then we're home. Kids ride their bikes. The smell of asphalt and grass and someone's barbecue down the street.

I'm finally back where I wanted to be. Everything is familiar and . . . I can't seem to make myself walk to the door. My mother watches me from the porch as I stand there with my silver suitcase.

"It's just a house," my mother says. "It hurts. And then sometimes it doesn't."

Sometimes.

We walk in and I hold my breath. Inside the house, nothing is how I remember it. It seems smaller. My dad's hospital bed is gone. His pills from the counter. His sweater from the hook. But his keys are still in the bowl by the door. His shoes are gone, but not the scuff marks on the wall from the place he would toe them off.

His chair is still by the window, but he isn't.

My heart hurts, but time has moved on.

My mother's arms wrap around me, wordless, and I realize that we both have been left with an empty chair. I finally stop measuring my pain against hers. They mix like ink in water and become the same hurt. Shared.

Eventually, I go to my room and my mother decides we should get takeout for dinner. She orders my dad's favorite dish and I wonder if it's habit or because she wants to remember him in the little ways.

In the back of my closet are my father's ashes. It's odd thinking about my larger-than-life father in a box that's so small. But really, it's only part of him. My mother buried most of his ashes at the center of a huge mausoleum that smells like dust and death and decay. And even though his headstone is in the rose garden, there isn't a universe where my father would have enjoyed being there.

The stillness that feels so different from every other memory of my father. It's quiet and reverent, with an immense sadness floating in the air and pressing down like a fog.

But my mother said that it was nice to have a place to visit.

Something about it just never felt like the goodbye I wanted for him. So now he sits inside cardboard and tape behind winter coats I never use.

I take off my clothes and stand in front of the shower, finally alone. The bathroom is starting to fill with steam. And I know it's stupid. But. Taking this shower feels like I'm losing the last little bit of King.

Will I still smell him on my skin?

I get in.

But I can't bear to wash the dirt from under my nails. Dirt that says I was there. On the trail. I did it.

I dry my hair and pull my father's list from my back pocket. It's folded and soft from sweat and time and me.

I can cross off the trail now. Even though he wasn't there, his memory still lives there. Above it, I rub a finger over *See the birds fly south from the beach*.

And I know what I want to do.

A day later, my mother drives me to the airport and tells me to have a safe flight. I forgot my earbuds, and I'm left listening to my own thoughts as I stare out at the clouds below.

I wonder if King is on a plane to Alaska. I pretend like I don't have a thousand things to tell my mother about. To disappoint her with.

When I land in Florida, I look at the blue cloudless sky and know today is a perfect day to say goodbye.

The box of my dad's ashes sits on the seat next to me in the Uber. *Patrick James* is written on top on beige masking tape that comes up at the edges. I run my fingers over the black Sharpie that spells his name.

I want to give my dad something he would appreciate.

A man with a belly that hangs over his shorts and cheeks that spill onto his neck tells me I'm not allowed to rent a Jet Ski and go out to the island because the land is protected. "What do you wanna do out there?"

"I wanna see the birds."

"Birds?" He looks confused.

"My parents got engaged there at dusk and the birds . . ."

He laughs. "People are weird. No one goes out there but kids getting high or biologists."

But he whispers to me that I can rent a rowboat.

I give him my credit card and paddle out. Rowing is much harder than it looks. It's a rhythm and I have none. When I finally get the boat to go in the direction I want, it's late afternoon. I jump out into the water and pull my boat ashore. The island is covered in plants and trees that are thick and look ominous, but there's a rock with people's names and dates on it. I read them as I wait for the sun to fade from the sky. I sit on the beach and I think.

I think about my dad's list of things to do before he died. I think about the way he talked about this beach. I swat at a bug that crawls up my leg and groan. I had imagined this moment going differently. I had imagined the blue sky fading into soft light and maybe piano music. Not the heat and the itchy sand and the weird noises coming from somewhere just beyond the trees.

"I'm here, Dad," I say to the sky. "I'm here and . . . I hope I'm not too late for your birds' migration." I find a spot between two rocks that looks like a good place and I dig a hole. There's no one to hear me talk at my dad, so I tell him all about the trail. The good parts, the bad parts, but not the parts about King. I keep those to myself.

When I set my dad's ashes in the hole, I look back at them. Was I supposed to spread them? I can't even honor my dad properly.

"Shit." I wipe at my forehead with the back of my hand and see it.

In the middle of several wildflowers is a poppy. Bright orange and open.

I'm not going anywhere. I promise.

My fingers wrap around the stem of the poppy and I pluck it from the earth. Because he was wrong. He left.

"You lied," I tell the box. "You are a *liar*."

Just like me. Just like King. Just like everyone, I guess.

I throw dirt over his ashes until I can't see the box anymore and then I toss the poppy on top.

"There."

I lie back on the ground, surrounded by my own carnage. Tears fall down my face and into my hair and ears uncomfortably. Grass and sand and sticks poke at my legs and back. I'm so angry. So hurt.

And so scared.

I'm scared that if I show someone how hurt I am, I'll never stop hurting. A hole of my own pain will open up and swallow me. I'm afraid of what's on the other side of this pain.

Afraid of the emptiness that means he's really gone.

But it's not these moments, the scheduled grieving days or holidays with empty chairs that hurt. It's the unexpected moments. The ones that sneak up on you from seemingly nowhere. The ones you're not prepared for. When you pick up your phone to call them because you want to tell them something, but then you remember they won't answer. When you get a glimpse of them from the corner of your eye.

Those moments are the ones with knives and teeth and poison.

The sky above me is a bright blue mottled with white clouds. I can see the moon, small and white in the sea of cerulean. Today is a perfect day to say goodbye. Anyone can see that. I will leave my father here and it will be perfect. My dad among the poppies. Something for just him and me.

Something that—if someone asked about it—would sound like a touching story. They might even give me the look I hate.

Even if the birds don't show.

"I hate this island," I tell the dirt covering my dad's box as I continue to cry. "I hate poppies. I hate blue skies and the ocean and especially the goddamn moon. I hate that you died. And I hate more than anything that you're not here to help me deal with it."

I should say goodbye to my dad and leave him here. It's a perfect day.

But what I hate more than anything is saying goodbye.

The sky changes to a soft yellow and I know the sun is finally setting. A whirling sound, like a swarm, fills the air. I hear chirping and suddenly the sky above is painted with black.

The birds. They flock in thick and steady streams. They circle above me and swoop down and my dad was right. It's beautiful. Stunning dark creatures against the pink sky like confetti spread out. I wish my dad could see it. I wish he and my mother could stand here and look up at the birds as they recommit to life with each other and feel like their love is countless and free like the birds.

Except . . . they aren't birds. They're bats. Millions of . . . bats.

Fucking bats. Did he know? Did my mother know? The birds

they thought they were lucky enough to see migrate are actually tiny, winged mammals.

Just fucking great.

Laughter bubbles up inside me, soft at first until it changes to full-on belly laughing. They were bats. My parents got engaged under a million bats. I consider digging my dad up, but somehow the bats seem more fitting than anything else.

"That's what you get for dying," I tell the mound of dirt with the poppy thrown on top of it. And I know this is right. This was supposed to happen all along.

Because, truthfully, I hate perfect days.

33

THE WORLD DOESN'T STOP. It marches on for hours and days.

Grief doesn't care about time.

I watch the sun rise and fall and rise and fall and rise from my father's chair. Days move past me in streaks of light and shadows that stretch and pull against the faded carpet. Trashy reality television keeps me company. Something I don't have to focus on, but that softly whispers to me that I'm not alone.

In my mind, I can hear my dad complain about the content of what I'm watching. And I do something I haven't really done since he died. I let myself be sad. During game shows with dad and daughter duos. During commercials for cereal. When my mom asks me if I want to get ice cream at his favorite place.

I read *The Call of the Wild*. I try to like it, but I don't. There isn't any kissing in it, and I tell my dad's memory that his favorite book is boring.

I stop asking my grief to make sense.

I tell my mother I want to get my GED.

She doesn't push or make comments about it. She just lets me breathe and be.

And I think about King.

When I close my eyes, I see the fractured light play against his skin as we sat on the bank of the river under the moon. I see him in the soft morning sky against the bright green of the trees. I see the hollow of the place between his jaw and his shoulder that was a perfect place for my head.

Our last conversation plays on a loop in my mind.

I wonder if he made it to Alaska. I wonder if it would make me happy or sad if he didn't.

I go to grief group and sit in plastic chairs and drink cups of lemonade and store-bought sugar cookies. Not with my mother, but with other people who have lost a parent. Some are old, some are younger, but all of them let me say, or not say, anything I want.

One particular day in group, I explode. It's about the dishes. How my dad would have never yelled at me about what side of the sink they go in and then it devolves into all the ways my mother is failing. I press on the pain like a bruise. I tell them that she thinks she hurts more than I do and I hate her for it. I hate her even when she's kind. They let me complain and cry and babble and say things I don't really mean, but I do.

And when I'm done, a woman with dark hair in braids hands me another tissue and says kindly, "I'm so sorry, Atlas. I feel for both of you. Especially your mother. I imagine it's hard for her to constantly be compared to your dad's perfect ghost."

She doesn't mean it as a reproach, only a possible reason for my mother to act the way she does.

But I can't unhear it. My dad's perfect ghost that has been frozen in time and is infallible. My hurt is fair, but so is hers.

All these things are honest. And for the first time, my grief is honest.

Things change slowly between us, but in the right ways.

My mother shakes her head and tells me my father would be *disappointed* in me.

When I say, "Yeah, well, he died," it's with anger instead of grief and she almost looks relieved.

We plan a girls' trip to New York and I cross it off my father's list.

I get a job at a coffee shop. It's not my calling in life, but it does help me save money and requires that I leave my house. My mother pretends not to be elated that I'm socializing. And I let her think I don't see it.

I smile at people, and laugh, and make friends with coworkers who don't know anything about me. I tell them the truth. About my dad, about King and Bear Creek and school. It feels . . . nice. Sometimes they give me looks of pity, sometimes they don't. I wait for the sting of my own embarrassment, but it never comes.

I'm growing, even if there is something missing.

Even if I still fall asleep in King's shirt that accidentally ended up in my things.

Joe stops by one afternoon.

I can't help but feel like it's a welfare check. Like he's making sure my mother and I haven't become shut-ins.

He stands on the porch, showered and shaved. Almost looking

like a completely different person except for his frown. "Outlaw."

My eyes look past him to his Jeep. Empty. I can't help the way my stomach swoops with disappointment. I was hoping to see King and the realization is surprising even to me.

"Well," Joe says, shaking his head. "That look tells me everything I need to know."

"What do you want?" I ask him as I lean against the doorjamb.

"We should talk."

I move to the side to let him in, but Joe shakes his head. "I don't want . . . Let's go for a walk."

"Joe," I complain. "I'm not walking anymore. Maybe never again. That's all I did on the trail." I point to the two rocking chairs on the porch that my mother had to have, but no one has ever used.

Joe looks like he wants to argue but thinks better of it and sits down in the chair. His eyes are on the driveway. "Sometimes I swear I think I'm gonna see him. Especially in those mountains."

I bite the inside of my cheek.

"That stupid bucket hat he always wore and a fishing pole in his hand." Joe sniffs.

We go quiet remembering different parts of my dad until eventually I say, "You tricked me."

He breathes heavily next to me and folds his hands together. His thumbs rub against each other. "Not everything is about you."

"What?"

Joe leans back and stares at the street like it has the answers.

278

"I don't mean to be a dick, but King and Books knowing your dad doesn't have anything to do with you."

"He's my *dad*."

"And he was Patrick to them. Just because he's one thing to you doesn't take anything away from anyone else's memory. You're not pissed about that, anyway, Outlaw. You're embarrassed." He says it like a fact, like saying the ocean is deep.

"Wasn't the whole point of the nicknames so that people didn't know about us?"

He laughs and shakes his head.

"You know the nicknames were your dad's idea? He read it in a book or some shit."

I laugh, because of course it was. My dad loved nicknames.

If you met him more than once, you got one. And he would say, "They aren't for them. They're for me. People remember the person who calls them something special and I want to be remembered."

But it wasn't until much later that I realized how wrong he was. Nicknames aren't just about someone knowing you well enough to call you something just between the two of you, or about remembering the man in the bucket hat who is generous with his smiles despite losing all his hair.

It's about something bigger.

Our names feel like permanent ties to who we are and the things that we've been told define us. But, without those names, you can be Freckles, the girl who makes the best cup of coffee. Not the girl with a shitty boyfriend. And you can be Patches, a nurse who laughs at my dad's jokes every day.

Not the nurse who slowly watches someone die.

Nicknames are important.

I think of my friends, Sugar, Books, and Junior.

And I think of King.

I feel my courage rise like the tide. Slow, but sure. "Can I . . . can I ask you something?"

Joe doesn't even look at me as he nods. "Yeah, King went to Alaska."

"Oh." I try to sort through the emotions that fire at me like bullets from a gun, wounding me. I settle on the biggest wound.

Missing him. Like wanting to touch a star in the sky. I can see his memory, but I can't hold it. It's a familiar ache.

"If you were worried about what happened with you on the trail—"

"I wasn't."

Now Joe looks at me. "Right." He reaches into his back pocket and pulls out a mostly empty bottle with golden liquid inside. Joe smiles as he holds it up to me. "Your dad and I had this tradition of sending each other the worst bottle of alcohol we could find. I was in Mexico in November, and . . . I knew your dad was in bad shape, but." Joe shakes his head. "I bought this bottle of questionable tequila, the kind they sell to kids on spring break and tourists. With the worm. I just thought, if I buy it, he can't die."

Joe clears his throat. "I drank most of that bottle last night. Fuck your dad for dying."

I take it from him; the petrified worm at the bottom looks like it's started to disintegrate. Without thinking, I unscrew the cap and take a drink.

"Hey," Joe complains, but it's not with any heat. "You can't take my alcohol. Damn it, Outlaw." He pulls it from my hands and recaps it before sliding it into his pocket again. "Sometimes you have to leave things where they are. Sometimes the smartest move is to know when to drink the whole bottle and walk away."

"I'm not going to call him," I say because I know he's talking about King. "I don't even have his number." My voice is soft and I look down at my palms when I say it, like I'll find something secret written there. My name? But all I'm left with is the faint scars on my hands.

"I'm not talking about him, Outlaw. I'm talking about your anger."

34

BOOKS FINDS ME SOME time before Halloween. There is no real autumn in California, just a day all the leaves decide to drop from their branches. Seasons aren't really a thing here.

I'm wearing a sweater in protest, as if I can demand fall with my protest.

Is it cold in Alaska? Is King wearing layers on top of layers?

I'm pulling shots when I see the name on the side of the cup. *Books.* I run my thumb over the letters as if I'm imagining them, but when I look up, he's standing at the counter. No hello, or smile; Books simply points to a seat by the window.

He stays for my entire shift, drinking the same cup of coffee.

When I'm done for the day, I make myself one, the kind that has a foam heart on top. I've been trying to decide if I'm the kind of person who likes sweet coffee.

Each step to Books feels important. Something I'm choosing. He knows it too, because he watches me until I'm sitting down in the chair across from him.

"Nice sweater." It's what he says instead of hello or where

the fuck have you been. It's so very Books that I can't even be upset.

I wrap two hands around the cup and hold it up to my mouth. "I'm pretending it's raining. If you want something bad enough, it will happen." I take a sip of my drink.

It tastes like someone melted a cake in my cup.

Books gives me a smile, as if he's been holding it in this whole time. "You're not a fan of the coffee."

I take a deep breath and really look at Books. The tan from his face has faded and he wears a maroon henley that looks worn in and cozy, but fake warm. This is California, after all. He's different here. Not the boy in the anime or band T-shirts, but someone older and softer. Someone who doesn't have to have the hard edges from before.

"I'm trying to figure out what I'm a fan of."

He takes a drink and I do the same, lifting my cup like my mirroring is unconscious.

"Did Joe tell you I was here?" I ask.

"No." He sets his mug down and licks his lips. "I haven't talked to Joe."

"Do you live around here?"

Books shakes his head. "I was looking for you."

Something about the way he says it makes me understand that he's not teasing. That he really was looking for me. I can't remember the last time I expected someone to come look for me.

"Why?" I ask.

Books takes a deep breath and makes a face like his next words pain him. "Because I *missed* you."

I'm so surprised I can't even speak. Books is the last person I would expect to miss me.

He frowns. "Has no one ever missed you before?"

"That's not—"

"I know," Books says, cutting me off. He sighs. "Me, Sugar, Junior . . . We all miss you."

He doesn't say King, but he doesn't have to.

My tongue runs across my teeth. "I had some shit to work out."

"Don't we all." This truth is accompanied with a little laugh.

And suddenly, I think I know why Books is here. My dad. Some kind of misplaced loyalty. "If you're here because you—"

"God, Maps. You really are an idiot."

If this is what Books is going to be like, all questions and accusations, I don't want to be here. My mouth opens to tell him it was nice to see him and make an excuse to go when he says, "Wanna go see a movie?" He hooks his thumb over his shoulder to the building across the courtyard from the coffee shop.

"A movie?" I repeat to him. "Like in a theater?"

"Yes, like on your phone, but *big*." His hands go wide in front of him like he's demonstrating the massive scale of a big screen.

No. I do not want to go to a theater.

"Just you and me," he tells me. "I promise."

It sounds ridiculous. I don't even really like movies. But.

I can be with Books without having to talk and much like everything with Books, I think he realizes that's about all I can handle right now.

"Why?"

"Because loneliness sucks." He doesn't point the word at me.

Instead he points it at the sky, like he and I are on the same side.

"When?"

He takes his phone out of his pocket and checks something. "There's one in twenty minutes."

I don't ask what the movie is. It doesn't really matter. Books and I get enormous sodas, small bags of candy, and a large popcorn to split.

When the movie is over, he asks me if I want to watch another. We watch three movies and are the last people to leave. Kids with brooms and a giant trashcan stand outside the theater, and the sky is black when we walk out. I expect him to suggest we make plans with Sugar or call Junior. Instead, he just says, "Next week? Same time?"

I agree and even as I'm leaving, I'm not really sure what I've just said yes to.

But it becomes our thing. Sitting in a theater without talking and binge eating candy and the occasional hot dog. "There's a joke about wieners somewhere in here," he says.

"Junior would know where to find it."

Books looks at me like I've actually made the joke. And maybe I have. It's the first time either of us has brought up Junior.

"You and him . . . ?" I ask.

Books looks at the door. "Yeah."

I want to know if they talk to Sugar. If they hang out and live close and if they see movies. I want to know if they know how King is. But I guess all my questions are stuck somewhere in the Sierras.

"We're working through the Marvel movies."

285

I smile. "Does he like them?"

Books gives me a serious look. "He asks questions the entire time."

Of course he does.

"Is he still with Joe?"

Books nods. "He's trying to get a place close to the college."

A fond smile cracks over my face. "He got in. I guess he figured out what a FAFSA was."

Being with Books isn't less lonely, but it makes me feel like we share something. We spend weekends this way, never the week. It's odd to see Books in clean clothes, in trendy pants and hoodies and Vans. People turn their heads as we walk past but he doesn't seem to notice. Here, he's handsome in a brooding way. I wonder if I'm different here too.

And sometime in November, Books asks what I'm doing for Thanksgiving. My mother and I have plans to go to her friend from grief group's house. It's important not to be alone on your first holiday without a loved one, even though the entire evening will be spent talking about the people who aren't there.

I don't want to go.

My therapist says it's okay to say that I'd rather do something else. She calls it *setting boundaries*. Which is basically just *not* doing something you don't want to do.

"Nothing," I tell Books, and it feels good.

He takes my phone and holds it to my face to unlock it. "Dinner is at three because apparently you have to eat all day on holidays." He types in his phone number and his address. "I hope you come, but if not, we should go to the movies on Black Friday." He pats my cheek. "Text me."

And I do.

I stand outside Books's house on Thanksgiving. There's a huge blow-up turkey on the lawn and I can't seem to figure out how I got here. Not here as in Books's house. Here as in an oddly comfortable friendship with him. The kind built on silence and lack of expectations. Books feels like a blanket I wear over my shoulders when I just want to be comfortable.

I laugh and think his nickname should have been Blanket.

Books has become *my person.*

The noises coming from the open red door are loud and chaotic. The exact opposite of my time with Books, but I think . . . I think this is what I need.

At the door, a face that looks like an older female Books greets me. "Maps!" She claps her hands together when she sees me. "I'm so glad you're here!"

I don't have time to marvel at the fact that she's called me Maps and not Atlas. I also have no idea what to call her.

"I'm Joey's mama, Millie."

Joey? Is that Books's real name? It's so . . . *normal.* "Nice to meet you, Millie."

As I walk into the noise, I can hear the football game and see several broad-chested men sitting at the edges of their seats. They pick at a tray of food sitting in front of them. They're all wearing black-and-silver football jerseys except for one in red-and-gold.

"Come on, you fucking ass—"

"Hey!" Millie shouts. "Watch your mouths!"

One of the men throws a tiny sausage at the man in red. "Your jersey is bad luck. Go outside till the game is over."

"Come on, man. They don't even play in Cal—"

But before I can hear the end of the conversation, I'm pulled into the kitchen. Books stands with two other women and he stuffs what looks like a sausage ball into his mouth. When he sees me, his eyes go wide. "Maps! You came."

He throws an arm around my shoulders and then turns me around. "Everyone, this is Maps."

"That's a weird name," a little girl playing a handheld video game and sitting on a bar stool says. She eats from an enormous plate of toffee.

"Your name is Diamond," a woman in a turkey sweater says to her. "So maybe don't make judgments." She turns to me. "I'm Elise, Joey's favorite aunt."

A second later, another woman takes me by the hand. "Come eat."

She shoves a plate with some kind of bread stuffed with meat and cheese at me.

"It's going to change your life," she says, smiling with pride. "Because it was made with love."

Millie rolls her eyes. "She didn't make it, she bought it at the bakery."

The other woman frowns. "Someone made it with love. Joey's friend will still think it's wonderful."

And I do.

I love everything about the day, even though it's not my family. I love the noise and the teasing and the food. I love the way Books's great-grandmother swats at all the grandkids because she can't hear them but gives them candy she keeps in her pocket. I love the way his uncles steal food from everyone's plate, even mine, and call it the uncle tax.

I'm so busy that I assume I won't have time to think about my dad, but I do. Almost constantly. Not in a way that makes me sad, but in the soft way that lives inside of memories and nostalgia.

It feels alive.

Almost happy.

And I think about King.

Books is sitting down at the table when his phone chimes. I look over his shoulder and see the name KING with a crown emoji next to it.

King:
Did she come?

Books takes a deep breath and his thumbs hover over the keyboard before typing one simple word.

Books:
No.

I can't tell if I'm happy or sad he said no. I can't even tell how I feel now that I know Books has been talking to King about me. Or maybe he's talking about someone else. Maybe King doesn't even remember me. Books slips the phone underneath his thigh as I move to sit next to him.

"Hey," he breathes and smiles, but it doesn't reach his eyes. He is decidedly not a master criminal.

"Hey."

"Sorry my family is . . ."

"Great," I finish for him. "They're great."

"Yeah."

Later we go to Books's room, and I see an entire wall of bookcases filled with manga and novels. I run my hands over the spines and I smile when I say his name. "Books."

He takes a breath. "I wanted to ask you something." He looks nervous, something Books doesn't usually look. "My boyfriend wants to come to the movies this week."

I've been waiting for this. I give him a smile. "Is your *boyfriend* someone I know?"

Books frowns. "Listen. Junior thought I was cheating on him, so I had to explain. About you. About the coffee shop. The movies."

"When did you tell him?"

Books looks guilty but not sorry. "After the first week. He made me take him to your store, but he promised not to go in."

"I'm not hiding," I say.

"You're not? Is that why I had to track you down?"

"I've been busy."

"You've been a ghost, Maps. No social media, no contact. I know you're mad—"

I scoff.

"You are. But Junior and Sugar didn't know."

Right. It was only King and Books. I've been a brat. I've been shitty and punishing everyone because I was hurt.

"I can't even figure out why you came to find me." I'm not

fishing when I say it, but now that it's out there, I wait for Books to answer.

"I came to find you because everyone was really hurting and I thought, if we were hurting, you probably were too."

I'm not sure how his words were meant, but they feel like charity. "We don't have to keep doing the movies. Really."

Books's brows pull together. "I want to. I *like* it."

"You don't have to hang out with me because you're worried."

He looks at me for a long moment and then says, "*I* was hurting too. I missed you."

It's honest, and vulnerable, but mostly, it's direct. Books doesn't have time to have his intentions misread.

Later that week I tell Books to invite his boyfriend.

And Sugar.

I'm nervous when we get to the theater, but I shouldn't be. Sugar and Junior stand with Books by the snack bar. Her faded green hair is now a bright purple, and she looks like a makeup tutorial come to life, complete with false lashes and gems around her eyes. Junior's hair has grown out and is in the beginning of twists that he plays with.

Nothing has changed.

And everything has.

"Hey," I say, and I wait. In the second it takes them to process that I'm standing there, I consider every worst-case scenario. They hate me. Books didn't tell them I was coming. They're here to yell at me.

But the second ends and both of them lunge forward. They

hug me and talk over each other, asking questions without giving me a moment to respond. I smile and for the first time since the Sierras it feels consuming. And a laugh escapes me. Books frowns and rolls his eyes.

"I do all the work and you're the happiest to see them."

Sugar is touching me. Fixing my hair or straighening my shirt. "You look so pretty, but you smell like coffee."

Junior comments on my lack of tan, telling me he didn't realize how pale I actually was. Everyone acts like no time has passed. Like I haven't spent months avoiding everyone.

When we order at the snack bar, Books and I do it together and Junior frowns. He leans over to Sugar. "That was weird, right?"

"Really weird. I didn't know they even talked."

Books and I don't say anything as we walk to the theater and sit down next to each other, the bag of popcorn in the middle. Books puts M&M's in it and I hand him half the pack of Red Vines. He puts two straws in the soda we ordered.

A tradition.

Like my dad and Joe and the bottle of liquor.

Junior raises his eyebrows at me and then looks down at our soda.

He whispers something to Books, who rolls his eyes and offers him a Red Vine.

The movie is a nice break; it allows me to collect my thoughts. Junior and Books hold hands and Sugar regularly tries to give me things. Her soda, more candy, a tissue when I cry.

We get coffee after.

"Have you seen Joe?" Sugar asks.

I nod. "He comes around to check on my mom and me."

"Lucky you," she jokes, but I am. I'm lucky to have Joe.

We spend the entire time laughing about nonsense and nothing. I tell them about the bats and the poppy. I mention the grief group. When we leave, Sugar holds me for a long time and whispers in my ear that she missed me. Junior squeezes my hand and tells me not to wait to call them again.

I don't. We make plans to meet in December. We walk through Christmas lights with hot cocoa and none of us talk about the thing that is missing. The person in Alaska.

King.

But I think of him constantly.

Two days before Christmas we all drive to the mountains. Not as far as our trail, but to a lookout where Books can park his car and we can pretend we're back there. We pass mulled wine back and forth. Books declines because he's driving.

Junior has brought an assortment of junk food and it reminds me of the trip to the gas station. He passes a bag of chips between us and when it's my turn to eat a wax-covered doughnut, he pulls it from my hands. "Oh, wait." His mouth is full, and he reaches into the back and pulls out grape candy. "For my grape monster."

He winks and I get teary eyed.

It's all the little ways.

The little ways we tell the truth all day without ever realizing it. A hundred ways we tell people who we are without ever speaking. A person only has to see.

These people *see* me.

They make loving me seem easy. It makes me want to let them.

My heart shatters under the pressure because not all the pieces of it are complete. Something is missing.

They ask if I'm crying about my dad, but I shake my head and tell them I miss King.

An odd truth.

I don't ask how he's doing in Alaska, but I can see they're all waiting for it.

Sugar pats my head and lets me say how awful King is for lying. For leaving. For never calling.

They pretend to agree, even Books, but I know they hear the truth. My heart is broken.

"You should tell him," Junior says.

He makes it sound so simple. So easy to just say those things.

But loving King has never felt like that.

35

IT'S NEW YEAR'S EVE.

The end of the year.

The most cliche ending of them all, but instead of being excited for the year to come, I can feel myself wanting to hold on to this one. Not because of me, but because my dad died on a cold March night in *this* year.

The thread of that memory has pulled itself across this calendar and with the strike of a clock, it will snap. My reality will turn to a timeline in which my father doesn't exist.

"You're going?"

My mother stands in the doorway of my room as I turn in front of the mirror.

Junior and his brand-new roommates are hosting a party. He promises it will change our lives. Sugar told him it sounded like a discount frat party and Junior didn't speak to her for two days.

"I think so."

She nods thoughtfully. "You look pretty."

Do I? I turn in the mirror and the sequins on my jacket catch the light. It's only a party. One Junior has made clear is important to him to which our attendance is mandatory. Even though he's been hard to get ahold of all week. All our friends have been. Taking hours to respond, busy with family or doing couple things.

"Even if you make that sad face all night long, you still have to come," he told me.

"Are you sure you don't want me to stay home?" I ask my mother for the millionth time.

"I can be sad all by myself, Atlas," my mother says. "You don't need to stay here to help with that. Be safe and have fun."

I'm out of excuses. Which is how I find myself at Junior's.

Loud music drifts over crisp winter air, and I pull my heavy sweater tighter around me. I'm sure it's already started to snow in the mountains, but here in the valley, it's freezing winter temperatures in the low fifties. I googled the weather in Alaska, because apparently I have no concept of self-preservation. It's too cold to even consider what King is wearing tonight.

I go into the party. I smile at strangers. I let them ask me about the name Junior uses for me and why I call their friend a weird name.

Sugar texts me a series of emojis and a picture of her by a pool. I think it's wildly irresponsible to let a bunch of young men rent a house with a pool. But when I mentioned it to Junior, he just said, "Thanks, Mom."

I smile and type back:

Maps:

Stay away from the pool. I'll be right there.

She texts back immediately.

Sugar:
There is a lot of booze here.

I head outside and find Books and Sugar sitting on long pool chairs. Sugar motions for me to sit with her and turns her attention back to Books, who lounges with his ankles crossed and a red cup in one hand and a joint in the other.

"What are you doing out here, Books? Shouldn't you be on boyfriend duty as Junior makes it his personal mission to greet every human here?" I ask.

"Do I look like I want to do that?" he asks me as he takes a hit off the joint in his hand.

I take a deep breath, watching the smoke from him float up to the black sky and shake off the memories of skin and starlight and King.

"You shouldn't smoke."

"Says the girl who carried around cigarettes."

I don't respond. He's gotten too close to casually mentioning King, and I'm not sure I'm ready for that.

The three of us sit by the pool in our shared comfort. Everyone else at this party knows each other or wants to know someone. No one cares about the three people who don't belong.

I wonder if the people here have heard we're the bad kids. Ones Junior met working on trails in the Sierras with complicated relationships to rules and authority.

"What do you want from next year?" I ask.

"Oh good. More questions," Books says with his eyes closed. "I want to stop answering questions next year."

"I want to move. Away from my family." Sugar says she wants freedom, but it's not true. We let her believe we agree with her.

"I want to move out too." Books takes a drink of his beer. "Fucking family."

"You gonna move in with Junior?" Sugar says and we smile.

Books makes a face but won't look at us in the eyes when he says, "It's way too early for that."

"What about you, Maps?" Sugar asks.

"I want to just move on from this year." I say it and realize I mean it. Not my dad, but the grief I feel, and King . . .

"You're being tragic," she tells me.

From behind me I hear Junior say, "That's kinda her thing."

"Is this a pep talk?" I ask and take Books's joint from him. The inhale hurts my lungs and makes me lightheaded. I don't know why I did that.

"You shouldn't smoke, Maps. It's gross," Books says as I hand him back *his* joint.

Junior takes it from Books's hand and the tip turns red in the dark, the paper crackling when he inhales. "No, not a pep talk," he says, holding in his hit. Then on his exhale, "It's permission. Aren't we all a little tragic?"

I make a noise. Sugar holds out her drink and I take a sip to get rid of the taste in my mouth. The four of us sit on the chairs, staring up at the sky, and I remember a different time when we all sat in a row staring out at the sky. The sounds from inside drift toward us swirled with music.

"I'm glad you're here," Sugar tells me, and I smile at her because I'm glad too.

And I let my mind wander to King for longer than I should. I replay all the moments I shouldn't. I ask myself what he's doing in Alaska. I even tell myself I'm going to ask Books.

But I don't.

Junior's phone chimes and he looks down at it. "Fuck," he says, and Books looks over to his phone, reading something on the screen.

Sugar and I look at each other, confused, until someone yells from inside the house.

"*Junior!*" It's said like a silly joke. "Your friend is here!"

Junior? They called him our name. *Junior.*

"No," Books says to the phone, and then looks at Junior. "Goddamn it." They stand up so fast I'm actually startled. Their backs are disappearing through the crowd. I grab the cup Books was holding so it doesn't tip over and . . .

. . . I'm curious, that's why I follow.

I barely hear Sugar calling my name as she follows me into the house and through the crowd of people and noise and music.

I'm curious but I shouldn't be, because deep down I know what I'm going to find. Deep in my heart. And even as Books and Junior step in front of the door, I already know who's standing there.

Cheeks flushed from the cold. Eyes seeming darker than before. My heart still in his hands.

King.

36

The end . . . again.

BOOKS IS MOVING TOWARD him, fast, and taking him by his arm. "What are you doing here?"

"What?" King smiles but looks confused. "You asked me to come."

"But—" King's face folds in confusion as Books stumbles over his words. "You never said. You said you were busy. You—"

"Books." King frowns at him like he's worried about his friend. "You okay?"

"Damn it," Books says, and in that second I watch King's face transform. A sudden realization.

"Maps." King is saying my name, but it sounds far away.

Everything is far away, and then suddenly it's not. Sound comes crashing back to me like the volume on the world has been turned up. King looks at Books and he knows.

His eyes find mine, like magnets that have been drawn together. His mouth is open in surprise. And for some odd reason, that hurts worse than seeing him here. The fact that this wasn't some sort of elaborate plan to see me again after all this time. He didn't expect this either.

Of course he didn't.

"Maps."

"I—" I set my drink on a nearby table and don't bother to check if it's upright or if it splattered onto the floor like my heart. "I'm going . . ." I have to get away. I walk back through the house, away from him, weaving through people, and I know that Junior is calling my name, but I have to leave. I can't stay here a second longer. I can . . . I'll walk all the way to my house if I have to.

And because my panic tells me that something is chasing me, I look back. I don't know what I hope to see. My life has become a series of *which will hurt the least* choices.

King is pushing through the crowd with his brows drawn into a frown.

"Fuck."

My steps are fast, but I know King is faster. *Please. No. Please. Please.*

I say it only to myself because I don't know if I can do this. I don't know if I will survive the boy who's responsible for the bleeding heart inside my chest. I'm out of the house and in the yard. Running from the thing I want the most because pride won't let me stand in front of him broken and embarrassed.

"Stop," I hear from behind me. It's frustrated, not a command, more like a . . . wish.

My feet hit the sidewalk, but then King is standing in front of me.

His arms are out, as if to stop me, and his chest moves up and down. His eyes never leave mine. They're wide and his throat works to swallow.

Finally, he whispers, "Stop." King studies me, as if there is some clue to what we need to talk about on my person. "*Maps.*"

Watching his lips form that syllable makes me ache. I want him to say it again. But he doesn't.

He stands on the street. The sunshine gone from his skin, and hair a little longer. It curls into the collar of the dark flannel shirt he's wearing. I can count all the ways he's different under the light from the lamppost instead of the light from a summer moon.

But the look in his eyes. That's the same.

It hurts to meet them, like pieces of jagged glass pressing against my heart, so I focus on his hands. He's holding the journal. Worn leather that's pockmarked from water and pages softened by touch. I want to reach out and open it because I know on those pages are words I want to read again.

And words I don't.

"You still have it." I'd hoped my voice would sound surprised, but all I can hear is the sadness in it.

"Yeah." He says it simply because of course he still has it. And I can feel my heart bend and break in that one word. Like the spine of a new book.

"Why?" I ask, but really I *hope*.

For what exactly, I'm not sure.

He runs his fingers over the word etched on the cover; the one I watched him carve with a knife in short static strokes as we sat under the stars. "I didn't want . . ."

But he trails off, leaving me wondering. He didn't want what? Anyone to know about what happened?

About how he shattered my heart into pieces that bled onto those pages without my permission?

He didn't want his lie to unravel?

He takes a step forward and practically whispers, "*Maps.*"

"It's Atlas."

Bang. The two words are like a shot fired into the dark, cracking against the quiet. Words I know will hurt him. The way he's hurt me. "People call me Atlas here," I repeat—justify.

There's something different in his eyes now. "I don't call you that."

No.

No, he called me something else. Something that meant something different, in a place where it felt like nothing meant anything—which made everything mean something.

"Please," he almost whispers. "Don't run. Not again."

I take a breath. It fogs in the air between him and me, and I watch it disappear into the night.

An ache settles in my chest as I consider how much he's changed. The memory of him has become faded.

His chest rises and falls with deep breaths as he pulls in the air around us. Pulls in me. But he's not touching me, only staring at me with eyes that change and darken and catch against the streetlight we stand under.

Leave. Leave. Leave.

I chant it in my mind, but I don't know if it's for him or me.

Maybe it's for whoever is strong enough.

"Maps, can we—can we talk?"

Talk. I don't want to talk. I don't want to be here. I'm not ready. My heart hasn't callused yet. It's still bleeding and broken and . . .

hurt.

"What do you want to talk about?" I ask, like I don't know what he could possibly mean.

King looks disappointed. "Come on," he says. "Don't do that."

And for some reason, this version of King breaks me the most. The one that refuses to let a lie replace the memory of the last time we saw each other.

"I didn't know you were going to be here," he tells me. "Why didn't you call me?"

There's an ache in his voice, and I hate it. *I'm* hurt. I'm the one who gets to be in pain. "I didn't know you were going to be here either."

Confusion snakes through his features before realization sets in. His eyes close and he lets out a soft groan. *"You didn't know."* He shakes his head and takes a step back, away from me. "I'm sorry. Really. I didn't realize that you— I wouldn't have chased you like I did. I shouldn't— This isn't an ambush. I'm— I'll go." He takes a breath, like *going* is the last thing he wants to do. "Happy New Year."

Happy *fucking* New Year? That's what he's saying to me. Like we can just leave. Abandon this. Abandon me again. My stomach turns and I understand that the last thing *I* want King to do is *go*. I march forward and I take his wrist and pull him toward me. King turns around, surprise making the colors in his eyes appear brighter.

"You're supposed to be in *Alaska*."

He runs his hands through his hair. "Alaska?"

"Why are you here? Are you back?" I flex my fingers from where I touched him.

King's brows pull together. "Is that what you wanted? Me to stay in Alaska forever?"

No. I didn't want to be left with the hole in my heart. "Joe said—"

"Joe said a lot of things."

My teeth grind against each other. "Why aren't you in Alaska, King?"

"Because I came back for the holidays." He throws the words at me. "I wanted to see my friends. I'm only here for a few days." He watches my face now, as I realize what he's telling me. "I didn't come back for you." He lets that sink in. "I can see you're thinking that. That's not why I'm here. I just wanted to be with my friends on New Year's."

Suddenly Junior's and Sugar's avoidance of me makes sense. The way it took Books a little longer to respond to texts all week. It's ridiculous. "You've *been* here."

King nods.

"No one . . ." I swallow. "No one told me."

"Maps." He takes a step forward; his breath fogs around my name. "I tried to find you. After. I talked to Joe. I . . . I wanted to—"

I wait to be angry, but all I can feel is the hollow between my ribs where it used to be. As if seeing him has replaced it.

"I needed the space."

He nods. "Yeah. I know."

"When I left Bear Creek I was so fucked up. So angry. You didn't *tell* me. I was walking around with this huge hole in my chest, and you pretended like you couldn't even see it."

He stands there, not denying or defending himself. He just takes it.

"And I'm not even mad. It's so much worse than mad. And now you're here, not in Alaska." Tears are cutting a path down my face. "You *hurt* me."

He lets out a breath and puts his hands in his pockets. "I . . . I never knew how to tell you about your dad. Half the time you were pretending he wasn't dead and the other half you weren't talking about him. It doesn't make what I did right, but . . . I'm still not sure what I should have done." He stares at the asphalt like if he looks hard enough, he can see what's buried underneath. "When you left, *I* was mad. I thought a hundred different times about what I would say to you if I ever saw you again. I was so angry at you. I yelled at your memory." I watch the roll of King's neck as he swallows down all his feelings. "And then one day I realized I was mad because it was the only thing I had left of you. My anger. And I was afraid I would lose that too."

I'm silent for a long time.

"My name is Henry. I'm the third, and Joe made a joke about me being a king. Which is why . . ." He waves his hand around. "I'm from here. I don't talk to my family. I've been on my own since I was seventeen. I met Joe. He gave me a different name and I . . . I liked being someone else. Not being Henry."

My breath stutters because I know what he's talking about.

306

I like being Maps. I like being someone else who doesn't carry Atlas's mistakes.

"I really liked getting to know you, Maps. Not because of your dad, but because you're funny and curious and smart. You ask questions and act like you really want to know the answer. You hate silence, beans, and the idea that you need people. You spend a ridiculous amount of time looking at the sky. When I think about you, it's always like that. With your face turned up."

"King."

"I've liked you since the moment I saw you crying at your dad's funeral. I'd never met someone like you before. So sure she's right, but doesn't care if she's wrong."

I can see the embarrassment on his face, the way these words cost him something. The way his teeth worry at his lip and his hands tighten and the knuckles turn white.

"Are you still mad at me?" I ask.

He shakes his head and his chest expands. I remember what it felt like to press my face against it. "No." It's soft. "I'm scared."

"Scared?"

"Scared you're gonna walk away and I won't see you again."

My eyes close and I tell a truth. "I don't know what to say."

"You don't have to say anything." He looks a little deflated, as if all his words were the thing he was holding in his chest and now that they're gone, he doesn't know what to do. "I'd settle for you letting me text you. And if you want to text me, you can. If not." He shrugs with a self-deprecating smile. "It can't hurt worse than it does right now."

I want to give him my number.

I want to talk to King.

I want King.

But my hurt is irrational.

"Okay," I tell him. I open my phone and he types in his number and I watch his hands shake and stumble over the keys.

When he hands it back, he says, "I . . . I really hope you use it." And he looks like he really does hope. With eyes that look like the river.

I hold my phone in my hand and King walks back to the house.

I press two letters and hit send.

Maps:

Hi.

I watch as King reads the text. His shoulders are hunched and he keeps his back to me.

King:

Hi.

His response lights up my screen and I smile.

King:

Wanna hang out?

37

KING AND I BEGIN slow at first.

We don't go back to the party, instead the two of us drive to an overlook. It starts to rain and the city is lost behind the pattering on the windshield. We're in our own little world. We talk about nothing, but it feels like everything. Between his words are looks that hold intention and breaths that feel like pressure being released. And when he drops me off, I kiss him, a soft and cautious thing, before running into the house.

I wait for him to text me, but three days pass in silence. I stare at my phone and wonder what I should say.

In my room I sit on my bed and press my phone against my chest.

Maps:

Hey

It's Maps

I watch the phone show delivered. I see bubbles appear. Disappear. Appear. Disappear. And I wonder if I'm going to get a response.

King:

I know.

I smile down at my phone and feel the tightness in my chest loosen. King texted back.

Maps:

I've been waiting for you to text me.

I drop my phone into my lap as soon as it's sent and press the heels of my hands into my eyes.

King:

I have typed out at least ten messages
to you every night.

Maps:

Oh yeah? What did they say?

King:

Some version of "hey what's up."
Mostly embarrassing things.

Maps:

I was hoping for something
more spicy.

King:

I don't even know . . . how do you want
me to respond to that?

Maps:

Nudes?

King:
JFC, Maps.

I stare at my phone forever. *Maps.* I can hear his voice say it.
Curl around the word.

Maps:
I miss you.

He tells me about his flight back to Alaska, about his work.
His roommate. I tell him about classes for my GED and actual
college applications. The next day he sends me a picture of an ice
chest at a convenience store and says,

King:
Is it weird that I'm craving
those gross ice pops from
Bear Creek?

It goes on like this. Just the little things that a person does
throughout their day. The quiet thoughts.

King:
I miss In-N-Out.
What do you think of this shirt?
This song reminded me of you.

And then one night while we're texting:

King:

Can I call you?

I don't want him to call. I don't want to hear his voice. I almost don't remember how much I loved it. But I text back,

Maps:

Yes.

"Hey." I answer on the third ring.

"Hey." His voice is tired and it sounds like he's lying down. But it's exactly as I remember it. Addicting. "My thumbs were getting tired."

"Oh yeah?" I say with a laugh.

"No." He takes a breath and his voice loses the teasing tone. "I just wanted to hear your voice."

I don't speak because hearing King say it makes everything I've been doing on a tiny screen feel real.

"Sorry if that's too much . . ."

My lips press closed to keep in all the things I want to say as I lie back on my bed and stare at my ceiling.

"Or, I guess I'm not sorry really."

I close my eyes and listen to King on the other end before asking, "Why didn't you text me?"

"Today?"

"After New Year's. I waited, but you never did."

There's a rustling on the other end as our silence stretches. "When you kissed me on New Year's, I didn't know if that was a one-time thing or, like—I spent a lot of time thinking about it and wondering if you even wanted me to text you."

"I did." And it's true. I always wanted a text from King, even when I shouldn't have.

"What're we doing, Maps? Just tell me so I can know this time."

"We're talking," I tell him.

He lets out a heavy breath. "Right."

"Are you going to stop texting me if I say nothing?"

The laugh that I hear is breathy and he waits forever to respond to me. And when he says, "No," I feel it in my chest.

Something about knowing King can't stop . . .

"I wouldn't stop either," I admit.

We talk on the phone. Sometimes we fall asleep. Sometimes we do more than talk, and we pretend we can touch each other despite the distance. But it becomes something I can't live without. I'm still too scared to ask when he's going to come back. *If* he's coming back. I don't want to ask about a future.

Long conversations that drift into the dark, where we're busy trying to figure out how Maps and King fit with Atlas and Henry.

On the anniversary of my dad's death, I plan nothing. Grief group says to do something to honor my dad. My mother makes reservations to eat at his favorite restaurant, so we push around our broccoli beef and try to tell stories that we think will make each other smile. Instead we just notice the empty chair at the table.

I think about Pidgeon saying *that sucks* and it makes me feel better. She would think this dinner sucks.

I text King.

Maps:

Today is the worst. I wish
I could hug you.

King:

Want to talk?

Maps:

No. But I want you to call anyway.

He doesn't say anything about today, and I can't help but feel a little disappointed that he hasn't. It's stupid, but I haven't even told him what today is, like he should just know. I'm punishing him for something that he doesn't even realize.

Maps:

Today is the day my dad died.

I don't even know what I expect him to send back, but he just says,

King:

Want me to call now?

I sigh down at my phone. I don't know what I wanted from him, but it wasn't this, and it wouldn't have mattered anyway. Because the truth is, I want my dad, and he's dead. I have to stop expecting people to be there for me when I don't even know how I want them to show up.

Maps:

Later.

I add a heart to the end of it and put my phone down. My mother and I sit on the couch to watch my dad's favorite western. His chair is empty. I don't know why, but I crawl into it. Fold my legs against it and run my hands over the arms. On the television, I hear someone say, "You're an outlaw." And I know that was just for me.

There's a knock at the door and I look to my mother. She takes a handful of popcorn and looks back at the television as she says, "You should get that."

I know what I'm going to find before I even open the door. My heart pounds as I wrap my fingers around the handle.

King stands on the porch wearing a white hooded sweatshirt that looks soft around his neck and makes him look tan. Like Summer King. It makes me want to curl up into it.

"What . . ."

"I want to hug you too."

I throw my arms around him and turn my face into his neck. The place that feels like it's just for me. He still smells the same. Feels the same.

My mother tells us to have a good time and not to stay out too late and we get into his car. I don't ask where we're going because it doesn't matter. King is here. With me. And that's enough.

But when he drives to the place where my dad's ashes are buried, I feel emotion sitting in my throat, waiting to break free. I don't let go of his hand, as if he'll disappear if I do.

The cemetery is closed so we park at the school next door, and I sit in the car with my hands in my lap after King has turned off the engine. He looks at me, waiting, like he has all the time in the universe.

"I went to that school," I tell him. "Every morning we would drive past this cemetery and he would tell me the same joke. *Atlas, people are dying to get in there.*" I mock my dad's voice when I say it and King smiles. I run my hands over the top of my jeans and I look out the windshield at the darkened cemetery. "I don't know if I can."

"You don't have to," he tells me.

And something about knowing that I won't disappoint him makes me feel like I *can* do it. Like I'm brave enough to do it.

"Okay," I say and wrap my fingers around the handle. I take a deep breath and step out of the car. We climb over the fence and King helps me down even though I don't need it. When he drops his hands, I take one of his in mine. This is what people who date do. This is how they do it.

His eyes are on the place where our fingers lock together and he gives me a shy smile. "Feels wrong to hold your hand in here," he says as we walk through the headstones.

"You're not taking my virtue," I tease.

I look at King, but he just squeezes my hand gently. He lifts it up to press his lips against my skin. Just a small reminder that he's here. He sees me.

Something about it makes my chest inflate. Not with air, but something else undefinable. He follows me toward the rose garden where my father is buried, and I see three figures standing there.

Junior holds up a bottle of alcohol and Books has a stack of clear cups in his hand. Sugar smiles and says, "Thought we would make a thing of it even though you never mentioned . . ."

I bite my cheek so I don't cry, but tears well anyway.

On my dad's headstone is a picture of him smiling, etched onto the marble. Before.

Before the cancer, before chemo, before time poisoned him.

Junior reads the inscription. "*He was beaten (he knew that), but he was not broken.* What does it mean?"

"It's from his favorite book. *The Call of the Wild.*"

The words stick to my mind. *Beaten not broken.* I never understood why he chose to put them on his headstone. To etch them into his eternity. I look for the hope in them that they always gave my father. I look for meaning in them.

Sugar lays a votive on my dad's grave and lights it. "I saw this on a TV show. Something about the candle lighting your way home. I don't really know, but it looked cool." She looks down at it. "Just in case."

It casts a faint yellow glow on the headstone and lights my dad's face.

Junior pours alcohol into the cups and Books hands them out. I open my mouth to say *thank you for doing this* when Junior speaks first.

"Hi, Mr. James. I'm a friend of your daughter's. We call her Maps."

I feel my brows pinch together and I stare at Junior.

"I met Maps at the camp your sadist best friend, Joe, runs. But I just wanted to tell you that you would be proud of Maps. It started out dicey—"

"Junior," I say. I don't understand what's happening.

"But she worked really hard. Took responsibility for herself and she grew a lot. I just thought you would want to know that she's doing well."

Before I can speak, Books goes next.

"Hi, Patrick. It's Books." He clears his throat. "I met your daughter. She is exactly like you said she was. She doesn't talk about you a lot, but I think that's because she misses you. Being her friend makes me miss you too. She asks questions just like you did. I hope wherever you are, you can see her, because I think you would be proud." Books clears his throat. "Or whatever."

I'm crying now. I can't help it. Watching the people I love talk to the person who left.

"I'm Sugar. And I just want you to know, Maps is gonna be okay. She's one of the toughest people I've ever met. I agree with Books and Junior. You'd be really proud of her."

"Hi, Patrick." My hand tightens in King's, and I look down at my father's headstone. "I met Outlaw. You were right, she's . . . something else. You did a good job with her, and you should be proud. She's everything you said. Joe is looking out for her, but I think Maps can take care of herself. Also, you were right about the other thing too. Thanks for changing my life."

"To Patrick James, Maps's dad," Sugar says, lifting her cup. "The river is a little colder without you."

"To Maps's dad," they all say.

I can barely take a drink.

Proud. Proud. Proud.

The words beat like a drum in my mind, and I hear my

father's voice in them. For so long the only thing I could hear was disappointment.

But now.

Somehow, these four people knew that I needed this. I needed him to be proud.

We only stay a little while longer, but it's enough. They have seen the biggest hurt in my heart, and they stayed. They honored it. They loved me anyway.

King sneaks in my window that night and falls asleep on my bed. In the morning my mother knocks on the door and asks if King is staying for breakfast.

We drink coffee and eat cereal and stare at each other in the morning like we did on the trail, but here it feels different. Like I'm seeing a whole new person.

"You look different here," he tells me.

"Good or bad?"

He taps a finger on the side of his mug thoughtfully. "Just different."

When he leaves for Alaska again, we stand with our foreheads pressed together. "I'll be back."

But another thing death steals from you is the belief that time is limitless. I don't trust that I'll see King again. I don't trust.

My hands bunch into his sweatshirt as he steps back from me, and I can see on his face that he doesn't want to go either.

I watch his car drive away and I tell myself it's fine. But when the door is shut, I cry. My dad's silver suitcase is still next to the door. I hear his voice: *"Every scratch and ding on it is a reminder of somewhere I've been. A time I said yes."*

And I pull the suitcase into my room.

38

A MONTH LATER I end up at King's. He picks me up from the airport and throws my silver suitcase into his truck. His apartment is a small one provided by the internship. A makeshift kitchen, one sofa shoved against a wall, a table with three chairs. Not even four. It's clean. Tidy . . . some people might even say empty.

There are two bedrooms: one for him and one for his roommate.

"Is your roommate gone?"

"For the weekend." He nods.

"So, no one is coming home?"

"No." He hesitates. "Do you want to watch a movie? Or . . ."

I look him directly in the eyes when I say it. "No. I don't want to watch a movie."

"Do you want something to drink?" He opens the mini-fridge, but I walk past him into his bedroom. Dark curtains hang over a window with a desk pushed under it. A white comforter is bunched up like King had just gotten out of bed and threw it to the side. Sketchbooks, novels, and clothes are strewn about, and suddenly King is bending down, trying to tidy his room.

"Sorry. I didn't know if— And I never make my bed."

I stop him.

The things in his hands drop and I smile. It's a predatory thing, and his eyes watch me with warning.

"Maps."

I step toward him, and he steps backward.

My lips are on his a second later and the ache I always feel when I'm with King is back. We kiss and find our way to the bed. Gently, King pulls off my shirt, but I claw at the fabric of his until it's over his head.

"Maps, wait."

I stop.

"I love you."

I smile, not because it's funny or doesn't mean anything, but because those three words are something King has been saying to me for a long time. Over and over in the whispers and touches and tears.

I know he loves me.

Because it's the thing he shouts between his words.

And as he kisses my skin in places I didn't know I could feel, he presses on scars I didn't know I had. He touches places in my heart that I thought had grown callous and I know there is nowhere I would rather be than with him.

He bites my shoulder, holds on to my hips, takes me into his mouth as we come together. He doesn't make me feel embarrassed for wanting him, only beautiful and strong.

And when the world shatters beneath me, King shatters too.

After, he kisses my bare skin. Shoulder, torso, the tops of my thighs. He goes to the kitchen and brings back two plastic water bottles. "Joe would be so mad," I laugh.

"Please don't talk about Joe right after we just did . . ."

"Filthy things on your bed?" I laugh.

He shakes his head and smiles. "None of those were filthy."

King offers to bring me something to eat, but I'm not hungry. We hold each other and stare at the ceiling. Tangled in each other and our thoughts.

"I wish I would have met you earlier," I tell him. "Not . . . not the way we did."

"I think it was perfect."

"You don't regret it?"

"Do you?"

I think about his question. About my dad dying, school, my mother, the trail. I remember everyone standing at my father's grave telling him that he would be proud of me, and for the first time, I understand that it doesn't really matter what my father's ghost thinks. *I'm* proud of me.

I survived.

There is still fight inside of me.

I was beaten, but I was not broken.

"When I came to Bear Creek, Junior and Sugar had this thing about the Popsicles that you and Books handed out."

He sits up and frowns at me.

"It's so stupid." I put my hand over my face, trying to hide.

"Tell me." He nudges.

"There's this whole hierarchy to the colors, apparently. And Books gave Junior a red one because red is the best color? I don't know. But he thought it was a sign that Books was into him."

King hums in understanding. "Everyone knows blue is the best color."

"And they thought you liked me because you gave me a blue one!"

He laughs, his face turning a bit pink.

"Did you? Is that why you never gave me yellow?"

"Maps, that's ridiculous. You think I just always saved a good Popsicle until you showed up?"

"Did you?"

He sits up. "Why were you always in my line? Never in Books's?"

"Why were you paying attention?"

King shakes his head, but doesn't say anything else, just traces the freckles on my legs with his fingers. Sitting next to the bed is King's journal, the one my father gave to him. I pick it up and run my hand over the cover. ATLAS.

"A collection of maps. That's what it means." He presses his lips onto my arm.

A memory from the trail lights in my brain. *An Atlas if you will.* "You knew. The whole time, you knew my name."

He doesn't bother to deny it, but he also shakes his head. "I knew of Atlas the Outlaw. But I got to know Maps."

I groan. And open it. "That's cheesy." But I love it. I feel it expanding against the walls of my heart.

Flipping through the journal, I see trails and all the different things King felt were important to write down about me. Things like, *bites lip after she lies* and *she cried today.*

"I didn't cry *that* much," I grumble.

He kisses my thigh. "You cried a lot. It felt like you needed it."

On the day of the panic attack, he just wrote, *doesn't like small spaces—let me hold her.*

My fingers move to the last page of the trail, but there's more writing.

Real journal entries. I skim through them, too afraid to read a whole passage, afraid of how I will bleed.

> *Couldn't sleep. I'm a fucking idiot. I should have told her.*

and

> *Books found her. He called but he won't tell me where she is.*

and

> *It's a coffee shop. Junior told me.*

and at the very end

> *I need to let Maps go.*

"I was gonna burn it," he says against my skin.

"Burn it?"

"Yeah." His eyes are sad. "New Year's seemed like a good time for a fresh start. That's why I had it. But then I saw you, like a sign. Like the cigarettes."

I close the book and hold it against my bare chest. "You love a sign."

"Yeah," he says, leaning back. "I guess."

I don't see any of Alaska. All three days are spent in King's room. We whisper secrets and let ourselves be greedy as we learn all the ways to unravel each other.

And when I leave, I know it's without my heart.

39

The beginning, again.

MY TINY APARTMENT IS by the river.

During the day I can hear people rafting, kids playing, and sometimes smell barbecue. She's not the peaceful river that my dad and I spent time going to. But at night, I can open the window and hear her. A constant. I know her water is from the snow on the Sierras, and for some reason, just knowing that makes me feel better.

My roommate is Junior, but *roommate* is generous. He's gone with Books most nights, and somehow he's found himself three new parents. Books's mom, Millie, my mom, and Joe. I expect him to be annoyed that they're always calling and checking in on him, but he just shakes his head and says, "I'll never be annoyed that someone loves me."

Books predictably still lives at home. He still complains about how his mother won't let him leave, but he's all talk. Wrapped up in Junior on his mom's couch is exactly where he wants to be.

Sugar goes to the big private college a few towns over, but she's at our school studying more days than she's not. "It's too loud over there. It smells like rich kid."

And King.

He's currently lying between my legs with his head resting on my stomach. We listen to the way the water moves across the land as I pretend to read a book for class and not notice the way his thumb slides across my skin.

Since he's come back from Alaska, we find ourselves like this most nights. Him tired from work, me tired from school, but neither of us willing to be apart from each other. We've already spent too much time that way.

King's phone dings on the bed next to us and he groans as he picks it up. His head falls back and he looks annoyed.

"What?"

"Everyone is getting pizza at that twenty-four-hour place down the street."

He means Books, Junior, and Sugar. They are *everyone*.

"Is Sugar bringing that guy?"

"We don't have to go."

We don't. We don't have to do anything because my friends will still be there. If I say no. If I say yes. King's eyes light as he watches me try to decide.

"We could stay here," he says as he presses a kiss to the skin on my leg.

I put my book onto the nightstand, which is just the silver suitcase, and King's eyes darken.

King and I go.

Me in the white hoodie I stole from King when I visited him in Alaska and never gave back. Him in his jacket. Our arms wrapped around each other.

We sit in a booth with red vinyl seats and drink soda despite it being one in the morning. Junior has three different slices of pizza because he can't decide which one he wants.

"If you could only have one topping of pizza for the rest of your life, what would it be?" I ask, plucking a sausage from his slice.

"You and these impossible questions," Sugar grumbles. "I'm pretty sure this is a form of torture under the Geneva Convention."

"I hope you never stop asking questions that I refuse to answer," Junior says, wiping sauce from Books's face with his thumb and then licking it off. "It's part of your annoying charm."

"I have a question," Sugar asks. "What's one thing you wish you could change without anyone getting mad? I'll go first: I would outlaw eating food off your boyfriend's face because it's gross."

"I'll go next," Junior tells her. "I know exactly what you ate off of Mallory with two Ls, so you do not get to call me *anything*."

Books leans back and rolls his eyes as Sugar and Junior argue across him. King picks up my hand and kisses the back of it. His lips find my ear and he whispers, "I would change coming here because I could still be alone with you."

Each time he kisses me, I think about all the things it took to bring me here.

In a place where my heart hurts in a good way. Where it's so full and love is familiar. The journey to this moment is something that I wouldn't trade.

I miss my dad, but I don't feel alone in that pain.

The person I've become in the places that he left has changed me. And I'm proud of the girl I am. The one whose scars say I've lived a life with a story. I'm not embarrassed to hurt or cry. And I've stopped feeling guilty of the moments when I don't do that.

I feel safe. My friends took the time to break down my walls. They pulled away all the things I had been using to stop the bleeding from my pain and they exposed the wound. Not so it could hurt, even though it did, but so that I could figure out how to heal.

And if I'd been able to see a map of my past year, I still would have taken this path. To Sugar, and Books, and Junior.

To my mother.

To King.

And I know if I was to look at a map of my life, I would see that I'm exactly where I want to be. So.

I close my eyes and I whisper a truth that I don't care if anyone is mad about.

"I wouldn't change anything."

And I wouldn't.

THE END

which is just another beginning.

ACKNOWLEDGMENTS

Writing a story, any story, requires so many people to help shape it. This book was particularly hard for me to see clearly. So many of my own stories are layered in these pages. My dad, my own struggles as a teen, my sense of home. When I got to the end of this book, I realized how many people helped me find my way to it. From editors and copyeditors and marketing teams and friends and agents.

Erica Sussman, if this book is any good at all, it's because of you. You saw this story and ever so patiently redirected me toward my own vision time after time when I went down the wrong path. I imagine it was similar to herding cats. I'm sorry, but mostly grateful.

Sarah Landis, my extraordinary agent, thank you for being my emergency contact. You did not agree to be listed, but that is your punishment for agreeing to sell my books. Thank you for reading SO many versions of this book and telling me that Atlas is special.

To the team at HarperCollins that worked on this book during a really intense season of change, I cannot tell you how much I appreciate all of you. Things evolve constantly but you were steady, and your eyes and talent are something I'm so thankful for!

To all the people who have inadvertently ended up in this

story. The teachers, continuation school educators, counselors, volunteers at community service and work projects who loved me and saw me as more than just an angry teen. You're all here.

Mr. C, who saw a kid who had been kicked out of high school and wasn't on track to graduate and told her *you can start a story any way you want.*

Mr. Axtell, who saw a student who told him to F off, and knew she needed help, not detention. Your memory is forever in my heart.

To my uncles and my dad, who spent countless summer nights with a beer in hand as they told stories laced with memories. In those moments I knew that there was magic in words.

To my mom. The strongest human I know. I love you and I am only strong because of your example.

To my children, who make me want to tell stories and to my husband, who always encourages me to do so. David, I can't do anything without you, and I don't want to, honestly. (Please don't tell Jin I said that.)

To my Dwyers. Thank you for loving me and for letting me be exactly who I am. I feel safe and loved because of you.

Stephanie Garber, whose brain I cannot live without. Stephanie Brubaker, whose opinion and laughter are two of my favorite things. Isabel Ibañez, who tells me I'm good even when I don't feel it. Rachel Griffin, who always sees the me I think no one else can. Adalyn Grace, who always reminds me to speak up, embrace my value, and fight for what I believe in (I know you would help me hide a body). Shelby Mahurin, for always answering my texts and taking my author photo. Jordan Gray, for reading and reminding me why I do this. Alexa Lach, thank you for reading and cheering and supporting me even when you don't have time or emotional support.

To my first readers/encouragers: Natalie Faria. My love and gratitude for you is endless. Jenn Wolfe. GAH. You don't even know how much I appreciate you! Lacey, Jacki, Morgan, Lisa, Christina. I LOVE YOU.

IF IT'S NOT WEIRD . . . MaLLory (Malor), Alex, Gretchen, Alexa. What would I do without your aggressive pep talks, deep conversations about craft and story, and hilariously perverted commentary. Die. I would probably die.

Susan Lee. BOOK TWO. Did we survive? Tell me later. Thank you for understanding my feelings about air travel and being my person after debut. Sasha Peyton Smith, thank you for always being a phone call away and always having the perfect reaction to everything. Akshaya Raman, I'm really sorry about the K-pop thing (this is a lie). I love you.

To Writing with the Soul, thank you for being the most supportive community that continually loves me and encourages me and inspires me. I love all of you! (ROUND ZERO.)

Adrienne Young, thank you for being my support human. Thank you for listening to all my self-doubt, watching all my annoying starts and stops, and having unending faith in my storytelling ability. On days when I can't see the end of the darkness, you remind me that the only way out is through. In our next life, I promise to have my shit together. No promises in this one. Sorry I keep leaving the fan on at the office.

To the game Bullshit—which we played nonstop in airports

during layovers, on beaches during rainstorms, and all over Thailand—and the people we played it with.

To the American River. Every rock, every tide, every bridge, every fish reminds me of my dad. This was my love letter to that place filled with childhood memories and adult emotions and eternal lessons. A reminder that everything keeps moving.

And last: to those of us who have lost a parent much much too soon. I love you. I see you. And I agree—it's the fucking worst. Life is colder without them, but they are the sunshine on our faces and the North Stars in the sky.